DEAD END

GWYN BENNETT

CHALKY DOG

ALSO BY GWYN BENNETT

DI Claire Falle series

Lonely Hearts

Home Help

Death Bond

The Dr Harrison Lane mysteries

Broken Angels

Beautiful Remains

Deadly Secrets

Innocent Dead

Perfect Beauties

Captive Heart

Winter Graves

Dark Whispers

The Saskia Monet series

The Stolen Ones

Secrets in the Blood

The Villagers

Published in 2024 by Chalky Dog Publishing

Dead-end

"The end of a road or passage through which no exit is possible, or a situation offering no prospects of progress or development."

PROLOGUE

When I look at my hands, they're covered in blood. I smell it too, the rich, iron-laden narrative of death slowly pooling on the ground beside me. I glance down at myself: my clothes are damp and crimson; my cheek sticky in the breeze from the open front door, bringing the sounds of faraway police sirens to my ears.

Six bullets to the chest and abdomen. No one can survive that.

My vision blurs and I feel myself slipping into unconsciousness.

Perhaps that's a good thing. An escape from this reality.

My eyelids flutter.

If I let them close, then I won't have to face up to what's next.

But I have to.

Hasn't this been all about justice?

Justice and revenge – and one terrible mistake.

I just never thought it would end this way.

1

6 WEEKS EARLIER

I must have been an absolute bitch in a previous existence, because my life right now is full of crap – literally! Ben, my two year old, has just filled his nappy as we were about to leave the house. I've got forty minutes to get him to the childminder and then make it to work for a meeting. I have to be on time. There's a promotion going and it's me or Mason Laing, who happens to be male and single without any responsibilities. I know I'm the most experienced, but 'my situation', as my boss calls it, is going to work against me.

That 'situation' is the other crap in my life: my husband Dylan, father to Ben, who walked out on us three months ago to move in with his personal trainer. What he doesn't realise is that she's more impressed with his bank balance than his six pack; and what she doesn't realise is that it's going to take a lot more than gym work to train him to be a responsible partner. The upshot though, is that I really, really need that promotion, otherwise I'm going to have to sell the house to give him his share and as it is, I can't afford the mortgage payments on my own. Dylan is happily bench-pressing his girlfriend while I'm struggling as a single, working mother.

One sniff and I can tell that I can't leave Ben as he is, so I quickly whip out his changing kit and try to do a hasty diaper switch, but oh no, that would be too easy. Wouldn't it! His little cheek is flushed, so I think he's got a molar trying to come through. The result is that his diaper isn't as straightforward as I'd hoped. The word poo-nami comes to mind: it's half-way up his back. I have to change his clothes too, which means running up and down the stairs and getting hotter by the minute with the exertion and stress. Thank goodness I remembered to do a full spray of deodorant and perfume earlier.

I'm smartly dressed for today, in a skirt and blouse with my power-woman blazer on. After the meeting, I'm due to do an interview with a hot-shot economist from one of the big banks. Some more doom-mongering about the state of the country's finances – as if we haven't all already noticed how expensive everything has got. He spends his days crunching data to help the rich get richer through their investments; I just need a miracle to make my meagre wages go further.

I'm on my knees in the hallway with a mountain of baby wipes and the only saving grace is that Ben thinks this is all highly amusing. How can I possibly get annoyed with that giggle? I sort him out, wash my hands and have us back on our way out the door again having lost only ten minutes, but it's still ten minutes I could have done without losing.

As I fix Ben into his car seat, I imagine Mason will be just finishing his leisurely double espresso and straightening his tie before sauntering out the door to the sports car he's recently bought. I *have* to do this. I have to make that meeting on time.

I virtually throw Ben at Jo when she answers the door. She's a total rock, takes it all in her stride and gets Ben to wave bye to Mummy as I virtually run back down the path. I nearly twist my ankle in the rush and when I get into the car and inspect my shoe, I can see I've scraped the side of it. The universe slinging more crap at me. I lick my finger and try to wipe away the scrape but my shoe isn't having any of it.

No time for worrying about the state of my footwear, I need to get on the road. It's a twenty minute drive if the traffic is reasonable. I have twenty-one minutes. I can do this.

I've been working for the regional newspaper since I left university, which, unbelievably, is nine years ago now. Where did that time go? I'm a senior reporter, but what I'd like is to be a correspondent – and the coveted crime beat is up for grabs. I've done my time, brought in plenty of front-page leads. But while my boss might talk the diversity buzzwords, he doesn't always put them into practice. The last two crime correspondents were men, and they've both left and gone to the nationals. I guess Pete's just quite old-fashioned, and I don't think it's malicious, but I think he genuinely believes crime is too dangerous for women.

I work hard, I write well, I find exclusives and I've got great contacts. This job should be mine. Admittedly, some mornings I've been a bit late for the editorial meetings. I've always been an owl, not a lark, but now mornings are a whole other story - and without doubt, the most stressful part of my day. B.C. (before children) I used to think that mothers I knew were poorly organised – I mean really, how long can it take to get yourself and a small person that you can pick up, ready and out the door? But hey, we all learn right? Add being a single parent to the equation, and I'm surprised I ever get to work at all, let alone on time.

So, I've been making a real effort to make sure I'm in work before 9 a.m. for the past few weeks. It's not been easy I can tell you. Today, though is critical. The meeting is to go through our forward planning for the next few months and I've got some great ideas for a crime series. I just need to get myself there so I can impress.

It's going well, the traffic lights are with me – three greens in a row – and now it's just the dual carriageway. Unfortunately, this is where my little dose of luck runs out. My positive mental attitude obviously means nothing to the traffic gods who are entertaining themselves creating mayhem for us mere mortals this Monday morning. The radio tells me that a broken-down van in one of the two lanes on the dual carriageway has caused a massive tailback, and I'm stuck right in the middle of it. I'm progressing slower than a slug – let alone a tortoise, and the minutes are ticking down in front of me.

'Shit, shit, shit!' I scream to myself and half-attempt to beat my head against the steering wheel. I don't, of course. Having the imprint of a car part on my forehead is not exactly going to encourage my boss that I'm the most responsible and mature member of his staff and therefore deserving of a promotion. Instead, I'm getting more and more anxious and my fingers are getting RSI the amount of tapping on the wheel I'm doing.

There must be a way around this. I've done this route a thousand times and I've always gone the same way, but one of the photographers at work told me there's a side route off the dual carriageway. I look around me. I know there are a couple of side roads coming up on the left – but which one is it?

I know we shouldn't use our phones while driving, but I am honestly going so slowly that it can't possibly be a danger. I'm virtually at a standstill. All the cars in front have merged into the one clear lane and I can now see down the left hand lane that there's a turning coming up.

I've just picked up my phone to open Google Maps when I notice a car come speeding down the left lane and past me. I drop the phone onto the passenger seat, thinking it might be the police, but it's a black BMW and it indicates left, heading up the turning. I go to pick up my phone again, trying to get it to open without putting it right in front of my face where it's obvious what I'm doing, but then another car speeds past. A silver Mercedes this time, and it too turns up the side road. That's got to be it. Two cars in just a few seconds. Smart, expensive cars too. They must know what they're doing.

I don't have time to lose. I look in my rear-view and side mirrors to make sure nobody else is haring down past me, and pull into the empty lane, pressing down on the accelerator and heading straight up the side road as fast as is safe. I can still do this.

The road is little more than a single lane in some places – I'm going to have to take it carefully in case something's coming down.

I'm surprised by how overgrown the roadside hedges and banks are. This clearly isn't a route many cars travel along – there's even debris from the trees on the road surface. Suddenly, I start to doubt myself. If I've gone up a dead end and I have to retrace my steps, this is going to be a disaster. There's nowhere to turn around – and there's no way I'm going to make it to work on time.

About a mile and a half in, there's a wall on the right-hand side. That's a good sign. I think. I hope. Indications that I'm heading back into inhabited territory. Surely I'm going to come to the outskirts of the village soon?

I come to a large, open gateway, which the road leads through. Is this a private property? I drive in anyway because I've got nothing to lose. I can't see a house or other buildings. I also still can't see the two cars. There's no way I've missed a turning off that lane, so they have to have gone this way.

Two hundred or so yards on and some large farm buildings appear. I'm not sure if this is a good sign or not. Perhaps the road leads straight past them and out to Upper-Retford. I glance at the clock on my dashboard. I've got less than ten minutes before the meeting starts. When I glance back up again at the road, I can see I'm heading straight between the outbuildings. I slow down, not sure whether there'll be people or vehicles around, but I see nothing. The place is deserted. But that's not what matters. What matters is that it's a dead end. The bloody road stops here, amid the big, warehouse-like barns, and what looks like a run-down farmhouse.

'Shit, shit, shit.' I close my eyes and try to calm myself but really I just want to cry with frustration.

Then I remember the two cars. Where have they gone? I can't see them parked in the yard. Is there a way out of here that I'm just missing?

I crawl forward in the car. The outbuildings' doors are open and I can see inside them. They're empty. Those cars had to go somewhere.

Then, as I reach the last barn, I see them and my hope evaporates. The black BMW and silver Mercedes have pulled inside and two men are standing talking. Probably a bloody estate agent showing a client round. What an idiot I am. Why didn't I just check on Google Maps?

I feel the hot prickle of tears in my eyes again. I can't keep doing this. I'm going to have to turn around and go all the way back down the lane and re-join the tailback. There's no way I'm going to make that meeting on time now.

All the fight is seeping out of me and as I'm about to reverse and turn the car around, I look back up at the warehouse and the cars. The men haven't seen me and it looks like they're arguing now. Probably come here for a quiet conversation and weren't expecting some idiot to follow them up a dead-end lane. The tall one looks familiar, but I'm not sure from where.

I get ready to leave but the short man lifts an arm and the one I think I recognise, strikes it away. Then he pulls something out of his trouser waistline. I can't see what it is clearly, but it flashes in the sunlight coming down through the holes in the rusted roof. Before the other man can react, the taller one seems to swipe at him and he falls to the floor, writhing and clutching at his throat. There's no mistaking what just happened. I can see the blood pumping out of him.

The attacker steps away and watches the man on the floor. I've forgotten to breathe. Transfixed. My heart is beating so fast and hard that I think they must be able to hear it. I grab for my phone and take a quick shot, reporter instincts kicking in. Then my survival instinct takes over.

I need to get out of here, before he sees me, and call the police. I push my foot on the accelerator, but I've forgotten that I'd put the car in reverse and I speed straight back and hit some empty steel drums stacked against the opposite barn. The noise of them falling is like an explosion. I don't need to look to know that the man has heard it and is now running towards me. I have to get away.

I slam the car into first gear and wheel spin back the way I came, looking in my rear-view mirror as I see the silver Mercedes screech out of the warehouse and on my tail. I've got no hope in my little Ford Fiesta – that thing will outrun me any day.

I fumble for my phone that I'd tossed onto the car seat next to me, but it's fallen into the passenger footwell along with my handbag. It must have been the jolt when I slammed into the drums. Not taking my eyes off the road, I lean down and stretch my arm to try and reach it. It's just beyond my fingertips.

The stone gateway is coming up and then I need to get down that narrow lane, and hope nothing is coming up the other way. I lean over again and just manage to touch my phone. I press down on the end, trying to flip it towards me.

At first it's too heavy for my fingertip so I give one final stretch, straining to keep my foot on the accelerator and the other one ready to break. At last, I reach it and try to flip it again. It works. I desperately grab it, coming back upright just as I hit a bend. I'm too tight, nearly hitting the bank, and brambles scrape along the side of my car. The sound of them squeaking and screeching along the metal makes me jump. The Mercedes can't be far behind.

I dial 999 on my mobile. It doesn't ring. 'Shit!' The road is in a dip so there's no reception and the trees can't help. They're blocking the signal.

I'm on a straight piece of road now and the Mercedes has just come round the bend behind me. I have to get back onto the main road before he reaches me. He wouldn't dare attack me in front of all those commuters sitting bored in the tailback.

The road seems to go on forever and every second he's gaining on me. I'm sure this lane wasn't as long when I drove up it.

At last, I see the end of the lane and the traffic is still there. I barely brake as I re-enter the dual carriageway and swerve into the clear left-hand lane. There might be police officers up where the van broke down. I see the Mercedes arrive on the dual carriageway behind me. He puts his foot down.

Then up ahead, I see a stationary police car behind the temporary sign telling everyone the lane is closed and to move into the right lane. I'm in such a panic now that I clip the lane closed sign, coming to a screeching halt behind the parked police car. Two officers look up shocked and then run towards me.

Where's the Mercedes? I twist around in my seat and see him force his way into the right-hand lane, crawling past me. It's him driving. The man who took out the knife. The one who slashed the other man's throat. For a brief second our eyes meet and I see the anger in his. Then he's blocked from my view by one of the traffic cops who has come round to my door and is banging on the window telling me to get out.

I'm not sure I can even stand, my legs are so shaky. My breathing is shallow and rapid. The police officer yanks my door open.

'Turn your engine off and get out of the car,' I hear him say, although it's distant. My head is whirring.

He's leaning in, turning my ignition off and I look at him for the first time.

'I just saw a man being murdered.'

2

It takes a good twenty minutes of explaining, tears, and then me remembering I'd taken a photograph, before the police officers start to believe me. The shot isn't great, but you can clearly see the two cars and beyond them, the man standing looking over the other on the ground.

When they see the photo, they step away and huddle together whispering. I hear one of them calling it in over his radio, and they ask me to get into their car and show them where it happened. I sit in the back, shaking by this time, the adrenaline worn off.

'I recognised the man,' I say, 'I'm sure I've seen him somewhere before.'

The two officers in front of me, one with a beard, the other older with grey hair, exchange a glance. What does that mean? What are they not telling me?

'Up there,' I say, pointing to the side road I'd gone up. We head slowly the wrong way down the closed dual carriageway lane, lights flashing. Only this time, I see the sign. It is partially hidden by tree branches and ivy, but it very definitely reads, *Dead End, Farm Access Only.*

'That's a dead end. Why did you go up there?' The older man, who isn't driving, turns and looks at me.

'I didn't see the sign,' I say, but that sounds pathetic. How could I not have seen the damned sign? I was focusing too much on being late and following those cars, that's why.

'You're a reporter, right?' the older officer continues. I see the bearded cop glancing at me in the rear-view mirror. 'So were you chasing a story?'

'No. I honestly thought it might be a shortcut. I was late for work.'

'Dead ends don't make for great shortcuts; everyone knows this just leads to the old Fullerton farm.'

'I didn't. I just saw two cars go up and thought they might know a good route round the traffic.'

The older officer gives me a piercing look and then turns back round to face the front, but not before he and beardy have given each other another knowing glance. Why don't they believe me? Do police officers have a default mode to suspect everyone? I've just witnessed a terrible crime. I'm doing my civic duty and yet I feel like the bad guy here.

We go round a bend and the stone gates loom up in front of us. I feel sick as we head through them. The image of a crumpled, bloody person on the floor of the barn flashes into my head. I push it away, but there's no escaping it. We travel the rest of the way in silence.

Beardy slows the car as we reach the buildings. 'Which one?' he asks me.

'Last one on the right.' I point it out. 'There's a black BMW in there too.'

When we pull up and look inside, and the car and man are both still there, I feel a perverse sense of relief. Now they have to believe me.

'Wait here,' the older officer orders me, and they both get out.

I don't need any further persuasion, all of a sudden this surreal nightmare I've been in has become so much more real.

I sit watching them walk into the barn but thoughts of what my editor might say when I tell him about my morning, prompt the reporter instincts in me to resurface. I pull my phone from my pocket and snap a couple of photos. This will be front-page news. The two cops walk towards the man on the floor and check for signs of life. From the amount of blood, I'm pretty certain there isn't much hope of that. Then, they turn and start walking back towards me. I quickly hide my phone. Beardy walks up to the car and opens the door.

'We're going to have to ask you to wait here for a few minutes please,' he says sternly.

'Who is it?' I ask, nodding towards the dead man.

'We can't release that information I'm afraid and I'd ask you not to report anything about this incident and who's involved because it could compromise our enquiries, not to mention upset his next of kin.'

I think he's about to say something else when another car comes rushing up behind us. It's unmarked but definitely something to do with the police because both officers look up and get ready to greet its occupant.

'Wait here,' I'm told again. The door is shut on me and I realise that it's designed so I can't open it from inside. I'm a prisoner. Am I a suspect?

I crane to see what's going on. A good-looking detective gets out of the new car and they shake his hand. I recognise him: Detective Sergeant Nicholas Barnes, of the serious crime division. I interviewed him a couple of times. His dad was a cop too – and was shot and died about a year ago. I did a piece on him and spoke to DS Barnes then, and I also interviewed him about the spate of spikings that had been going on in clubs around the area. Loads of mostly girls had been injected with date rape drugs, the next step up from slipping something in their drinks. Sick.

The three of them are deep in discussion. Older guy is pointing to where the victim is, then they all look up and over towards me. Beardy shakes his head. That guy definitely doesn't like me. They then edge slightly closer to the scene, but not up to it. I've watched enough TV cop dramas and documentaries to know that they don't want to contaminate the murder scene.

There's another quick discussion and then DS Barnes asks the two cops something and the two of them are on their radios while he approaches the victim alone after putting on some plastic overshoes and a pair of latex gloves. It looks as though he's searching the victim. Probably looking for ID. He seems to find something and slips it into an evidence bag. Then he sees something on the floor a few feet away from the victim, looks up, perhaps hoping to catch the two cops' attention but they're still talking. I watch as he gets another evidence bag out and slips the object into it. I keep snapping away on my phone, all great action shots for my lead story later.

Finally, he takes the gloves and overshoes off and walks towards me. *Shit*, he's seen my phone. He might not like me taking images. I quickly email myself the photos I've just taken and delete them all from my phone apart from the original one I took when the murder happened. The whoosh of the outgoing email sounds and I delete the 'sent' email from my phone, just as the car door is yanked open and DS Barnes climbs in.

'Hi,' he holds out his hand politely, 'I'm Detective Sergeant Nicholas Barnes.' He narrows his eyes and studies me. 'I think we've met before, haven't we?'

'Yes, Abigail Murphy, I'm a reporter with the *Evening News*,' I say.

Even though I'm still in a bit of shock, I can't help but feel a little frisson of something. He's sitting close. I can smell his aftershave, which is nice, and he's even better looking than I remembered. Is it because I've just been scared for my life, or perhaps it's just that I've been single for a few months.

'I'm really sorry, but I'm going to need your phone I'm afraid.' He looks at me. 'For evidence.'

'What evidence?'

'It will show data for when you were here – and did I see you taking pictures? This is a crime scene and we haven't informed the next of kin.'

'No, no photos – I was going to, but I only took that one when it first happened.' I lie and hope that I managed to delete everything properly. I know they can access deleted stuff, but if they don't suspect me, then it's unlikely that they'll go looking for it. The email I sent the photos to isn't an account on my phone.

'OK, but I'm sorry, it's protocol.' He holds out his hand.

I can see he isn't going to let me keep it. I hate the thought of not having my phone – but at least I've got the photos.

I hand it over.

'Thanks. I understand that you followed the two cars up here?' the DS asks.

'Yes. I thought it might be a shortcut to work.'

'Even though it's a dead end?' he queries. 'Look, you're not going to get into any trouble if you tell us that you were on a story and were following them. It's important that we have the full facts.'

'I wasn't. I'm not. I didn't even know who they were – although I do recognise Mercedes man.' My mind is scrambling to start functioning again after the earlier life-and-death road race. DS Barnes is sitting watching me. 'Honestly,' I add, beginning to feel like I'm back at school and someone's accused me of stealing another kid's pencil case.

Then it hits me. I know who Mercedes man is.

'Oh my God, it was Stuart Porter wasn't it?'

He raises his eyebrows. 'As you know, Ms Murphy, I am unable to confirm any details at present because this is a fast-moving inquiry. Can you please tell me exactly what you witnessed here today?'

'It is Stuart Porter!' I exclaim, the image of his scowling face as he drove past me earlier, coming to my mind.

I may not be able to read road signs, but I do know that this is big news. Stuart Porter is the head of finance and resources for the council. He has a squeaky-clean public image, I'd never in a million years have thought he'd kill a man. My mind is working on overdrive now. Why, what would drive him to do that? And then it hits me. There have been rumours that somebody in public office has been running a corruption racket, but nobody has ever been able to find out who. Could that someone be Stuart Porter? Now I get why the police think I might have been interested in the two cars.

DS Barnes is sitting quietly studying me, waiting for me to speak.

'I was genuinely in a hurry to get to work... I know there's a side road off the dual carriageway that can take me round the other side of Upper-Retford, but I just wasn't sure where, and after seeing two cars go up this road, I thought it might be the one.'

His face is impassive as he listens.

'When I got here, I realised it looked like a dead end but I couldn't see the two cars so I wondered if I was missing something. Then I saw them parked in there.' I nod at the barn where the BMW still sits. 'Both the cars were parked in there and the two men were arguing.'

'Did you hear what they were saying?'

'No. I had my window up. The shorter man lifted his arm and Stuart hit it away, then seemed to pull a knife out from his trouser waistline and slashed him across his neck. He stepped back and watched as the man bled.'

'Did it look like the victim was pleading for his life?'

'I'm not sure. Possibly.'

'But Mercedes man was definitely the aggressor?'

'From what I could see, yes.'

'Did you see the victim with a weapon?'

'I'm not sure. I think he had something in his hand when Stuart hit his arm.'

'I've found a mobile phone a few feet away, could it be that?'

'Maybe. It was too far away to be sure,'

'But he definitely hit something out of his hand?'

'Yes.'

The only object I can see is the phone.'

'Then yes, that must be it.'

'OK, did it look like he was showing him something on his phone, or trying to make a phone call?'

'I'm not sure, the victim just seemed to take the phone out of his pocket and then Stuart hit it away and attacked him.'

'OK, so the tall man hit the shorter man's mobile out of

his hand and then slashed at his throat. What happened next?'

'He stood and watched him and then I panicked and tried to drive away but I'd forgotten I'd put my car into reverse and I knocked those steel drums over.' I nod towards the pile of scattered drums. 'That's when he saw me and started to chase me. I drove as fast as I could back to the dual carriageway and found the traffic police.'

'What happened to the man in the Mercedes?'

I note that Barnes has carefully not used Stuart's name because that would confirm his identity.

'He pushed into the queue of traffic and drove past me.'

'Did someone tip you off about this?'

'No absolutely not! I've told you, I honestly thought it was a way around the backlog.'

'The Upper-Retford road is further up the carriageway, past the broken down van,' DS Barnes says to me, not taking his eyes from my face.

'Right,' is all I can say in return. That's information which is no good to me now.

'And you didn't hear anything that they were saying? You're a reporter and a senior council executive is arguing with a man in a remote location, and you don't wind down your window?'

I shake my head and with a sinking feeling, think that this is exactly what my editor is going to say to me. You can bet that Mason would have. I see the crime correspondent job disappearing from my future CV.

'No. I didn't. Like I said, I didn't realise who they were at first.'

But there is still the photo – that was initiative. My editor will definitely want that.

'Can I have my mobile phone back?' I say to Barnes. 'I

really do need to call work and let them know why I'm not there.'

DS Barnes considers me for a few more moments. 'I'm afraid that this is an active murder investigation. We will need to keep your phone for a little while. You're welcome to use mine to call anyone you need to – but I am going to have to ask you not to report anything that you've witnessed here today. You appreciate that it could compromise our investigation, and the apprehension of the murder suspect.'

I nod. I feel like I want to cry now. This is so not how today was supposed to have panned out.

DS Barnes's face softens. 'This must have been a big shock to you?' he says gently.

I nod again and dig my nails into my palm. I will not cry in front of him.

Barnes hands over his mobile phone, unlocked, but he doesn't leave the car. He stays sitting next to me, looking out the window as though he's not really listening in to my conversation or checking that I don't look at anything else on his phone.

I look at the time. The meeting will be over now and everyone will be at their desks or out on the day's stories. I dial the direct line to my editor.

'Pete, it's Abbie.'

'Where the hell are you? You're supposed to be interviewing Jonathon Brunner. I've had to give it to someone else; you weren't even answering your mobile.'

'Sorry, I've been... I've been involved in an incident and I can't talk right now but I'll explain it all later.'

'An incident? What sort of incident?'

'I can't go into any details.'

'Are you OK?'

'Yes. Thanks. I'm fine. I'll call you as soon as I'm able to.'

'You coming in today?'

'I don't know…'

'Bloody hell, you're not giving me much to work on here. Fine. Get in as soon as you can.'

Pete put the phone down and I could imagine him swearing to himself in his office. There was no way that DS Barnes didn't hear that whole conversation – Pete didn't exactly have the quietest telephone voice. I hand Barnes's phone back to him.

'Thanks.'

'Is there not anyone else you want to call? Your husband?' Barnes looks at me surprised.

I shake my head. 'We're separated. I'm good.'

I've got until 5 p.m. to get all this sorted out so that I can go and pick up Ben. Surely they won't keep me locked in this police car until then.

'How long is this all going to take?' I ask DS Barnes.

'I'm not sure. That will depend,' he replies.

'Have you arrested Stuart Porter?'

'You know I can't answer that,' he says to me.

I sigh.

'If you have any questions, or you think of something else,' he hesitates and I can feel his eyes roaming over every inch of my face, 'or need anything, even if it's just to talk to someone, you can call me.'

He hands me a business card and I look up into his eyes; they're sympathetic and he gives me a reassuring smile.

Behind us I hear sirens coming up the track. The cavalry has finally arrived. DS Barnes gives me one final look over, and I catch his eyes sweeping over my legs and up. Then, he is gone.

. . .

Detective Inspector Conor Roberts cuts quite an imposing figure. He's tall, well-built and has an air of quiet calm about him. I reckon he must be about fifty. I've not met him before and he takes me in with the practised eyes of a well-seasoned detective. He arrived with another detective, a younger guy with black hair. DS Barnes handed over the evidence bags to the younger detective, and they had a conversation before Barnes left, giving me a final glance of reassurance. Now, DI Roberts is on the back seat beside me, his head nearly brushing up against the roof of the car. He's had to sit at a slant so that his long legs aren't jammed into the driver's seat in front.

'What were you doing coming up here?' he asks me.

I wonder how many more times someone is going to ask me that question. I tell him. He doesn't look as if he believes me either.

'You do understand that if you withhold information that could be pertinent to this inquiry, then that is a criminal offence. You won't be able to publish it.'

'I know. I am telling you the truth,' I'm getting irritated now. What does he take me for and why won't they believe me? I stare back at him, clenching my jaw.

'OK. What did you see?' he asks now.

'I've told DS Barnes everything,' I push back, annoyed.

'DS Barnes is not the officer in charge of this investigation, I am,' Roberts replies, deftly putting me and Barnes in our places. 'If you don't mind, I'd like to hear the account from you,' he softens slightly.

I'm not sure I like DI Conor Roberts – he's certainly not as sympathetic as Barnes, but I tell him my story. The same as I told Barnes and the traffic cops. He listens, frowning.

'So the tall man attacked the shorter man when he pulled his mobile phone from his pocket?' he clarifies.

'Yes. He slashed at his throat with a knife.'

DI Roberts nods thoughtfully.

'And you didn't know who they were when you followed them?'

I shake my head.

'I understand that we have your mobile phone and we will have to obtain information from that to verify your statement. I'll need the code please to access your phone.'

'What!' I'm incredulous now. 'You think I'm involved in this somehow?'

'I didn't say that Mrs Murphy. I said it is to verify your statement because if this goes to trial, the defence will try to dispute the course of events. We will also need to access that photograph you took,' he pauses, 'You are of course welcome to seek legal advice at any time.'

He's a cool customer, and doesn't bat an eyelid at me. I have a quick internal debate as to whether to give them the code to my phone, or refuse. I know they're going to have a damned good nose through everything. It's obvious they think I somehow knew about this meeting, but bearing in mind they all think I'm already lying to them about why I was here, I don't think withholding it is going to do me any favours. They've got smart programmes that break into these devices anyway. I give it to him and he thanks me and asks me to wait in the car, and someone will drive me back to my vehicle and then on to the station, where I can give a full statement.

I'm getting sick of sitting in this damned police car, but I'm writing the story in my head while I wait. I watch the forensics crew arrive, the hushed conversations between detectives, and try to figure out how I can get in touch with Pete to tip him off about the story. I can see the headline in tomorrow's paper with my by-line underneath.

It's boring and getting quite stuffy in this car. I look for DS Barnes, but his car still hasn't returned and he's nowhere to be seen. I watch the forensic team setting up and then my mind wanders to thinking about what might be on my phone that I'm going to find embarrassing. There's nothing I can think of. I've always been careful not to keep any digital records of informants, so I know there's nothing like that on my phone. I'm so glad I was able to delete the sent email with the photographs in time. All they'll find is a ton of photos of Ben in various poses and the email trail between my friend, Julia, and I, as we bemoan our lives. I think I might have made a few threats to castrate Dylan and poison his floozy Harper, but I'm hoping that the police – if they read them – will view them in the light they were intended. I'm just a cheated-on woman who has found herself in the wrong place at the wrong time. I know I shouldn't have missed that dead-end sign, but I was stressed. The silver lining is that I'm right at the centre of one of the biggest stories we've had in years and I'm going to make sure that I turn this into an opportunity to get that promotion Ben and I really need.

3

———

It's nearly midnight and I'm standing in my kitchen sucking an ice cube made of wine. It had seemed like a great idea when the incredibly smug TV health expert suggested it. Rather than feel like you have to drink a whole bottle of wine quickly when you live on your own, freeze some in ice cube trays and use it for cooking. She'd gone on to remind us all just how many calories there are in the average glass, while sitting serene, slim, and sexy on the *Good Morning* sofa.

I've had the day from hell, stuffed a quick McDonald's on the way home after picking Ben up late from the childminder, and now I'm slurping the only wine I have in my house from an ice cube tray like some mad alley cat.

They took me to the police station after making me sit in the damned car for ages. I was quizzed again about why I'd driven up the road and what I knew about the two individuals in the cars. By this time, the police were using their names. I already knew that the killer was Stuart Porter, and it turned out that the murdered man was Jordan Christie, a local accountant. There was a big operation to arrest Porter, who had tried to do a runner, but only got as far as a service station on the M20 heading towards Dover.

DI Conor Roberts and his sidekick, who I learned is Detective Sergeant Tony Fuller, came to talk to me again. They were a little more conciliatory this time round, although I wouldn't go so far as to say they were warm. DI Roberts said that the photograph on my phone of Porter wasn't good enough to identify him. They were going to ask me to come back in for an identification parade either tomorrow or the day after. Because Porter is a well-known local figure, my testimony was going to be crucial and I had to be absolutely sure about what I saw and that it was him.

Even after I'd given my statement, they'd kept hold of me. I tried to complain at one point but they said it could compromise their investigation if they allowed me to leave. I guessed that they wanted to have me where they could keep an eye on me – they wanted Porter arrested and their comms briefed and ready before I filed a story. I should have called the paper to ask for a lawyer to get me out, but by the time I'd gotten over the shock of everything and instead got annoyed enough to start demanding to see a legal representative, they'd obviously found Porter getting his motorway cuppa and let me go anyway.

As soon as I was out, I called Pete, but I was too late: the paper had gone to print. He wasn't overly impressed with me. Said he'd get Mason on to the story tomorrow and I was just to send over whatever I had and they could do some social media posts and put it on the website in the meantime. I know I can kiss goodbye to that promotion, but I'm so tired after today that I don't even have the energy to stress about money and my career tonight.

The only thing to cheer me up in my crappy day comes in the form of an email from my best friend Julia. I've known Julia about twelve years B.C. (before children) We'd gone to university together. She's a rock, and has been there for me through everything with Dylan, but the downside is that she now lives about a hundred miles away and so we don't get to see each other as often as we'd like. Julia's husband Oscar has done rather well for himself as a software developer, and they've recently had their third child so she's on maternity leave and contemplating giving up work to become a full-time mum. But after today's email, she might have changed her mind.

To: Abbie
  From: Julia
  Hi how's things?

Oscar's been away on his business trip for only one day (he's not back for another three), I have a headache, two naked children – one of whom has a very snotty nose that keeps on being wiped on everything but the tissues I give him. Meanwhile baby James is upstairs having finally gone to sleep fed up with the sound of his own crying. Oscar left saying that as the decorators have now finished, everything should be nice and easy while he's away and wasn't it a great idea to get them in whilst I'm at home on maternity leave so that I can oversee it all!

We have a new carpet going into the living room tomorrow which means that everything from that room is now in the dining room, leaving the kids with very little play room, and it's just started raining. The cat is at least safe from having his tail pulled because there are a million hiding places for him, and I've absolutely no room in which to swing him.

Oscar's parting words were, 'I'm only a phone call away if you need me'. What the bloody hell use does he think being on the end of a phone is?

I want to go back to work!

Rant over. Hope you're good. Gotta go as I can hear the baby crying and he hasn't had his millionth feed of the day yet, plus I'd better find some clothes for the other two before they go completely feral. Speak soon.

Julia

She makes me smile, but then I feel guilty because I'd only started feeling better because she sounded like she was having a bad day too. I go to write back and tell her I've just witnessed a murder but if I know Julia, the second she reads it she'll be on the phone asking if I'm OK. It will be good to talk to her, but just not now. I'm all out of wanting to talk about it. I've recounted that stupid decision to go up the dead-end road so many times that I shall no doubt be muttering it in my sleep.

It's now half past midnight, and I'm out of wine ice cubes. I've been up since half six, Ben will be awake again at quarter to seven and I'll need to go into work and try to regain some semblance of my career. It's time I started to think about bed.

Wandering into the kitchen to get a glass of water, I nearly go flying as my foot slips on a little plastic figure. I give a little yelp as it digs into the soft skin of my foot arch. The kitchen floor resembles a scene from a spaghetti western. There are discarded bodies of little plastic people all over the place, some lying next to the cars they had been driving, others abandoned midway across the wooden floor. I gather up the plastic bodies ready to return them to the playbox, but as I stand up straight again I think I see a movement out in the back garden. My heart freezes and my stomach flips.

I turn off the light and stare out into the darkness.

Nothing.

Nothing but the pounding in my chest.

I'm probably just being paranoid. It was either a fox or an owl. I still double check the locks on the door and windows. Maybe I should have left the little plastic men out all over the floor, just in case someone did break in. That would stop them in their tracks.

I almost have to drag myself upstairs. You know the feeling – it's not that you don't want to sleep, it's just the thought of having to take off your make-up and clothes, when all you want is to be carried upstairs and placed under your duvet like a baby. I decide to do the undressing bit first, peeling everything off and leaving it in a pile on my bedroom chair – the pile which is standing about two feet tall and in danger of toppling the chair over. I catch sight of myself in the mirror accidentally. Not good.

Why is it that after you've had a baby your belly button seems to be about two-feet deeper. Mine has become a black hole, swallowing everything that dares go near it. I know my skin has stretched, expanding over the giant bump that was Ben, but they never tell you about how your belly button is going to change. Why couldn't we have been designed like a slinky toy with an ever-expanding middle that can be pulled but always goes back into its neat, coiled shape?

Ten years B.C., my girlfriends and I held Ann Summers' parties, now all we want are botox or liposuction parties. Where has all that energy we had gone? What happened to us?

Before I go to sleep I check on Ben one last time. He's on his side with his teddy tucked under his chin. I need the reassurance of his breathing and so I wait in the silence listening for the tiny little breaths to raise his body ever so slightly and let it fall again. I tuck his blankets in around him and sneak out of his room, narrowly avoiding the interactive Muck from Bob the Builder. I bumped into him once before and believe me, at midnight in a quiet house he's got a very loud voice.

Finally, I crawl into bed, but that fleeting image I thought I saw in the garden still has me on tenterhooks and keeps my eyes from closing. I heave myself back out of bed and for a few moments stand peering around the edge of the curtain into the dark night. I know what I witnessed today will have disturbed my subconscious mind. I tell myself that it's over. That it has nothing to do with me and the killer has been arrested.

Maybe it's my active imagination, or maybe it's the heightened sense of danger you get from being a mother, but it takes me a while longer to fall asleep as I wrestle with a grey shadow of foreboding.

4

I 'm woken by Ben calling for me. For a blissful few
moments, I've forgotten the trauma of yesterday, and
then it returns. I can feel my heart beat faster at the
memory and the resulting impact it's had on my promotion
chances. The alarm hasn't gone off yet so I sleepily stagger
into Ben's room and pick him up out of his cot to give him a
cuddle before we go downstairs. I bury my face into him and
breathe him in. He's my world. Nothing else matters but
him. I'll find a way forward for us both. Perhaps it's time I
looked at another job. I've been toying with the idea of
public relations for a while. Regular hours and generally
better pay. It's just when you're a serious journalist it's a bit
like crossing to the dark side, going from reporter of the
news and facts, to spin doctor and word massager. But, I'd
do it for Ben.

We have breakfast and as I'm getting his lunchbox ready
to take to Jo's, I listen to the local radio to see how they're
reporting 'my' story. They just quote the press release that
was issued late yesterday afternoon by DCI Henry Kennedy,

DI Roberts's boss. It's so frustrating that I was there, I saw it all before anyone else, and yet I didn't get to break the story.

I grind my teeth and look out the kitchen window into the garden. The fleeting image of the shadow out there last night comes back to me. My imagination has sharpened its edges, made it man-shaped now. A big man in dark clothes, striding across my garden. I give myself a mental slap and push it out of my mind. Instead, I attempt to transplant an adorable fox in there instead, a nice mummy fox searching for some food for her babies, just like you see on cute Christmas ads. But no matter how hard I try, the man shadow takes form with dark eyes and a menacing look.

Once Ben has finished flinging his breakfast on the floor, I clear up and we head upstairs so I can shower. Perhaps the water will help me cleanse the fear from my skin where it seems to have oozed out of my pores and dried like sea salt.

I'm getting used to never taking a shower or going to the toilet without the door being open. It's the only way I can hear and see Ben. He plays in his push-along car, stair gate latched, whilst I wash. This way I can be sure he's safe and he doesn't panic that I've disappeared.

Putting on my make-up can be a real challenge because Ben invariably wanders off with something when I'm not looking. This morning, I am so on it. The second I see his little pudgy hand reach up to grab something, I whip it away. He gives me a look with his big blue eyes, which makes me feel guilty and so I offer up a soft brush that I'm not using as a consolation. I'm relieved when he takes it happily, but the relief doesn't last long.

Teeth cleaning time. 'No!' he shrieks as soon as he sees the brush and clamps his lips firmly together.

I just don't have the time for this. I have to get to work. I start by trying to persuade him by opening my mouth, brushing my teeth and making silly 'aaggh' noises, but he's not having any of it. I plead with him, but the concept of urgency is not yet in his toddler brain. All the time, I can feel myself getting more and more wound up.

Eventually I resort to telling him that unless he cleans his teeth he won't be able to eat any more food, especially ice cream, because all his teeth will fall out – but only after they've hurt a lot. His little face creases into worry and he takes his toothbrush, opening his little mouth with a quiver.

Now I feel like the world's worst mother. Why can't I be like Kanga in Winnie the Pooh, all hugs and soft voices to baby Roo? She'd never lose her patience and resort to telling threatening lies to her innocent child. Nobody ever tells you that being a mother will involve so much guilt.

My guilt trip isn't over yet. When we make it to the hallway, I already know what's coming. He doesn't want his shoes on. His body goes limp and then rigid all in the same defiant second, before launching into a sideways roll on my lap, followed by a head-first lurch. Luckily I'm ready for every manoeuvre but the effort of holding on to him means I can't even begin to try to get the damned shoes on his little scrunched-up feet. We battle a while until eventually I have no choice but to hold him down on the sofa and forcibly put his shoes on. He starts to cry. That's it. I feel even more guilty, but I'm doing it for Ben. He doesn't realise it, but if I don't get to work on time then we can kiss goodbye to our nice house. I'm feeling sorry for myself now too. Why can't I just get up, get him ready and out the door without all the battles. Why is it all so hard? I fight back tears and bundle our bags and Ben out of the door.

When we get outside, the guilt and frustration of my everyday are forgotten as I see a police car drive slowly past. The officer inside has his head turned, clearly looking at us.

Yesterday comes rushing back to me. Are they here because they still think I was tailing Porter and Christie and know more than I was letting on?

Ben tugging my hand distracts me. I hoist him onto my right hip. He's my world and I'm all he's got. I kiss his soft cheek and squeeze him to me as the police car glides off down the road.

THE IRONY IS THAT TODAY, I actually make it to work slightly early, but Mason is already in, tapping away on his computer keyboard.

'Hey Murph,' he calls out to me as soon as he spots me. 'Come spill your guts about yesterday, I can quote you as a witness.'

Quote me as a witness. It should be my story, my by-line.

'In a minute,' I shout back. I'm going to talk to Pete first.

I see Pete watching me through his office window. I walk straight in.

'Hi,' I say, trying to judge his mood.

'How you doing?' he asks. He actually looks a little concerned.

'I'm fine, but obviously I'd like to be involved in the story seeing as I was there.' I don't waste time on small talk.

Pete takes a big breath in and leans forward onto his desk. 'Thought you'd say that, but you realise it's not straightforward, right?'

I fold my arms over my chest, defiant and defensive. 'In what way?'

'I have a duty of care, Abbie. You have witnessed a murder carried out by a very public figure who is going to be desperately trying to save his reputation and attempt to get off this charge. You don't seriously think I'd let you go noseying around into what went on between him and his accountant do you? You've got a little boy at home to think about.'

I'm briefly speechless. I can see he genuinely means it. Genuinely thinks that I could be putting myself in danger.

'Besides,' he continues, 'the police have been on to me. They don't want you publicly being seen to be doing anything with this story because it could jeopardise your testimony and therefore their case. They have a point – and quite frankly I think quite a few people would like to see Porter banged away for a long time if it's him who's been embezzling public money.'

'So, that's a definite no then...'

'Mason is running with it. Nothing's stopping you helping Mason behind the scenes – you can tell him everything you can and give us the inside scoop. It's common sense Abbie, you know it! Also, I have to ask you, were you investigating Porter? Have you been looking into the council corruption story already? I don't get why else you'd have been there that day and the police seem to think that one of our team has been making enquiries?'

'No. I accidentally went up a dead-end road thinking it was a route around the traffic. I didn't even know it was Porter.'

I can see from the way Pete is looking at me that he's not 100 percent convinced. I'm absolutely fuming inside. I get up to leave and then feel emboldened. 'Have you made a decision about the crime correspondent's position?'

'I have. I'm doing you a favour Abbie. That role needs irregular and long hours, visiting places that you wouldn't choose to go to.'

'Right!' I say. 'Thanks for the favour!'

'Abbie... Abbie...' Pete calls after me, but I'm out of there.

I don't care if he thinks I'm being rude. I slam his office door shut, making half the newsroom and ads team look up. I want to scream and shout and kick and punch, and then cry. Instead, I walk straight to the coffee machine to hit the caffeine.

I feel like a burning coil inside. I'm angry and frustrated. Maybe I could take Pete to the employment tribunal – he as good as said that he wasn't giving me the role because I was a woman and a mother. If that isn't discrimination, then what is? One thing's for sure, I'm not giving them the photos I took. Why should I let Mason get all the credit?

'You alright Abs?' Tessa from classified ads has come up to me as I'm waiting for my coffee. She clearly can't see the smoke coming out my ears, otherwise she'd leave well alone.

'I'm fine, thanks Tessa,' I say back and try to smile at her but my mouth muscles are refusing to bend the corner of my lips upwards.

'You must be scared after what happened yesterday,' she continues.

This woman is totally reading me wrong.

'I'd be terrified he'd come after me too. I hope the police are giving you some protection,' she continues.

'Who is going to come after me? Porter has been banged up,' I tell her. Is she trying to scare me?

'Yeah, but he's bound to have criminal friends, right? Aren't you the only witness?'

'There's photographic evidence too,' I tell her. 'It's not just down to me.'

'Oh that's a relief,' she says and smiles at me, unconvincingly. 'Still, it must have been a big shock to have seen it.'

'It was,' is all I say back.

She is clearly hoping I'll expand and give her the gory

details. My coffee has finally finished dribbling out of the machine. I can escape her nosy sympathy. 'I'd better get on with some work now,' I add and head over to my desk.

Of course she's right, I am the only witness and Porter must be a nasty piece of work. But I'd assumed that with the photograph, his car having been caught on the traffic camera when he left and came back onto the dual carriageway, and the fact they can probably trace his mobile phone, then surely the police have enough with or without me. If not, then they'd have offered me some kind of witness protection, wouldn't they?

'Y'alright Murph?'

Bloody Mason has walked up to my desk.

'You shaken up after yesterday? Must have been a real shock, but what were you doing up that road anyway? It's a dead-end right?'

'I thought it was the Upper-Retford turning.'

'That's about a mile further on,' Mason replies.

'I know that now.' The temperature of the angry furnace inside of me jumps up a few centigrade.

'Look, I guess Pete's told you about the crime correspondent job,' he has lowered his voice. 'I know you were going for that too and so just wanted to make sure there were no hard feelings. I think you'd have been great for it, but it's easier for me. You know, I only have a cactus to worry about getting home for.'

I look at him and can see he's genuinely trying to make the peace. I'm still angry, still worried about how I'm going to pay the bills going forward but, bizarrely, since Pete told me, an unexpected sliver of relief has also appeared. I wanted the job, I know I could do it, but maybe it would have been too much. My mind goes back to this morning and the stress of just getting out the door. I'd have really struggled with juggling care for Ben and been constantly feeling guilty about not being there with him. Perhaps Pete did do me a favour, but I'm not going to let him know that. I still think he'd have given it to Mason even if I wasn't a single mom.

'No worries Mason, wrong timing for me. Congratulations.' I don't want him to know I'm upset.

His face un-creases with relief.

'Cheers Murph,' he beams, and heads back to his desk.

I feel sick, but determined. It's time for me to do some job hunting and so I log onto my computer, ignore the emailed press releases that I've been sent to write up for the news, and start looking in the recruitment section for PR and communications roles. There are a couple and so I log into my personal emails and send the links to myself.

'Tell Pete I'm going to skip today's meeting,' I say to Mason when he gets up to go to the editorial meeting. Pete won't argue with me. He knows he's pissed me off and as half the meeting is going to be talking about what happened yesterday, I don't want to be there. In fact, I don't want to be in this office at all, but I can't just walk out.

I email Julia. I still haven't told her about yesterday, but she always cheers me up.

To: Julia

From: Abbie

How's it going today?

How are things?Is the carpet down yet?

I'm grateful that she instantly replies.

·   ·   ·

To: Abbie

From: Julia

Re: How's it going today?

Carpet fitters are currently hammering away in the sitting room, in between requests for cups of tea. I'm trying to keep Lucy and James entertained in the kitchen, but Lucy keeps wanting to go help. I'd give anything to be able to go back to work and have a whole day to myself without any nappies, washing, crying, sick — or decorating!

Besides that we're all fine. Hope you're well. Call me when you can. I need some adult conversation!

JULIA IS ACTUALLY A VERY good venture capitalist. Trained as an accountant and quickly proved that she has a good eye for detail as well as the gut instincts to spot a great new idea. She's supposed to have three months maternity leave and then get back into the fray, but at this rate she's going to be calling up and asking to go back to work early.

You'd like Julia – she's one of those women who everyone adores, no edges to her, just naturally friendly and capable. I can't call her from here, but I'm going to ring her when I get home and tell her what's been going on. I text her back and let her know.

I take my last sip of coffee and it's back to reality for me.

I spend the rest of the day job hunting or writing up extremely boring news stories. It's like Pete has me on desk duty. Does he think it will keep me out of trouble, or is he thinking he's doing me a favour and giving me an easy day? I decide to leave half an hour early so I can pop into the supermarket before picking up Ben as we're running low on food.

Somewhere about halfway round the supermarket I feel

absolutely shattered. I've almost gone into a bit of a trance. I'm sure yesterday and the resulting shock are a big reason, but I'm also convinced the lights they have in these places have some kind of soporific effect. I'm in the tea and coffee aisles when my eyes start to get heavy, and I begin to yawn every thirty seconds. Of course it could also be the effect of having wandered into warmer climes from the frozen wastelands of the chiller cabinets, but whatever it is, I feel exhausted.

I can barely get through the cleaning items and toilet roll aisle to the wine section, it's absolute purgatory, but the thought of a delicious bottle of malbec pushes me on. I think I deserve a proper glass of wine after yesterday. I pick up a *Thomas and Friends* comic for Ben too, to ease my conscience.

The checkouts are all busy so we're queuing six people deep. I'm almost asleep on my feet when I'm suddenly cured by a handsome thirty-something man coming and standing behind me. Julia keeps telling me I need to get dating again and I confess that it has been on my mind lately. He's definitely single because despite the absence of a wedding ring, (which isn't always a guarantee they're not married or committed), his basket is filled with ready-made meals and quantities that clearly suggest a single person. Southern fried chicken, steak and ready-prepared mashed potato, but no veg. No self-respecting wife or partner would let him eat that.

I swish my hair a little and I'm quick to get the *Next Customer* sign ready for him. He thanks me. He even sounds alright. I'm doing everything I can, holding in my stomach, smiling sweetly at everyone, and I make an effort to strike up a rapport with the checkout assistant so he thinks I'm nice...

'Catchy isn't it?' says the grey-haired smiley woman scanning my food.

'Sorry?' She's caught me unawares.

'The *Thomas the Tank* music. Watch it with my grandson and I always end up humming it after.'

Oh no.

I look at 'him', and he's smiling at me.

Oh no, no, no. I've been humming the theme tune to my son's favourite TV show like some demented mother, and all the time I thought I was wowing him with my sparkling personality and subtle goddess flirting. I'm mortified. I leave as rapidly as I can, that bottle of wine definitely on the agenda for when I get home.

5

———

I've slept lighter since becoming a mother. I guess your sub-conscious listens out for signs of your child being in distress or danger, having been trained by their hungry crying. In my early twenties, I could have slept through an earthquake. Tonight, I'm woken at just gone midnight by a noise, but it's not Ben.

I wake up with a jolt, my heart thumping in my chest.

What was that?

Ben's monitor is just static, but I slip out of bed and cross to his room to be sure. He's there lying in his cot and I wait a moment to see the reassuring rise and fall of his breathing. Before I leave, I sweep the shadows in the room to check there's nobody or nothing in there with him.

I stand on the landing and listen down the stairs. I hear the fridge click on in the silence. A gentle whirr as it works to maintain the right temperature.

I'm just about to go back to bed when I hear it again. It sounds like something at the back door.

For a moment I'm paralysed with fear. A thousand scenarios running through my mind – none of them good.

Could the shadow man from last night now be at my back door, trying to get in?

I instantly switch into protective-mummy-mode and run into my room, grabbing the staple gun from where I've hidden it so Ben can't get it. It's one of those industrial-strength staplers that shoot out big, razor-sharp metal staples like an automatic gun. The guy who fitted our WiFi when we moved in forgot it. I did report it but they never collected it and I keep it as a weapon for just this type of occasion. If anyone is trying to break into my house, they'll get a salvo of staples shot in their face.

I don't want to call the police if I'm just being paranoid, but I keep my finger poised over the house phone's call button. I've already typed in the emergency number.

Slowly I creep down the stairs, listening and peering around the ground floor as it comes into view. The back door is to the right of the stairs through the kitchen door so I can't see it from here. I put my back against the wall and peer around the door frame.

There's definitely someone there. A figure dressed in black.

My heart is thumping in my chest and I forget to breath. It's only after my thumb has pressed the call button and the operator asks me what service I need, that I gasp 'police' and give them my address.

The woman on the other end is very calm and reassuring as I tell her that someone is breaking into my house, but I can feel my breathing shallow and rapid as I peer round the door frame again to see where he is. He has some kind of a tool and has cut a hole in the back door's window pane. A black leather-gloved hand is reaching through fumbling for the door lock inside. It's just one of those that you turn. He's going to be in here any minute.

I can't let that happen.

I run into the kitchen screaming at the top of my voice and fire staples at his hand.

'Go away!' I scream.

The first staple hits the wooden door frame, and then the second one ricochets off the glass. As the third one releases, he's realised what's going on and pulls his hand back and the staple thuds into the door where his hand had been. He looks at me, but I can't see anything of him except the whites of his eyes and a logo of a yellow frog on his black woollen hat. His face is covered by what seems to be a black scarf, but I can't be sure about anything, because he's gone.

I see him run across the garden and leap up the side wall and over it. Whoever he is, he's fit and he's long gone before I remember I've left the emergency line operator still hanging on my phone. She insists on staying on the line with me until the response team has arrived.

I go around turning every light on downstairs, holding my staple gun like a revolver as I sweep each room to make sure nobody else has managed to get in another way.

Why was he here? Why break into my house? Was he here to steal something or hurt us? Tessa from advertising's words come back to me. Could this have anything to do with yesterday? Have I have put us in danger?

I go upstairs and check Ben again and remember to put my dressing gown on. I don't want to open the door to the police in my PJs. By the time I've got back downstairs, I can see the blue flashing lights coming through my curtains. I put the stapler away – I don't want them confiscating it as a dangerous weapon, and open the front door as two uniformed officers are walking up the path. My legs have started to feel shaky.

'Mrs Murphy, are you OK? We've received a report of a break-in,' The first one says to me.

'I'm fine. He was in the back garden, trying to get in the back door.'

My bravery evaporates now that they're here and I want to cry. My throat feels tight and there's a burning at the back of my eyes.

'Can you show us?'

I lead the two officers through to the back.

'There a side gate?' one of them says immediately on seeing the back door.

'Yes, but it's locked and the garden is fully enclosed, he jumped over that wall.' I point to where the black-clad figure jumped up and over. One of them heads straight back out the front door and goes to investigate what's over the other side of the wall. The other one stays with me.

'Did you get a look at him?'

'He was totally covered. I couldn't see his face, and he was wearing gloves, but his woollen hat had a yellow frog logo on it.'

'You ever had break-ins like this around here before?'

'No. I witnessed a murder yesterday. You don't think it's related to that, do you?'

'Murder?'

'Yes, the Stuart Porter one,' I add.

His face changes slightly, but it's hard to read.

'OK, doesn't sound like we'll get any forensics off this door. Probably just an opportunist, but I'll flag it up to DI Roberts. He's lead on that case.'

The other officer returns, breathless. 'Nothing.' he says to his colleague.

'The dog unit is at another incident right now, or we'd

call them over to see if they can track him. I don't think there's much more we can do now.'

I give a little nod.

'Do you have anything you can cover the door with?'

We all turn and look at my back-door window which has a neat round circle taken out of the glass.

'A piece of ply or board?' the officer adds. 'You could call out an emergency glazier but they'll charge an arm and a leg at this time of night. You just need something to tide you over until morning.' He walks over to it again and then turns, frowning. 'What are the staples for?'

My brain whizzes. Should I come clean or make up an excuse? I decide on simplicity. 'I've got a staple gun I was doing some DIY with, I picked that up to try to stop him coming in. He had his hand through.'

'Good thinking,' the officer says to me, much to my relief.

Both their radios come alive with a request for back-up – there's some fight going on in town.

'Will you be OK? Can you call someone?' he asks me.

I can see he's itching to answer the call. There's nothing they can do here and DIY is not their remit.

'I'll be fine, thank you.'

'We'll have someone contact you in the morning, take a statement,' he says as they head back out the front door.

When I close it, I stand for a minute, listening to their car pull away and the flashing blue of their lights disappear from the street.

Silence. I'm alone again and I suddenly feel scared. I've got to board up that hole. There's no way I'm ever going to get any sleep unless I can be sure he can't get back in easily.

I grab the tool kit under the stairs. What can I use to cover the hole? We don't have pieces of ply just lying around, but there's a tray my parents had given me years ago. It's stained and I was thinking about throwing it out, but I'd put it under the stairs as I was quite attached to it. I cannibalise it, ripping off the surround so that I'm left with just the board of the tray. It's the perfect size. We've got little tacks and nails, so I use those to gently fix it in place, being careful not to break any more glass and not to be too noisy and wake Ben up.

Then I stand back and look at my handiwork. It's covered it, at least. It will have to do.

But it won't do. It won't do at all. If he can make a hole in that window, he can make a hole in another one. How do I know he's not going to come back in an hour when I've gone to bed, and try to get in through the patio doors, or a window? My stomach knots and twists with anxiety. I've got to protect Ben. I start crying at this point. I feel very alone and I'm very afraid.

I contemplate phoning Dylan. He's Ben's father, even if he couldn't care about protecting me, perhaps he'll come over and help guard Ben? But then I remind myself of the fact that he's barely even visited his son since he left. Does he really care that much?

What if Stuart Porter has sent round someone to kill me, to stop me testifying against him? What if Tessa is right and I'm in danger?

I start pacing round the kitchen. Maybe I should grab Ben and go and check into a hotel? But what if he follows me there? People can still get murdered in hotel rooms, right? I'd be in a strange place and I think I'd feel more vulnerable. Besides, I don't have much money. I'd probably be able to afford one night but then we'd have to come home again.

My parents are over two hundred miles away, Julia is a

hundred miles away. I could get in the car and drive to hers but she's got enough on her plate – and what if he followed me there? Then I'd be putting her and her kids in danger.

Am I going crazy? Have the last two days turned me into a paranoid emotional wreck? I know I'm tired and I know someone has just tried to break into my house so my nerves are bound to be on edge. I don't even have my mobile phone still. If he cuts the house line then I'm totally isolated.

My mind goes back to sitting in the police car at the murder scene. The sympathetic eyes of DS Nicholas Barnes. He gave me his card, told me to call him if I needed anything. Does that stretch to one a.m. in the morning?

The paranoid thoughts are getting worse. Every murder and thriller movie I've ever seen and book I've ever read are throwing up scenarios in my mind.

I dial DS Barnes's number.

'Hello...' He sounds like he's not asleep, although I'm probably kidding myself.

'DS Barnes, it's Abigail Murphy.'

'Hi. Are you OK?' I can hear the concern in his voice straight away, and it's exactly what I need right now.

'I've just had someone try to break into the house.'

'Have you dialled 999?'

'Yes, they've been. He's gone and they had to leave. Could this be related to Stuart Porter? Are we in danger? I don't know what to think anymore...'

'Give me your address. I'll come over now.'

'Are you sure? It's nearly half one.'

'I'm sure. You're scared. I'm not leaving you alone like this. I'll come and make sure they've gone and your house is secure.'

'Thank you...' I can barely get the words out because my

throat has filled with the effort of holding down tears. 'I'm at twenty-three Rose Stone Avenue.'

'I'll be fifteen minutes.'

I collapse onto one of the kitchen chairs in relief. What is happening to me? And could we be in serious danger?

6

———

DS Nicholas Barnes is true to his word. Fifteen minutes after calling him, he is at my front door.

'Are you OK? Where were they trying to get in?'

'Round the back, they jumped over the wall.'

'OK, I'll do a quick walk around first,' he says to me and immediately jogs off round the side of the house. He's got jeans and a T-shirt on which shows up his muscular arms, legs, and chest. I feel instantly reassured.

I have to confess that in the fifteen minutes before he came, I did go upstairs, clean my teeth again and try to tidy myself up without looking like I'd just put make up on again because he was coming round. I also pulled on some jeans and a top. It was one thing being in my dressing gown when the emergency responders came, but it felt odd to open the door to DS Barnes that way. All the time I'd been on high alert, looking out the window into the dark garden, listening for any sounds, and I think I must have checked in on Ben about ten times.

It doesn't take long for DS Barnes to come back.

'No signs,' he says. 'I suspect they're long gone. Probably frightened off when the other officers arrived.'

'They made a hole in the back door glass,' I tell him, opening the front door and showing him in.

He walks into the kitchen with me and immediately goes and looks at the damage. The tray I've used to cover the hole looks incongruous. It has brightly coloured puppy dogs all over it. Innocence thrust into a crime scene.

'How did you scare him off, was it the officers arriving?'

'I shot staples at him,' I say almost apologetically, although really, I feel quite proud of myself.

Nick raises an eyebrow. 'Well done. Have you got anyone who can stay here with you tonight?'

'Do you think he'll come back...?'

'It's possible. This door isn't secure, and we don't know why he was here and how motivated he is.'

That knots my stomach up all over again. 'Do you think this is related to what I witnessed?' I ask him outright, looking directly in his eyes. I need an honest answer.

He hesitates. 'It's possibly just a coincidence, Porter is safely locked up. Unless you do have other evidence which could be used against him here?'

I shake my head. 'Honestly, I wasn't following them. I was late and thought it would be a shortcut. Why does it matter so much to the police if I was investigating him anyway?'

DS Barnes sighs and gives me a long hard stare, creasing his mouth in thought. I get the feeling there's something he's not telling me, and he avoids my question. I'm a journalist, I get that a lot with people. They think the second they've said something to me, I'm going to go and put it in the paper. I also get the impression he thinks I'm holding out on him.

'If you want, I can stay on your sofa tonight. I don't like the idea of leaving you on your own. Tomorrow morning you can get the door fixed and put in some extra security.'

'Thank you,' I reply weakly. A wave of relief washes over me. I'd had visions of sitting up all night armed with my stapler and a carving knife, watching the door and patrolling the other rooms in the house. Now, I might actually be able to get some sleep and most importantly, know that Ben is going to be safe. I'm suddenly feeling exhausted. 'I'm sorry to have called you so late.'

'It's fine. I never get to sleep until well after midnight.'

'Can I get you anything DS Barnes?' I ask him.

'Nick, call me Nick. No, I'm good. You get upstairs, you must be tired. I'll be fine.'

I could hug the man I'm so relieved that he's here and taking charge. But I don't. Instead, I leave him as he settles down on the sofa and I take myself back to bed.

I FEEL TIRED, but I can't fall asleep straight away. You don't go through that much of an adrenaline surge and then immediately relax. I lie in bed for what feels like forever, running over the last forty-eight hours in my head over and over again. At some point sleep gives me a merciful release – but not for long.

Ben's baby monitor lurches into action and I'm suddenly awake again, heart pounding to the sounds of my son calling for me. I race across the landing to his room, panicking that I'll find someone else in there with him, but when I push the door open all I see is Ben.

'Mumma, mumma!' he says, arms open for me to pick him up.

I wonder what's woken him?

I pick him up and creep out of his room. As we cross the landing, the light in the downstairs hall goes on and I see a shadow against the wall at the bottom of the stairs.

'Abigail!'

It's Nick.

'Is everything alright?'

'I think it's just Ben having a bad dream,' I reply.

Ben is even more alert now that he's heard another voice and cranes to see where it's coming from.

'Do you need me to come up to check around?' Nick asks.

My house is only two bedrooms and a bathroom. I know there was nobody in my room, or Ben's, so I push the bathroom door open with my foot and peer around the door.

'It's OK, we're fine,' I finally reply.

'OK. Goodnight then,' Nick answers and the light turns back off downstairs.

I carry Ben into my bed – there is no way he's going to settle in his own now. It's just coming up to 5 a.m. and he looks wide awake. Usually if he's allowed into bed with Mummy he soon curls up with his back to me, snuggling in as close as he can, disappearing off into sleep, sheltered and cocooned from nightmares. But not this morning.

This morning he rolls around and sits up, lies back down again and bounces around for about half an hour. He then turns his attentions to me. I'm just drifting off to sleep and a little finger grabs my eyelids trying to lift them up. Next, he flings himself at me, trying to sleep on my head so that I nearly suffocate. Then it's a finger in my ear or up my nose. This goes on and on until finally, he falls back to sleep, pushed in so close to me that he's nearly shoving me out of bed. Fifteen minutes later, the alarm goes off. It's six forty-five. Good morning Wednesday.

I manage to slip out of bed and into the shower without waking Ben, who is of course now extremely tired and fast asleep after his early morning mummy-poking, but at least it enables me to get myself going and ready. When we both go downstairs, Nick is still eyes closed on the sofa. The guy looks hot even when he's asleep. But seeing him lying there makes me realise that the sofa isn't all that large – he must have had an uncomfortable night's sleep, as well as a disturbed one. I really do appreciate his being here.

I don't wake him, and instead go into the kitchen and put some coffee on as well as make Ben some breakfast. I feel like I've got a dry hangover, even though I only had two glasses of wine last night. My head is fuzzy and pounding with the disturbed night. I stare at the puppy dogs on the door and decide that I'm going to email Pete and tell him I've got to work from home today. I toy with the idea of not taking Ben to Jo's, but decide against it because I know I'll never get any work done if he's here with me. I'm also going to have to probably crash out for a nap at some point – I'm not sure I'm going to be able to get through the day.

'Morning,' Nick's voice comes from behind me.

I turn and smile. 'Morning. Thank you so much for this,' I say to him. 'I really do appreciate it and I'm sorry if the sofa was uncomfortable.'

He smiles back and pushes his hands through his hair. 'It was fine. I've slept in far worse places, believe me.'

'Coffee?' I offer.

He nods. 'I've got a good guy who can come and fit you with new locks and a security system, do you want his number?'

'Please,' I say.

'Tell him that I suggested you call him, he owes me a favour so he should come out quickly for you.'

I'M surprised at just how quick Nick's guy does come. Nick offers to stay at the house while I take Ben to Jo's and by the time I've got back, Denzil is there working on the back door.

'I've got to head off and into work,' Nick says to me the second I get back. 'Denzil will sort you out and I'll call you later to check everything is OK.'

'Thank you so much for everything,' I say as he disappears out the front door. I wish he didn't have to go. He raises a hand to show he's heard me and is gone. Even though Denzil's in the house, I feel like a security blanket has just been taken from me.

'I can do you a couple of locks on here to make it harder for anyone to open the door, but you need some locks on them windows too.' Denzil nods at the window above my sink. 'If I was you, I'd be putting in a proper security system with an alarm.'

'They're expensive though aren't they?' I say to him.

'Depends what you want, if you wanna be wired up to some monitoring station or not. You can get a camera that alerts you if someone goes into a room for about twenty quid on Amazon. Don't need to be expensive, but gives peace of mind.'

'Thanks,' I say, 'I'll have a look. Yes please to window locks. If you could ensure all the windows and doors are secure, I'd appreciate it.'

'Sure. Nick's told me mates' rates too,' Denzil adds with a wink.

I silently thank Nick again in my head. My fast-declining bank balance will be grateful. There's just no way I can afford a fully wired-up security system right now.

I'm just making Denzil his third cup of tea when the phone goes. I don't recognise the number.

'Mrs Murphy, it's DI Conor Roberts, do you have a moment?'

He must be checking up on me after last night's break-in.

'Yes of course,' I say amenably.

'I've got your mobile phone here for you, we've finished with it. Plus, we'd like you to come into the station to take part in an identity parade please, to pick out the person you saw on Monday?'

'OK, right, yes sure.'

'Will you be free at two p.m. this afternoon?'

'Yes that's fine. Do you know about the attempted break-in at my house last night?' I have to ask. I'm quite shocked he hasn't mentioned it.

There's a few moments of silence. 'No. I hadn't been made aware. Did you report it? Did officers attend?'

'Yes, he ran off.'

'Right, I'll look into it.'

And that was it. No sympathy, no discussion. He just says he'll see me at two. Definitely not the warm type. Definitely not the type to turn up in the middle of the night and sleep on your sofa to make sure you're safe.

By eleven-thirty, Denzil is done. He explains all the keys to me and says he'll send his bill on. I happily wave him off and then turn back to an empty house. The silence hits me like a pillow thump in the face. I'm good alone, I will happily spend time in my own company and don't have to always be surrounded by people, but the last forty-eight hours have unnerved me. I want to seek others like the lone wildebeest on the tundra who doesn't want to be the straggler. The easy one for the lions to pick off. Yet I really don't want to have to go into work. I'm still annoyed with Pete – and I don't want to have to watch Mason writing my story. I do what I always do: I call Julia and tell her about my Monday morning.

'Oh my word! Why didn't you call me? You must have been so scared!'

Then I tell her about the attempted break-in last night.

'Holy crap Abs, I'd be a wreck. Do you think it's connected? Are the police giving you any protection?'

'I don't know, and nothing official. There is one really nice detective who stayed at the house last night...'

'Oh yeah?'

'Not like that! He stayed on the sofa. The back door wasn't secure and he didn't want to leave us on our own. He is rather tasty though.'

'And you're going to identify this killer guy later today?'

'Yeah.'

'You make sure you ask them, they can offer witness protection and stuff like that can't they?'

'I'll speak to them.'

'You know you're always welcome here if you want to get away.'

'Thank you, but I think you've got enough on your plate.'

'Oh, all's fine here. Everything has returned to a scene of calm utopia today – because Oscar's due home of course! He'll walk in the door and the baby will be happily gurgling in clean clothes on the brand-new carpet, and his siblings quietly playing with their toys like a scene from *Mary Poppins*. I'll have done the three loads of washing and Ziggy cat will stroll in as though he hasn't been missing since yesterday lunchtime when he ran off upset by the carpet fitters. Oscar'll think it's been like this all the time. So I'd love it if you came and actually Oscar might appreciate it too as otherwise there might be another murder for you to witness if he dares tell me how lucky I am to be able to stay at home with the kids while he has to go and work away, staying in a hotel room and eating out every night!'

I giggle. Julia can always lighten my mood.

'Ah, if only. But I've basically had to take today off work and I can't push my luck too far.'

'Let me know how the ID parade goes, you gonna have to walk up and down in front of them to pick out the right one?'

'I'm not sure, I hope not...' The thought hadn't actually crossed my mind and makes my stomach squirm with nerves.

THANKFULLY, I discover that the ID parade is no longer like those we watch in the movies. Modern technology means it's all done on video now.

'This is VIPER technology, video ID parade electronic recording, which means you don't have to get anywhere near the accused,' the young guy from the ID unit is explaining to me. I haven't even seen DI Roberts yet, but I'm told he's coming soon. 'The film lasts about three minutes and you should watch it at least twice. There'll be eight men on the video, looking direct to camera and then turning left and right. We will be recording the session and you're to say if you see the man who you believe killed Jordan Christie. The defence solicitor will be watching and DI Roberts and DS Fuller will also be there.'

All sounds pretty straight forward to me and I sign some forms before being shown into the room. DI Roberts arrives at this point, closely followed by DS Fuller.

I hadn't really looked at Fuller yesterday, most of my interaction was with Roberts. He's got jet black hair and clear pale skin that is already showing the hint of regrowth from where he has shaved this morning. He's younger than Roberts, a good fifteen or twenty years younger. Slim build, but wiry and fit, and although he's probably nearly six feet, he looks shorter than that up against his tall colleague.

'Mrs Murphy, thank you for coming in,' DI Roberts says to me, formally shaking my hand. Maybe that's his style, old school, slightly stand-offish. Perhaps it's not that he just doesn't like me. 'Here's your phone,' he adds, handing me my mobile.

'Thanks.' I take it with a surge of relief and joy. How attached we are to these things.

'I looked into that attempted burglary last night, we'll get a statement off you later but at present there's nothing to link it to the case, although it is a bit of a coincidence so we need to be aware.'

'Am I likely to be in danger with this?' I ask him directly.

'We've not got any reason to think so, Mrs Murphy, but if anything like that happens again I want you to call me.'

'I rang DS Barnes, he came and helped,' I tell him.

There's no missing the muscles flexing in his jaw as it tightens and the glance that he and Fuller exchange. What have they got against Nick? Roberts was short about him at the murder scene, saying he was in charge of the case not DS Barnes. He's clearly not a fan. Or maybe it's jealousy.

'I had his card,' I say, hoping he gets the hint that Nick had been the only one who could be bothered to give me one and be there when I needed him.

'I'll give you my number...' Roberts says, just as the door opens and a couple of others come into the room. That's the signal that we're ready to start the video ID parade and he doesn't get to finish his sentence.

The ID parade is a doddle. Takes five seconds to recognise him. Stuart Porter. He is number five. They've tried to find men who look similar to Stuart, but his face, staring at me when he drove past, is indelibly marked in my head. There are various mutterings and hushed conversations and DI Roberts walks me to the exit.

'Thank you for your time,' he says to me. 'If anything else comes to mind, or you have reason to be concerned, then please call me directly.' He hands over his card.

What does he mean if anything else comes to mind? He's still convinced that I'm lying about not investigating Porter before Monday, I'm sure of it.

'We'll up the patrols around your neighbourhood,' he adds, 'but any signs that someone might be attempting to break in again, dial 999.'

'I will,' I say, taking the offered card. As I walk away, I can feel his eyes burning into my back. There is definitely something about that man I don't like, and I think the feeling is mutual.

Dylan's family were horrified when he walked out on us, my mother-in-law Cheryl particularly. After all, Ben is their grandson too. I get a phone call from her once every couple of weeks. It's usually after she's tried unsuccessfully to speak to her son, who never answers her phone calls and when he does, pretends he either has to go into a meeting or the signal is failing. I suppose his lack of love towards his mother should have been a warning sign to me.

Today Cheryl decides to call. She's one of those women who talk loudly on the phone so you need to keep the receiver about six inches away from your ear to avoid being deafened. Usually she's had a glass or two of vino while cooking her dinner, which explains the volume issue.

'How are you both? How's my little boy?' she immediately asks as soon as I pick up, without saying hello or announcing who she is.

'Cheryl,' I exclaim, midway through cooking our own dinners. 'Ben's playing with his *Thomas the Tank* set at the moment.' The Thomas and Friends train set was a present from Cheryl and Joe, Dylan's father. He doesn't say much Joe. One of those blokes you always get the impression would rather be tinkering in his shed on his own, or pottering around the garden – anywhere other than having to make idle chatter.

'Is he out of nappies yet?' She has asked me that question virtually every single phone call we've had since Ben was six months. She's convinced that her children were out of nappies by one year old. Personally, I can't see Dylan ever having been able to contain himself at that age – he's still full of shit now!

'No, not yet, next year Cheryl.'

The conversation carries on but I get the impression she's holding something back, that something has upset her. Then she just comes right out with it.

'So, have you seen Dylan?'

'No,' I reply, 'he's not been to see Ben for nearly a month.'

'He's been away you know', she volunteers, 'with *her*.'

Her is of course the one he's now living with. She was his personal trainer at the gym. I'd met her a couple of times – before I knew she was sleeping with my husband. Harper Rodriguez. I can't deny she's got a fit body, but she's not got any real shape to her. At least I've got boobs. Although it appears they weren't impressive enough to keep Dylan. Truth is, I don't think he was ready to settle down even though he'd been the one to ask me to marry him. When we were able to travel and go out and be just a couple things were fine, but as soon as Ben came along, he started to drift. His loss. One day he'll regret leaving his son.

Cheryl hates Harper the harpy, as we call her, because she's broken up Cheryl's grandson's family, and to be honest

I can't see the harpy ever wanting children, especially as Dylan doesn't seem to want the one he already has.

Cheryl is going to miss me as her daughter in law. I phoned her, made sure she got all the birthday, Christmas and Mothers' Day cards and pressies she was entitled to. She'll not be getting that from *her*.

Every time that Cheryl rings, I secretly hope for some news that it's all gone wrong for Dylan, all come crashing down on him. That she's dumped him, or that one day a great big heavy weight has landed straight on his and his personal trainer's heads in the gym. As you can see, I've learnt to deal with this situation as a mature adult – I'm not bitter or harbouring any feelings of revenge at all!

I make the mistake of telling Cheryl about my last forty-eight hours of hell and it takes all my skills of persuasion to get her off the phone so that Ben and I can eat our dinners. It's the reason I've not rung my own Mum and Dad. They'd only worry themselves sick.

After the ID parade, it does feel like I've got a bit of closure. They're going to contact me about the trial at some point, but these things take time. I hope that will be the end of it for a while and we can get life back to normal. It's only the image of the gloved hand coming through my door last night, that keeps a niggling fear in the back of my mind.

I GET Ben to bed and by nine o'clock, I'm sitting at my kitchen table surrounded by bank statements, bills, and my calculator. I have one column for outgoings and one for incomings. They very clearly don't match up. I've not had a penny from Dylan since he left. Whenever I've brought the subject up he says, 'We'll discuss it', only of course we never do. I know I could take him to court, but as somebody else in my boat recently said to me, if you go after him for the money he's going to want his pound of flesh. We haven't seen him for a month; I feel sad for Ben, but I think asking for money would make Dylan come round for the wrong reasons.

There are times I've felt like killing Dylan, times like this when I'm sitting alone in the evening contemplating financial ruin. He's no doubt out having a good time with 'her' – no responsibilities, no worries. I know this feeling doesn't fit with my 'non-bitter, I'm going to get over him' promise, but what the hell. Every now and then there's an anger that builds up inside of me and I wish I could just punch him, or worse. I won't, of course, but it can't stop me thinking about it.

I have several unread emails from the loan company I'm already with, offering me new deals, so I look through those. I also check out the credit card balance transfer deals online. I decide to increase the loan amount and the loan repayment period so that it's costing me less each month, that way I can pay off the more expensive debts like the credit card bill which is screaming at me from where it's propped up in the fruit bowl.

It's frightening just how quickly you can run up debts. They don't take into account your change in circumstance. Based on my current earnings and previous credit record, I could easily go out and spend tens of thousands of pounds on credit cards and overdrafts. The banks seem to do everything in their power to get you into debt, increasing your limit if you're paying credit bills off monthly, and all in the hope that you'll spend over what you can afford so that you have to start paying them interest. Then, when you can least afford it, they hit you with the extra charges. I'm convinced they want us to be irresponsible, to get worried at the end of every month. And if we struggle to pay back, then it's more money for them, and if you can't pay, that's when they get nasty. I'm amazed the banks haven't brought back debtors schemes where those people who can't afford to pay their credit bills are put to work mailing out 'upgrade to platinum card' offers to other unsuspecting customers.

I don't want to get stressed about it. I'll call up the loan company tomorrow. Apparently, I can borrow another fifteen thousand if I want to. Mexico is looking a real possibility.

I start on the remainders of my wine and decamp to the sofa in the sitting room. The wine is red, so I convince myself it's good for me. Of course that's not what the latest 'expert research' says. I read something over the weekend which claims a glass of wine can increase your chance of breast cancer. I prefer to believe the reports that say it's good for your heart and the antioxidants are actually cancer preventative. They're a bit like horoscopes, all these scientific reports; you can pick and choose which ones you want to believe. If we listened to every one that came out, we wouldn't eat or drink a thing. I'm going to drink my red wine and enjoy it – the scientists can go study something else.

I'm feeling quite relaxed and the image of Nick Barnes lying on the sofa this morning comes into my mind. He'd texted earlier to check everything had gone OK with Denzil and told me to text or call anytime if I was worried. I'm thinking about how nice it would be to have him sitting here next to me, when suddenly a loud roar comes from Ben's baby monitor. My heart lurches and I jump off the sofa, nearly spilling my wine.

In seconds I am racing upstairs, listening out for anything else, but just as I reach the landing I realise what it is. Ben has an animal shapes jigsaw puzzle which makes a noise each time you put the right animal into its hole. The pieces are light sensitive and he's left them out so as darkness has fallen, they've reacted. As I reach his bedroom the elephant is already joining in the fun and I quickly gather them all and take them downstairs. Ben is fast asleep, oblivious to everything.

8

———

I head to bed quite early and fall asleep quickly out of sheer exhaustion. I've left the lights on downstairs and kept all the doors open so that I'll hear anything. The previous night means I am on edge but in the end I can't keep my eyes open and I slip into a fitful sleep. It's the sound of my mobile ringing which wakes me. It's not even midnight but I don't recognise the number. Sleepily I answer it and put my phone to my ear.

'Hello?'

'If you want that boy of yours to grow up, withdraw your statement to police. You're a lying bitch.' The voice is slightly muffled but there's no mistaking what they said. It yanks me into consciousness.

The phone goes dead.

I turn icy cold and my stomach twists. I almost throw up, dry retching.

I scrabble out of bed and across the landing to Ben's room.

He's fine. Asleep. Oblivious.

I rush back to my room and grab the stapler, then head

downstairs, checking every window and door. There's no sign that anybody has come in.

My heart is still beating wildly and I feel breathless. What do I do? It seems wrong to ring 999 – after all nothing has happened, it was just a phone call. Perhaps I should call DI Roberts, but I can't see him going out of his way to help me. I press dial on DS Barnes's number. He said he doesn't sleep until after midnight and I know he's looking out for our best interests. I just hope it doesn't get him into trouble with Roberts.

'Abbie, is everything OK?' he answers.

'I'm sorry to call you so late again.' I hear my voice, it's got the tone of slight panic. 'But I just had a threatening phone call on my mobile. They said they'd hurt Ben if I don't withdraw my statement. I don't know what to do. Should I call DI Roberts?'

'There's probably not much he can do. They'll almost certainly have used a burner phone. Do you have the number?'

I read it out to him and hear him scribble it down.

'I'm scared. What if they try to hurt Ben? Maybe I should withdraw.'

'Nine times out of ten these are just idle threats, they're trying their luck. Leave it with me a moment, I'll call you back.' He ends the call and I'm left staring at my phone, wishing he was here and not just a voice in my ear.

I'm totally wired. There's no way I'm going to get to sleep now. I get up and go and check on Ben again before heading downstairs, still clutching my staple gun. My mobile rings. It's DS Barnes calling back.

'It's a burner and it's offline already. We've no way of tracing it apart from trying to work out roughly what area they were calling from.'

'I don't know what to do,' I say to him, tears welling up now. When you have a small human being to look after, you realise just how vulnerable you can be.

'They're trying to scare you; this reaction is exactly what they want.'

'I know, but I can't risk it. I can't risk Ben.'

'Has DI Roberts suggested any support for you?'

'No, he just said to call him. I suppose I should have, I don't want you getting into any trouble.'

'You won't get me into trouble, don't worry about me, but you should ring him in the morning.'

'Yeah. Yeah I'll do that,' I say.

The static hangs between us, a frisson of unspoken thoughts.

'Look, I'm more than happy to sleep on your sofa again if it would make you feel better. It's not exactly official protection, but if it helps...'

My heart leaps at the offer but I try not to sound too eager. 'I couldn't ask you to do that again, especially as the sofa can't be comfortable.'

'It's fine. I'm happy to if it helps, at least until you get something else in place.'

The prospect of him being in my house is a thoroughly pleasant one. The prospect of having weeks, or months even of this stress, is most certainly not. I hear what he's saying about it being an idle threat, but I'm not willing to do this if it in any way puts Ben in danger.

'Thank you,' I say, and I immediately go and make myself presentable for when he gets here.

. . .

DS Nick Barnes arrives twenty minutes later and this time he's carrying a small bag. 'Brought my work clothes,' he explains to me.

I've also prepped a bit better this time, and have a properly kitted-out duvet and pillow for him. I'll get a towel later.

'How you doing?' he asks me when we're in the kitchen.

'Been better,' I reply and I can't help looking into his eyes. They draw me in. 'Do you want to go straight to sleep or would you like a glass of wine?' I reach for the half bottle I'd saved. I'd only managed to drink a tiny sip earlier before Ben's jigsaw puzzle interrupted me. I could really do with a drink now – anything to relax me.

DS Barnes studies me a moment and then gives a sympathetic smile. 'A small glass of wine won't hurt,' he says.

I do hope he's not looking at me like a sad case who needs some form of counselling, even if it is over a glass of wine, which unfortunately will be small as half a bottle is all I've got left.

I'm not sure if it's because I've now designated the sitting room area his bedroom, but we choose to sit on the high chairs at the breakfast bar in the kitchen to drink our wine.

'I'm really sorry you're having to go through this,' he says to me.

'It's not your fault.' I smile at him but then quickly have to look away because I'm finding myself too attracted to him for my own good.

'You know...' Nick begins, 'my dad was investigating the corruption in the council and I believe that's why he was killed. He suggested to me that Stuart Porter was behind it all, and a week later he was dead.'

I look back at his face, shocked. He's looking down at his glass of wine.

'You mean, you think Stuart Porter killed your dad?'

He gives a little nod of his head. 'No evidence of course, so I've never been able to prove it. But he has to be stopped. As long as we have him in custody then he can't go round hurting anyone else.'

'But he must have people working for him. Who was it that called me?'

'Was it male or female?'

'Male.'

Nick nods. 'Young sounding?'

I try to think back to the voice that woke me up. 'Yes, I'd say so. A young man. He'd tried to hide his voice a bit, but I caught the local accent.'

'Probably his son then. He's twenty-three. He's full of bluff. Wouldn't have the balls to go through with anything. Always been in his dad's shadow.'

I make a mental note to research Stuart Porter's son tomorrow and see if I can find any audio clips of him.

'Is that why you're not on this case? Because they think you have a conflict of interest?'

'Yeah...' Nick looks up and away and I get the feeling he's got something else to tell me but isn't yet ready to share it. He changes the subject. 'So, when did you and Ben's dad split up?'

'Three months ago.' I look at him and he's watching me closely. Neither of us turn away. 'It hadn't been great for a while. He was having an affair.'

'Ah, that's crap, sorry. It must be hard being on your own with a little one.'

'It's...' I don't want to make it sound like I'm not coping. 'It's taking adjustment,' I say to him. 'But we're better off without him. In all honesty, Dylan not being here hasn't made a huge difference apart from I don't get to share the bills anymore.'

I imagine how I'd be feeling now if it was Dylan sitting in front of me and not Nick. I wouldn't be feeling anywhere near as secure. There's something professional and calming about Nick which relaxes me. I guess that comes with his job. Dylan's a food buyer for a supermarket chain – not quite the same heroic quality to the role.

'Well we'd better get some sleep as it's work in the morning,' he says to me and we both get up, taking our glasses.

I head towards my dishwasher, but Nick turns towards the sink and that results in us virtually bumping into each other.

'Sorry,' he says looking at me. He's centimetres from me now. I can smell him. A heady mix of man and aftershave which merge into an intoxicating cloud that ensnares me and sends my hormones raging. I'm frozen. We're both staring at each other and there's no doubting that he fancies me as much as I do him.

I hear him place the glass onto the counter and then feel his lips on mine. My glass goes down and I curve into him, arching and willing him on, every sensation in my body heading south between my legs like some mass migration. *Shit*, he's such a good kisser, so much more passionate than Dylan.

Then suddenly it ends.

'Oh my God, I'm so sorry.' He suddenly backs away from me as though I've electrocuted him. 'That is just so unprofessional of me, I apologise. I shouldn't have done that.'

'It's OK,' I try to say, but I can see from the look on his face that he's horrified.

'No, no it's not OK. I'm here to help you, you're feeling vulnerable and I'm taking advantage. I am just so sorry.'

'You're not taking advantage. I am not complaining,' I say it more firmly this time and he stops and looks at me. I can see the battle of will on his face.

'Thank you, but this isn't the right time. For you. It was unfair of me. I really shouldn't have.'

I can see his mind's made up. Ever the protector. I go to bed wishing he'd ravaged me, but at least I now know he likes me. Nick Barnes has given me something far more pleasant to think about than Stuart Porter.

9

———————

leep was a tumble of fear and pleasure, dark shadows and blazing heroes. At least I do get some sleep with Nick in the house.

When I head down in the morning, I'm a little nervous in case last night has put him off helping us. Do I just carry on as though nothing happened?

Ben is the most wonderful ice breaker. He's sucking on his toast when Nick comes into the kitchen and chatters happily to him with a big smile on his face before offering up a soggy strip of his breakfast for Nick to eat. Nick pretends to eat it.

'Would you like a slightly less soggy piece of your own?' I ask him.

'Well, that might be nice, thanks.'

I turn to push some bread down in the toaster.

'I am sorry about last night. I shouldn't have taken advantage of you like that Abigail. I want to help you and that was selfish of me.'

'Honestly, it was fine,' I tell him again, but I can see he's beating himself up about it.

'You should ring DI Roberts this morning and report that phone call so he can investigate it officially. I can look into it too but he's running the inquiry and so you need to get it logged.'

'I will.' The toast pops up and I hand it to him. 'Coffee?'

'Please.'

'Do you think I should be worried?'

'I think you need to be on your guard, but as long as we can keep Stuart Porter locked up I'm sure you're both safe. He's a white-collar criminal. Gets his money from embezzling, bribing, and doing deals with backhanders. He's not a drugs dealer with a gang of desperate criminals working for him.'

'But he's a killer. He's proven that.'

'Yes. He has, but at the moment he's in a prison cell where hopefully we can keep him.'

I sigh, out of relief, not because I'm sad. Knowing Porter is locked up and having Nick around, takes the tension from my body. I realise I'm more relaxed when Nick is around – and although he's obviously still feeling guilty about last night, he has chilled a bit too. By the time he's had a shower and is ready for work, I really don't want him to go.

As he leaves, he reminds me to ring DI Roberts – and promises to call me later to check up on us.

I lock the door after he's gone and immediately dial DI Roberts's number.

'I had a threatening phone call last night. They've said they'll hurt Ben if I don't withdraw my testimony.'

'Mrs Murphy,' he says, he hasn't quite got round to calling me Abigail and actually I'm quite relieved he's not so familiar. 'Has anything else happened? Anyone come back round the house?'

'No but they knew my number.'

'Is it the same one you use for work?'

'Yes.'

'Then that's easy for anyone to obtain. I'm not dismissing this – we have to take it seriously – but the chances are it's someone who knows Stuart and they're just trying to scare you off.'

'I know they're trying to scare me off but I can't risk anything happening to my son.'

'I know.'

Does he though? Does he understand, or is he only thinking about his conviction success rate?

'How do you know the attempted burglary wasn't them too?'

'We can move you to a new address if you'd feel safer?'

I think about the implications of that for a moment.

'I don't see what that would achieve. I've got to work and Ben can't be stuck inside for weeks on end, so they'd just find us again.' What I really want is for this all to just be over, for us to be able to get on with our lives. 'Do you really still need me now anyway? If I didn't testify, haven't you got enough to convict him without me?'

'Not really Mrs Murphy, no. You were the only witness to the killing. He's arguing self-defence and your testimony conflicts with that.'

'That's just not true.'

'As you said.'

'But my son's life could be in danger.'

'I'll arrange for round-the-clock surveillance of your house until we can be sure that these are just empty threats. Do you have the number they called from? We can try to trace the call.'

I give him the number but I know what they'll find because Nick's already checked it out. I end the phone call with DI Roberts, not really feeling much better. I can't work out what he thinks of me. It's almost like he doesn't believe anything I say to him. Or perhaps he doesn't care. All he wants is his conviction. That's all well and good for him, but it's not his son's life on the line.

MY MIND IS BUZZING. What should I do? First thing is I do what every mother would: I don't let Ben out of my sight. I call up Pete and tell him that I'm not coming into work for a bit. He's sympathetic, tells me to take the rest of the week off but to keep him informed.

I let Jo know Ben isn't coming, and he and I enjoy some time together. I get the paints out and he draws pictures, or at least he scribbles in paint. By late morning I can tell he's tired and so we withdraw to the sofa. Ben watches Thomas and Friends and I get my laptop out. I start doing what I should have done two days ago: I begin researching Stuart Porter and his family.

His online reputation is impeccable. I read speeches he's made about how important it is that the council looks after taxpayers' money and gives transparent value. He preaches about the importance of family and how honoured he is to be serving his local community. There are photographs of him, his wife, Samantha, and their two sons, Jacob and Leo. Jacob is the eldest; he's twenty-two in the photo, and his brother Leo is seventeen. I switch my focus to Jacob but there's very little of him online. I try TikTok in the hope he's on there, but nothing comes up. The only way I'm going to hear his voice is if I speak to him. So, I find out where he works.

Jacob Porter is an estate agent. I go into my iPhone settings and turn 'Show my caller ID' off. I don't want him knowing it's me. I've done my prep – I've seen a house that he's down as being the agent for and so I can ask a question if needs be, but my heartbeat has got faster and my stomach feels tight when I dial.

A woman answers and so I ask to speak to Jacob Porter. She asks me to hold a moment while she transfers me and I hear some inane hold music come on. Twenty seconds later, Jacob says, 'Hello, how can I help?'

I have my hand over the mouthpiece so he can't hear a thing, but instantly I can tell that the caller this morning is not the same as the voice I'm hearing now. It wasn't Jacob Porter. I hang up.

My heart is beating hard and fast now and I give myself a couple of minutes to calm down. Perhaps it was the younger son. He'd be 18 now. I search online for anything about Leo Porter, but find nothing. He doesn't even seem to have a social media presence. I hit a brick wall with him. Then another thought comes to my mind. Could it have been Stuart who called me? You hear about mobile phones getting smuggled into prisons on a regular basis. It's not beyond the realms of possibility that it could have been Stuart himself.

I go back online and search for video clips of him. There are several. I play as many as I can find, but none of them sound like my caller. Stuart is older, his voice deeper. At first I'm relieved, but then I wonder who else it could be – and how dangerous they are.

10

———

I'm just putting together some lunch for Ben and I when my mobile rings. It's Dylan.

'What's going on Abbie? Mum tells me you saw a murder and now you've had someone try to break into the house. Is Ben OK?'

I feel a flood of mixed emotions at hearing his voice. Part of me wants to tell him everything, ask him to come round – the part of me that hears the familiarity in his voice, our shared history. Our shared parentage. The other half of me wants to tell him where to get off, ringing me up with his false concern. He hasn't even bothered to find out if we're dead or alive, or more to the point, if Ben is OK, for the past month. He walked out and abandoned all his parental responsibilities. Now he wants to play Dad?

'We're fine, but I had a threatening phone call this morning,' I tell him. Let's make him feel just a teensy bit of guilt. 'I'm keeping Ben here with me until I figure out what's going on.'

'Shit Abs. You've got to walk away. Tell the cops you're not going to testify.'

Dylan was never someone with any kind of sense of civic responsibility. I also note that he doesn't offer to take Ben to keep him safe somewhere.

'It's an option,' I concede.

'An option? Sounds like it's the only bloody choice. You can't put my son's life at risk.'

'Your son's life?' I feel the anger bubble up.

'Don't start. I know I've not been to see him. I didn't think you wanted me around. I was trying to put some distance between us.'

'It was you who didn't want to be around Dylan. Remember?'

'Look I didn't call to argue. I rang because I was concerned about you both. Do you need me to get you anything? I've got to take my car into the garage this morning and it's going to be in for a couple of days, but if I'm still on your insurance I can drive yours and get some supplies in for you? Maybe tomorrow morning?'

Does he actually want to help or does he just want to use my car? I quickly run over the pros and cons in my head. It could be an opportunity to get him to put his hand in his pocket for once – it's not like he can't afford to.

'Actually there are a few things we need. I'm running low on nappies and stuff.'

'OK. I can come over before work and pick the car up, then bring everything you need after work. But you've got to think about Ben's safety, Abbie. You need to knock this witness business on the head.'

He has got a point. I just don't know how serious this all is. Perhaps we're all overreacting. Neither Nick nor DI Roberts seem to think it's too serious. But what if our lives really are in danger? I cross to the sitting-room window and look out. There's no sign of any police presence. Is DI

Roberts really going to provide surveillance, or was that all just to fob me off?

My phone rings again and I'm almost too nervous to answer it, but as I look at it, I see *DS Barnes*.

'Hi, how are you doing? Everything OK?' he asks. He's talking quietly and it sounds like he might be at work.

'We're fine thank you. No other threats, but I don't think it was Jacob Porter who called me.'

'How do you know?'

'I called him up at work. It wasn't the same voice.'

'Abbie you need to be careful. Leave the investigating to us OK?'

'It's fine, I didn't say anything and withheld my number. He won't know it was me.'

'Please, don't do anything else. Contacting the family could compromise the inquiry and more importantly, your safety.'

I hear the concern in his voice. 'OK,' is all I say.

'I've gotta go, keep safe,' he replies.

I don't miss the difference in how I feel when Nick puts down the phone compared to when Dylan did it. I also need to listen to Nick; he knows what he's talking about.

After lunch, Ben and I play with his train set. Or at least, I set it all up for him, putting together the interlocking tracks and he makes little chuff chuff and choo choo noises as he pushes them around it. I do a little bit of work – or at least attempt to. My mind just isn't focusing. There's an email from Mason asking if I'm getting any inside info on the investigation, anything that I can share with him for a story that won't impact the case against Stuart.

As journalists, we know that certain things have to be kept out of the public domain while there's an active investigation that's going to end up in court with someone already charged. If we print something that the defence solicitors could say the jurors might have read, and therefore they can't be impartial having arrived with pre-conceived views on Stuart, then he gets to walk free – and we get into trouble.

I ignore Mason's email for now. I'm still smarting, and his email signature saying 'Crime Correspondent' rubs salt into the wound. I appreciate that he and his cactus have a completely different lifestyle to Ben and I, and that makes it a whole heap easier for him to manage the hours, but it's frustrating. I know I'd have been good at that job. Right now though, that isn't my main concern – and aside from Stuart Porter, my priority has to be finding a higher paid job in PR.

My eyes are constantly drawn to the window, peering out as though I expect to see some cowboy dressed in black with a black hat, gun holster and bullet belt, walking down the road coming to get us. A mean grin on his face as he spins his Colt 45 guns on his forefingers. This time, what I do see is a police car parked across the road. It must be the surveillance DI Roberts promised – finally. It feels better to know that they're close, that someone is watching the house, albeit only the front. But is that enough?

By half four, I need to start thinking about Ben's dinner. He generally eats between five-thirty and six-thirty. On the days I'm at work, I re-heat something I'd put in the freezer for him for speed. Today, I take a couple of chicken breasts out the freezer and I'm going to make him one of his favourites: shredded chicken in a creamy cheese sauce with pasta. He loves it and it's easy for him to eat. I'll do some peas too.

I've just hoisted Ben into his chair and put his dinner in front of him, his little blue eyes lighting up at the plate of food, when there's a thump on the doormat in the hall. I leave Ben in his highchair in the kitchen, and go to look to see what it is.

It's a brown mass with something white.

I tentatively walk a bit closer.

It's a great big dead rat. Someone's put a bloody rat through my letterbox.

I get a bit closer – I'm not squeamish and there's something with it.

A note.

I pull the note from out of the elastic band round its neck and open it.

Next time it will be a petrol bomb. Withdraw your lies and don't tell the police why.

News stories about whole families being burned alive in their beds flash through my brain. Even if I secure the doors and windows, we won't be safe inside. I open the front door and look outside for the police car to tell them. It's not there. It's gone. So much for the 24/7 surveillance that DI Roberts promised. Where are they? I can't even rely on them to help me.

I feel sick as I shut the door and return to Ben. His innocent, smiling face, smeared in pasta sauce, beams at me. I go to him, kissing his soft hair, and breathe him in.

He's forever a part of me. My world. Nothing matters except him and his safety, and the only one who can protect him is me.

He's oblivious to the stress and turmoil spinning around inside me.

I have to keep him safe. That's all that matters. Dylan's words ring around my head. I realise I'm shaking again as I dial DI Roberts.

'I'm sorry but I'm withdrawing my statement and the identification. I can't do this.'

There's silence for a few moments on the phone before he speaks. 'Has something else happened Mrs Murphy? You do realise that if you are being coerced into this, you can still be summonsed to appear in court, this is a case of public interest.'

'I just want to withdraw,' I say firmly. 'I don't want to be a part of this anymore.'

'There is another alternative, we can apply for you to go into the witness protection programme.'

'And will that be as effective as your 24/7 surveillance because there's a distinct lack of a patrol car parked outside.'

'It isn't there?'

'Nope. Isn't there.'

'Let me make some calls, please don't rush into this decision.'

'I'm not rushing into it. I've made up my mind DI Roberts. I don't want to be involved with this anymore. I have to think about what's best for my son and I.'

'Very well Mrs Murphy. I'll be back in touch. I need to find out what's happened with the surveillance and then perhaps we can talk about this face to face? In the meantime, if you have any reason to be concerned for your safety, then call me or dial 999 if it's urgent. Will you do that, please?'

As SOON AS I'm off the phone, I get a carrier bag and use it to pick up the rat, turning it inside-out to seal it inside. I chuck it out the back door. I'll deal with it later. I keep the note, but it's almost as though it's going to poison us or burst into flames, I don't touch it and use a glove. I put it in a plastic folder sleeve and place it in my desk drawer, far away from us. If there's any forensic evidence on it then it will be preserved – but right now, I'm not planning on handing it over to the police. The phone call made it clear that I wasn't to tell them why I was withdrawing my statement.

I return to Ben and take him upstairs for a bath. I need our routine, something *normal* to help me get through this. My life has been turned upside down since that stupid split-second decision. If only I could relive that moment, just sit in that traffic jam and be patient for five minutes more. But, hindsight is as useless as regret. All we can do is learn from it and move forward. I can't change what's done.

I've literally just got Ben into his pyjamas when my mobile phone rings. I'm expecting it to be DI Roberts, trying to persuade me not to withdraw, or to at least explain where his police protection was. But there's no caller ID.

I stop breathing.

'Did you get the message bitch?'

'Yes. I've withdrawn. I've told the police I'm not testifying.'

'Wise decision.'

They hang up.

I sit there staring at my phone, my heart banging in my chest, a searing pain in my gut.

Is that it now? Can I put this nightmare behind me?

Are we finally safe?

11

───────

Considering my evening started with a dead rat on my doormat and a death threat, it ends up a whole heap better. Ben and I go downstairs for him to watch his bedtime TV and have his glass of milk and some biscuits. I pick at my chicken pasta I felt too sick to eat it earlier.

I sit with Ben, just enjoying watching him. He's sipping at his milk but hasn't touched the little pot of biscuits I'd put out for him. Motherhood is a roller coaster of balancing devotion and guilt, even on a good day – which this isn't. Those biscuits suddenly start looking tempting and Ben's ignoring them, not interested. I've always been a comfort eater and so I reach out and take one. One of its companions quickly follows. I eat another and then another until finally there is just one left.

Right on cue, Ben gets up from the floor where he's been transfixed by his favourite engine, totally unaware of the theft that's been going on behind his back, walks over and looks at the virtually empty pot of his mini chocolate Digestives. He looks at it and then at me and back again. I crumble under the interrogative stare of a disappointed eighteen-month-old.

'Oh sweetheart, I'm sorry!' I watch as he puts the single biscuit into his mouth. 'I didn't think you wanted them.'

'More... more,' he replies, holding out his little pot like a modern day Oliver Twist. The thing is, I know there are no more, not only in the packet, but in the house. We are totally out of biscuits.

'I'm sorry honey, there aren't any more.'

He turns back to the TV, crestfallen. Now I feel wracked with guilt. If there is a god in heaven, then I expect to see the girth of my thighs increase three-fold. I start writing the shopping list for Dylan and make sure that mini chocolate Digestives are on it.

After teeth cleaning, I put Ben to bed and have just switched on the baby monitor, comforted by his little voice chatting away to his teddy, when there's a knock on the door. I freeze. The familiar twisting in my stomach returns and I peer round the curtain of the sitting room window to see who it is.

It's Nick. DS Barnes. I hope he hasn't come round to try to persuade me not to withdraw my statement.

'Hi,' I say and immediately notice he's carrying an Amazon box.

'Hi, you OK?'

'Yeah, do you want to come in?'

'After your threatening phone call and your night visitor, I thought you might feel a bit more secure with these,' he says, looking at me with concern. He steps into the house, wiping his feet on the mat. 'I got you some cameras that link up to your phone. Thought it would give you some peace of mind.' He hands over the box.

I peer over his shoulder into the street. That police car

still hasn't returned, but it doesn't matter now that Nick's here.

'Thank you so much, you didn't have to do that. How much do I owe you?'

'Nothing, I don't want anything. It's a gift. I know it's tough when you're a single parent. My dad brought me up alone after Mum died of cancer when I was a kid.'

'I'm sorry,' I say and our eyes connect, a moment of mutual sympathy and empathy.

He has gorgeous eyes.

'Would you like a drink?' I offer, distracting myself. 'Sorry it's only tea or coffee.'

'A tea is fine,' he says, I can help you get those cameras set up. I've got some at home, they're pretty easy.'

'Thank you, I really would appreciate that.'

We head through into the kitchen and it's then that I realise he may not know.

'Do you know that I've withdrawn my statement?'

I can see he had no idea. A wave of surprise washes over him and he stops dead.

'No, I didn't realise. I've been on another case, out the office all day. Why?'

Should I tell him the truth? They told me I wasn't to tell the police, but if Nick's not on the case, does that count? Nick's watching me, eyes narrowed.

'Abbie has something happened?'

'I just told DI Roberts that I didn't want to go ahead. I'm worried about Ben's safety.'

Nick is still studying me.

'Did they threaten you again?'

I give a little nod and look down.

'What did they do Abbie? Is Ben OK?'

I look back up instantly, 'Oh yes, he's fine. They said not to tell the police.'

'I won't tell DI Roberts if you don't want me to, but you shouldn't have to deal with this on your own.' Nick's voice has softened.

I concede.

'I had a dead rat with another threat put through my door this afternoon. They said they'd petrol bomb the house.'

His forehead is furrowed.

'How did DI Roberts take that?'

'I think he understood. Said he'd call me but that they could still force me to testify if they thought I'd been threatened or something.'

'Yes, you're a material witness and you've given a statement that you have sworn to be true. I expect they'll be running around like blue-arsed flies trying to see if they've still got a strong enough case without you. Porter's brief is already saying it was self-defence.'

'I know and I'm sorry, but I just can't do this anymore. It's Ben I'm worried about.'

I turn away and fill up the kettle to think. So does Nick.

'You know, even though you've said you won't testify now, he might still see you as a threat. There's nothing stopping you from changing your mind before the trial.'

I look up, startled. 'You mean he might still try to kill me or hurt Ben?'

'Maybe.'

I lean on the kitchen counter and take a few deep breaths. Suddenly Nick is beside me.

'I'm sorry Abbie, I didn't mean to scare you, but I don't want you thinking everything is going to just be OK. Stuart Porter is a dangerous man.'

He reaches out and puts his hand on my arm for reassurance. I desperately wish he'd just take me in his arms and hug me. I'm not a weak woman, but right now I could do with a hug from a strong, caring man.

As if he senses that he might be about to step over the line like he did last night, Nick moves away.

'Let's get these cameras set up. I'll put one in the hall facing the front door, one here in the kitchen so you can see the back door, and one in the sitting room facing the patio doors. That should cover you.'

I swallow down tears and nod. I pour the water on the tea bags and spend longer than needed stirring them and finishing off the tea.

'I'm sorry I don't have any biscuits or anything,' I say as I put his mug of tea down next to him.

'Do you need me to get you anything?' he asks, looking up from programming the camera.

'No, thanks. My ex has offered. He's getting us supplies tomorrow. I'm going to have the rest of the week off work and then we need to get back to normal. Somehow.'

'OK, that's good… I didn't think you saw him anymore?'

I detect a slight note of disappointment in his voice.

'We don't. But his mother rang and told him what happened. Although actually if I know him, I think he's only doing it because he wants to borrow my car. His is in the garage.'

'That's nice of him,' Nick says, sarcastically.

He's watching me now.

'I've only agreed to it because I don't need my car for a couple of days and believe you me, he will be making a big shopping trip.' I smile at him. 'Seeing Dylan is not something I want to do.'

I don't want him in any way thinking that I want to get

back together with Dylan. Nick is the one I want, but it's obvious he's made up his mind that last night was a mistake.

WITHIN HALF AN HOUR, Nick has all three cameras working. He shows me how they'll record everything, but I can set them up so that movement and sound will alert me on my phone with the SeeCam app, and I will also be able to hear and speak.

He then downs his mug of tea and says, 'I'd better go.'

But I don't want him to go. Every time that man walks out the door, I feel bereft. I want him. I want him to stay. Every cell in my body is attracted to him. It sure has been a long time since I entertained a man. Nick's been gone three months and things had got really sour a few months before that. No wonder my loins are longing! But this man is not going to want to make a move on me because he's too damned honourable.

'Do you have to go?' I ask.

He looks away from me and sighs. 'You should sleep better with the cameras – you won't need me here.'

'I want you here,' I say to him, walking up to where he's leaning against the counter and pushing my body against his as I reach up and kiss him.

'Abbie, this isn't right,' he protests, holding me back.

'Why? You're not directly related to the case and I am making a conscious choice to do this. You're not taking advantage. This is me making the move.'

'I just—'

But he can't finish his sentence because my lips are on his again. For a couple of seconds I fear he's going to reject me, but then I feel his body give in with a groan and his kisses become hungry. I feel his tongue searching deep into my mouth, exploring every inch, the smell of him enveloping me. I close my eyes and allow myself to be possessed. His hands hold my face and I open my eyes to see him looking at me.

'Are you sure?' he asks.

I nod. Within seconds he is kissing me again. I can feel his arousal, and then I realise he's undone the buttons on my top and his hand is gently caressing my breast. I head for his trouser fly and within minutes we are on each other. I forget everything else but this moment. Tonight, Nick won't be sleeping on the sofa.

12

I have to say that I'd been really stressed about Dylan coming round, but spending the night with Nick has totally put that into perspective. We didn't get a great deal of sleep, but the shut eye that I did get was deep. I felt safe and secure wrapped in his arms. Nick was mindful of both Ben and Dylan's impending arrival, and so slipped off early in the morning. For the first time in ages, I feel like I am on cloud nine.

I'd not seen Dylan for a month and it's weird, looking at the face that had been in my life every day for so many years, but is now a stranger to me. It doesn't make me feel good, putting a damper on last night, but not quite extinguishing that fire. I've put on my favourite jeans and top – the one that I choose when I want to be casual but look good – and done my make-up and hair. I want him to see what he's lost and feel it. I don't think it particularly worked.

'Benny boy,' he says to Ben, picking him up.

I hate him calling him Benny. His name is Ben, Benjamin if he has to use a longer version, but not Benny.

Ben is pleased to see him, but it takes a few moments for him to register who he is. That at least gives me something to gloat about.

'Can't stay as I've got to get to a meeting and it's an hour's drive, but you're alright yeah?'

'Yeah,' I say back.

'Thanks for the loan of the car,' he says, spying the car keys in my hand.

So, he was just doing this to use my car. The tight-fisted miser probably didn't want to put his hand in his pocket to pay for a loan car while his was in the garage.

'Here's our shopping list.' I wave a piece of paper at him. 'I've taken a photo of it too in case it gets lost and can WhatsApp that to you.' I know the games he plays.

'Ah yeah, sure. Blimey that's a lot of stuff.'

I stare at him, not saying a word. He gets the message.

'No problem. See you about half six. I'll pick this lot up on the way back.'

'Great,' is all I say as I hold the front door open for him. When I close it, I don't feel anywhere near the sense of loss that I'd felt this morning when Nick had gone. I'm not a mess about the fact the man who is supposed to be my husband has just walked out the door and is with another woman.

That's good. That's real progress. In fact, I feel like a complete mug for lending him my car. It's obvious that he only came here because he needs it, but at least I'm going to get some shopping out of it.

There are no threats on my hall doormat this morning – and I love the new cameras linked to my phone. Things are looking up, getting back to normal.

While Ben plays with his breakfast, I log onto my online

subscription to the *Evening News* and see what my colleagues are unearthing while I'm away.

Mason's got the lead again. *Culture of Corruption* is the headline. He's been digging deeper into what's been going on at the council. Seems like there's been money disappearing for years. No wonder our potholes never get filled – they've run out of money by the time it gets to doing anything to help the taxpayers. According to Mason, the police have been looking into widespread corruption that involves multi-million pound contracts and services.

I can feel the itch inside of me – that reporter itch that makes me want to get back to work and get involved. I love Ben, more than anything in the world. But I do also love having a career. I've just got to make that career work better for us. There's no way we can maintain our lifestyle without a boost in my pay packet. Which means moving over from being a low-paid reporter to the dark side of PR. I know I have to do it for Ben.

For a few moments I allow myself to fantasise about a new life. One where I don't have to worry about money, where I can come home and relax with my son, and where maybe, just maybe, I could call myself DS Nick Barnes' girlfriend. I'm not sure what's more attractive, thinking about him in bed or sharing the bills!

I click away from the juicy stories on my laptop and take another look at the job ads. These couple of days off are the perfect time to be searching.

DYLAN TEXTS me with queries about a couple of things I've put on my list, but seems to manage to get the bulk of it because he turns up at 6.40 p.m. with five carrier bags full of shopping, plus four packs of nappies.

'Can't stay,' he says as he hoists them into the hallway. 'That lot cost me a bloody fortune by the way.'

I guess that the harpy is on his back about when he's going to be home. I can't imagine that she's overly happy he's round here and borrowing my car. Bet she doesn't know he's bought shopping for us.

'I'll bring your car back tomorrow after work,' he says and starts walking down the path. 'You should get those brakes seen to, they're feeling a bit soft.'

So, he borrows my car and then complains about it, but doesn't for one second think that if there is an issue with it, then maybe he should put his hand in his pocket to help and keep his son safe. No of course, silly me. That's all my responsibility! I don't think the brakes are soft anyway, it's been driving perfectly fine for me. It's just him and the way he drives. No wonder his car is in the garage, he thrashes it sometimes.

I put my anger into hauling the shopping bags into the kitchen. A satisfying clink clink tells me he did actually buy the wine I wrote down too.

I had texted Nick earlier to see if he wanted to come round for dinner but he said he wouldn't be able to make it over until about 9 pm due to a work commitment and so we should eat without him as he'll grab something while he's out.

Ben and I have spaghetti bolognese for dinner. I make enough that there's some leftovers which I can freeze for quick meals for Ben another day. I've had to put some of the other fresh food in the freezer too as Nick obviously didn't look at the sell-by dates on them when he picked them up. I've planned our meals over the next week which means I won't need to go shopping again now for a while.

I'm just clearing things away into the dishwasher while Ben plays on the floor with his Lego people and cars, when there's a knock on the door. I'm so wary now that I peer at who it is from the sitting room window before I open up. I can see it's two uniformed police officers. They must be checking in on me. Ever since I told DI Roberts that there was no squad car outside, there's been one parked there constantly.

'Mrs Murphy?'

'Yes.'

'Would it be possible to come in please?' the female police officer asks me, gently.

'Why? What's this about?'

I'm getting a bad vibe. They've got sympathy written all over their faces.

'Can we go inside?' She nudges and so I open the door and let them in.

'Take a seat, I'll just get my son,' I tell them. I go into the kitchen and hoist Ben, and as many Lego people and toys as I can, into my arms and join the two officers.

She gives me another sympathetic smile. What's going on?

'Do you own a blue Ford Fiesta?' She asks me and reads out the registration plate.

'Yes...'

'I'm very sorry to inform you that your car was involved in an accident earlier this evening. Your husband, Dylan Murphy, has been taken to the general hospital in a serious condition.'

'What? How? What happened?'

'Witnesses say that it appears Mr Murphy lost control of the car when he came to a bend on the Elftown Road. The vehicle was going too fast and consequently left the road and hit some trees. Mr Murphy has sustained serious head injuries.'

'Oh my god!'

'You are the registered keeper of the vehicle, did your husband often drive it?'

'We're separated. He borrowed it this morning. Is he going to be OK?' I can barely think straight. 'Was another car involved? Did he swerve to avoid something?'

'There are accident investigators at the scene and the car and crash site will be checked thoroughly. Would you like us to take you to the hospital to see your husband?'

'Yes, yes I need to speak to him.'

They exchange a glance but I barely notice it.

'I need to bring Ben. Let me get a bag ready.'

They help me to gather my things. I know I need nappies, but I forget the wipes until she thankfully reminds me. Ben is already yawning but he perks up when he realises we're going out.

'Have you got your keys? Is the house all locked up?' the male police officer asks me as we're about to go out. Shit. I nearly walked out without my keys. He must be used to delivering bad news and seeing people completely lose it. I rush back into the kitchen to check the back door is locked and to pick up the house keys which are with my mobile phone. Nearly forgot that too! This is all so crazy. I'm in my house, my body, but this is not my life. It can't be.

13

The second I see him, I realise that Dylan is not going to be able to tell me what happened. His head and face are a mess. Most of his head is under bandages and what I can see of his face is swollen and purple. He's not even conscious.

'He has sustained a major trauma to his brain. We've scanned him and we're just waiting on the consultant to come and advise on the next steps,' the nurse is saying by my side.

Her words barely register. I'm staring at the broken body of the man I married, the man who over the last few months I have so many times wished bad things would happen to him, and now it has. He's unrecognisable. I can tell by the state of him and the way the nurse is talking, that even if he does survive, it's going to be massively life changing. I feel guilt. I feel sadness. I feel sympathy and I feel shock.

I hug Ben to me. He's oblivious to the fact that the person lying on the bed in front of us is his father and I'm so glad. This is a trauma I don't want him to register or remember. I try to keep him distracted.

'Shall I take your little boy for a few minutes?' the nurse asks me, smiling kindly. She's a bit younger than my mother and her face lights up when she smiles. Ben doesn't complain when she opens her arms to him and I hand him over.

'Mummy will be just a minute,' I tell him. The nurse is already chatting away to him about some pictures they have which she's going to show him.

I turn back to Dylan and tentatively reach out for his hand.

'Dylan, it's me, Abbie. I'm so sorry...' I don't finish. Sorry for the fact your life is all but over? Sorry that you did this in my car on the way home from getting our shopping? Sorry that we're not even living together anymore, that our relationship had grown so distant? I am sorry for all of it. But sorry isn't going to help either of us now.

The curtain sweeps back with the scrape of metal rings on metal pole. A man in a suit is there with another doctor in a white coat behind him.

'Mrs Murphy?' he asks.

I nod.

'Christian Glazer, I'm the neurological consultant here and I've been looking at your husband's scans.'

I hold my breath and listen.

'He has damage to the frontal areas of his brain, with swelling throughout and a major fracture to his skull. We are going to do what we can to help him, but I think that you need to be realistic about the outcome. Mr Murphy also has broken ribs, one of which punctured a lung, and has broken his collarbone. The impact on his body has been catastrophic. I assure you, we will do everything we can, but the damage to his brain may be life limiting.'

Life limiting! I look at this man I've never met, telling me that my husband is basically unlikely to survive. I trust him because he's a doctor, a consultant. I'm sure they will do their best. But I feel like I'm not really here, as though I'm watching an episode of *Casualty*, *ER*, or *Grey's Anatomy*.

'Thank you,' I whisper. It's my voice but I have no control over the output.

'We're going to make him as comfortable as possible, and presuming he has a stable night, he'll be going into surgery first thing in the morning. Any questions?'

I shake my head.

'OK then. My colleagues will be asking you to fill in some forms prior to surgery as you're the legal next of kin. I'll speak to you again in the morning.'

He is gone, but his shadow in a white coat stays behind.

'I'm terribly sorry Mrs Murphy, I know this is a big shock for you, but we need to get some forms completed as Mr Glazer said.'

I look up at the face of a young doctor. He looks to be in his mid-twenties, at a guess. Tired, probably overworked, and learning on the job how to deal with people at the extreme end of personal trauma.

'OK,' is all I can say in response.

He takes me through the consent form for the operation, and then produces a Do Not Resuscitate form.

'I know this isn't something you want to have to think about, but we need to know what your wishes are, and what Mr Murphy is likely to want. There is a possibility he will go into cardiac arrest on the operating table. Bearing in mind his injuries, do you want him to be resuscitated?'

'Yes. Yes of course. He's only thirty-four,' I say, horrified. 'We have to give him a chance.'

The young doctor has clearly not mastered the art of hiding his thoughts from his face yet, because I see a look that tells me he thinks Dylan doesn't stand a chance, DNR or no DNR.

WHEN I GET HOME I put Ben into bed, and then head straight for the kitchen and one of the bottles of wine that Dylan had bought. I touch the bottle and think about him picking it up for me earlier.

I ring his mother first, taking a huge gulp of wine before I dial her number and steel myself for the emotional trauma I'm just about to impart.

'Cheryl, it's Abbie,' I say.

'Hello darling, how's our little man?'

I pause, thinking how I would feel in her shoes if it was Ben.

'Abbie is everything OK? You sound a little... upset.'

'I'm really sorry Cheryl, is Joe there?'

She pauses before answering and I know that a cold fist of fear has just grasped her heart and is squeezing it tight. 'Yes,' she says, but not with the usual Cheryl enthusiasm.

'I'm really sorry, but Dylan has been involved in a car accident.' I pause because there's a noise that comes from the other end of the line. I cannot, and don't want to, imagine what it must be like to hear that your child is seriously injured or dying. 'He has serious head injuries. They're going to operate on him tomorrow morning but he may not survive.'

I hear muffled sobs and voices and Joe takes the phone. 'Abbie, what's going on?' He says to me, fear raising his voice. I repeat what I've just told Cheryl.

'We'll drive up tomorrow,' he says. I hear the practised masculine control in his delivery. The man wants to sob like his wife, but he'll wait until he's off the phone. 'Which hospital?' he asks.

I give them all the details I can, and our conversation ends.

My house is silence. I know that theirs is anything but.

I sit at the kitchen island, finishing the glass I'd poured, and then pour myself another one. I call my parents, filling them in on what's happened, and I hear the relief in my mother's voice that it's not me and Ben in that hospital bed.

Afterwards, I text Nick and say it's probably not a good idea for him to come over tonight. I'm not going to be good company. I know Dylan has been a shit to me over the last year, but I spent a chunk of my life loving him, and we created Ben together. To see him all broken up like that is incredibly shocking and upsetting. Plus, he's still technically my husband so to be with another man while he's lying in hospital near death after driving my car, feels like the worst kind of betrayal.

Nick calls and I hear his concern, but I reassure him. I just need some time to let this all sink in.

I sit and drink some more, lost in the memories of the last eight years Dylan and I spent together, interspersed with violent flashes of his swollen bloodied face in the hospital bed.

It's gone eleven o'clock when there's a hammering on my front door. I'm instantly rigid with terror. Dylan's accident had totally taken my mind off the events of the last few days, but now that panic returns in a hurricane of already raw emotion. I grab my phone, ready to call for help, and tentatively go into the hallway.

'Abigail, Abigail! I know you're in there. Open up. Where's Dylan?'

It's the harpy. I'd totally forgotten about her. She won't

be given any information or allowed hospital access because she's not a relative. I open the door.

Her face is wild and ravaged by stress; rivulets of tears have torn through her make-up.

'Where is he? Someone said there'd been an accident but nobody will tell me anything. I've been texting and calling him.'

I've wanted to scratch this woman's eyes out and pull out every strand of her bleached blond hair for ruining my marriage, but now the human in me can't be angry. In front of me is a woman hollowed out and embrittled by the emotional fear which can only come from loving someone and knowing you might be about to lose them. There's no faking this. Her complete vulnerability melts the hatred.

'He was in a car accident,' I tell her. 'He's in a critical condition with head injuries. They're going to operate on him tomorrow but...' I don't finish. I can't because my throat has tightened too hard to let the words out.

'I need to see him,' she says standing on my garden path, the tears streaking down her face glistening in the light from my hallway. She looks like a lost child and I'm the person with all the control and answers.

'He's unconscious,' I tell her. I don't need to let this woman who stole my husband anywhere near him, but somehow I feel like it's the right thing. 'Maybe after his operation tomorrow. Give me your number,' I add.

I type her phone number into my phone.

She's crumpled now. The fight, the indignation, and the desperation, have spilled out of her onto my garden path and she looks beat.

'Will he be OK?' she asks me now. Her voice tiny and afraid.

I don't know the answer to that question, but if I'm

honest with myself I don't think he will be. All I can do is tell her what the consultant said. 'They said we need to be realistic and that the damage may be life limiting. It's certainly going to be life changing.'

I watch as the bottom falls out of her world. I feel shocked and upset, but I've already mourned the loss of Dylan. He's a man from my past, a past where our connection had soured and withered, whereas her loss is unfolding now. It's visceral. I realise in this moment that she does really love him.

'Please call me,' is all she says in response. She drags herself back to her car and I watch from the corner of the sitting room window as she just stays there, sobbing. I turn away, unable to watch any longer.

Sitting in the shadows thinking about someone else's grief makes me realise just how tired I am. Not physically, but emotionally. It's been one hell of a rollercoaster week.

14

—————

Every day this week has brought new trauma into my life. This morning it comes in the form of DI Conor Roberts. I called the hospital and was told that Dylan was in theatre and that a doctor would call me after the operation. I let Cheryl and Harper know, then tried to carry on as though life is normal.

When the knock sounds on my front door, I expect it to be Harper again, until the tall frame of DI Roberts becomes visible.

'Mrs Murphy, would it be alright to come in please?'

I open the door. I'm not in the mood to have him try to persuade me to not withdraw my testimony. My mind is made up. I've got other things to be worrying about now.

'I'm not changing my mind,' I say to him. I don't have any fight in me to stop him coming in.

'I'm very sorry about your husband,' he says as we walk through to the kitchen.

It catches me unawares and I turn to look at him. But I guess police talk.

'Do you want a drink?' I ask, not acknowledging his

sympathy. There's something about this man and his manner which irritate me. It's the way he watches me, like he never believes a word I say.

'A coffee would be great, thanks.' He settles himself onto one of the tall chairs at the kitchen island. 'How have you been? Any other issues and threats?' he asks me.

I can feel his eyes boring into my back as I put the coffee into the cafetière.

'No.'

'I was contacted by the accident investigation team this morning.'

I spin round and look at him, feeling that he's about to say something big.

'They told me that your brake line was cut. Your husband's crash yesterday wasn't an accident.'

The kettle clicks off but I'm oblivious.

I hadn't even thought of that possibility.

'Why? How? I thought he'd just been driving too fast and misjudged the bend and lost control?'

'How is relatively easy for someone who knows what they're doing. The why is a little harder. Why was your husband driving your car yesterday? I thought that the pair of you were separated.'

'We are, but he called because he'd heard about the threats and said his car was in the garage and asked if he could borrow mine. He bought me some shopping.' Dylan's words as he left earlier yesterday come back to me. 'He said the brakes were soft that afternoon. But they'd been fine for me, I just thought that was him not used to my car after driving his.'

DI Roberts sits watching me.

'Do you think that I should have been in that car?! Whoever did this was trying to kill me?'

'I'm concerned that might be the case, yes. Bearing in mind the threats you've received.'

'But I did what they asked. I withdrew.'

'Perhaps that message hadn't got through?'

'Ben could have been in that car.'

My legs feel weak and my stomach sick. I walk over to the kitchen table and sit on one of the chairs. DI Roberts gets up and finishes the coffee making while the enormity of what he's just said sinks in.

'We've been looking into who could have been threatening you, but this takes it to a new level.'

'Does *he* know I've withdrawn my statement?'

'Stuart Porter's solicitor has been informed, yes.'

'When? When was he told?'

'Thursday.'

'So they knew. They knew before Dylan took my car. Before the accident.' Nick's words about me still being a threat come to my mind.

'We'll launch an attempted murder inquiry into your husband's accident. We also need to think about whether you and Ben require any additional protection.'

'Well, that didn't work out well last time did it?' I fling back at him.

'I've looked into that too. There was a major incident and unfortunately all available officers were called on to attend. We need to put something more formal in place going forward. This is the time that you really need to—'

He doesn't finish his sentence because my mobile phone rings. I stare at the number that's come up. I recognise the area code as being where the hospital is located.'

'I think it's the hospital,' I say and answer.

'Mrs Murphy, it's Christian Glazier, your husband's neurosurgeon. I've just come out of the operating theatre and I think you should come to the hospital. I'm really sorry but your husband's injuries are worse than we'd anticipated. We lost him twice in theatre and his breathing is now assisted. We need to talk about the next steps.'

'I'll be there in half an hour,' is all I'm capable of saying.

DI Roberts is sitting motionless, watching me when I end the phone call.

'I need to get to the hospital and I have to call his parents.' I obviously don't need to explain any further.

'I'll drive you,' DI Roberts says to me.

I think I mumble thank you. This is all surreal.

I go and gather Ben's things, throwing some toys and extra diapers into his changing bag, while DI Roberts watches over him downstairs. We have to use Ben's old car seat again as his current one is in my car. It's not ideal but it does the job. DI Roberts fixes it in and I choose to sit in the back with my son. I need to be close to him, to know he's safe.

I don't remember the journey, other than that on the way to the hospital, I call Cheryl and Joe. They're en-route, about an hour away. I don't ring Harper. I'm unable to deal with anything more right now.

Nothing about the next two hours stays in my head. As humans, we can block out the emotion and memories of events like this. It happened for me after childbirth. I know that this protective mechanism goes wrong with extreme and prolonged trauma – that's why people get PTSD – but these two hours will become just a blur in my lifetime's memories.

Dylan is effectively brain dead. His brain was badly damaged and sustained severe swelling, bleeding, and clotting, which means that he will never regain consciousness and has even lost the basic ability to breathe.

Mr Glazier tells me this in one of those pastel-coloured family rooms where the chairs are comfortable and the walls carry paintings and photographs of nature, as though any of it can help relieve the traumatic news that gets told in here.

Cheryl and Joe arrive in a tightly packed shell of restrained emotion. Mr Glazier patiently repeats the prognosis and tells us that we need to give permission for the machine that's keeping him alive to be turned off.

He looks at us all and then bows his head and waits for his words to sink in. I can see he doesn't want to pressure us.

'How can you be absolutely sure he's not got any chance,' I ask.

'I can show you the scans of his brain; there is extensive damage which has been made worse by a series of blood clots from the trauma. He's technically now already brain dead, it's only the respirator that's keeping him alive.'

There are a few moments of silence when the only sound is Ben's breathing as he concentrates on turning the pages in a book he's reading.

'If it's the best for him,' I say to Mr Glazier, and look to Cheryl and Joe.

Joe is cradling his wife, their hands grasping each other's. He nods at me.

'Thank you,' Mr Glazier says to us. 'I know that this is a hard decision, but it's the right one for Dylan. I'll get the forms for you to sign.'

'Mumma, Mumma...' Ben has toddled up to me to show me his book, his eyes alight. I pick him up and hug him to me until he struggles for freedom.

It really is just us now. Ben's oblivious to the fact I've just signed his father's death warrant. The man I had once loved, body and soul, will be no more. I've said the words but they still haven't fully sunk in.

I kiss Ben's soft cheek and let him go.

DI Robert's words come back to me, the thought that the car accident was meant for me and Ben hits me again in the guts. I am not going to let anything happen to my little boy. Stuart Porter has shown his hand. If he is still going to come after us despite me withdrawing my testimony, then I am going to make damned sure I take him, and anyone else working with him, down.

15

Saturday was just one big blur. I spoke to Cheryl and Joe about Harper, and we agreed that she should be allowed to come and say goodbye to Dylan. I didn't want to be there when that happened and I used Ben as my excuse to go home.

I am so grateful to Nick for getting those three cameras. It gives me great peace of mind to know that nobody has entered my house while I wasn't there. When I shut the door, I feel safe, cocooned from the nightmare of the past week. Sitting with Ben watching *Thomas and Friends* and then an episode of *Pingu*, I can pretend that none of it has happened. I didn't witness a murder and receive death threats, and my estranged husband wasn't killed in a staged accident meant for me.

But I'm not one of those women who can passively shut the world out. Everyone thinks that I've been investigating Stuart Porter and his illegal dealings, maybe it's about time I did. I have to do something which will ensure he gets locked away for good.

First, once Ben is in bed, I telephone my parents and tell

them the news, then I call Julia. I don't tell her at first. I want to hear about normal life; I want one of her updates that make me smile before I shatter it all with my misery.

'Are you still married to Oscar?' I say as she picks up the phone.

Julia giggles. 'Only just. It's one of the other males in my household who is making my life a misery today.'

'Baby James isn't puking again is he?'

'Oh no, he's fine now, it's George. He's decided that he simply isn't getting enough Mummy time. My demanding five-year-old has now taken to doing baby impersonations in an attempt to get my attention, as clearly that's been working for his brother. Last night he decided he wasn't going to bed, refused to stay in bed or even attempt to go to sleep. Oscar and I both tried to settle him but at one in the morning it ended up with me screaming at George to go to sleep and then him lying on his bed, crying his eyes out and cowering away from scary mummy. Oscar had to come in and negotiate a peace deal between us. Tonight he's already been downstairs twice. Can't we just keep them in high-walled cots until they're eighteen? What do you do with Ben when he won't go to sleep? Any useful suggestions apart from shackles, handcuffs, or the cupboard under the stairs?'

'A few glasses of wine help.' I smile down the phone at her, relieved by the normality of our conversation.

'For me or George?' she comes back, giggling. 'Anyways, how are things with you? Has everything settled down now?'

I take a deep breath and tell her about Dylan.

'Oh my god, Abs, I don't know what to say. I'm just... shit! And here's me moaning about George not sleeping. I just can't believe it!'

'It's fine Julia, it's nice to hear about the usual stuff. I need that right now.'

'What are you going to do? You must be terrified. What are the police doing?'

I stand up and cross to the sitting-room window looking out on the street. I've been checking constantly, and they're still there.

'There's a patrol car parked outside watching my house,' I tell Julia. 'They're hoping that will be a deterrent. DS Nick Barnes has put cameras inside so I can see all the doors and the app alerts me if someone moves around inside.'

'Bloody hell Abs, you're under siege. The police need to get that bloke to stop this. They must know it's him.'

'I think they're working on it.'

There's silence between us for a few moments.

'You know you're both always welcome here,' Julia says gently. 'Really, we'd be happy to have you and help you get away from this nightmare. I'd love to have the company.'

'Thank you, but I can't leave right now. We need to go into the hospital tomorrow as Dylan's machine is going to be turned off. Then I want to make sure that Stuart Porter did know I'd withdrawn my testimony. If he's still coming after me even though I've said I won't testify against him, then I'm going to do my absolute best to make sure he gets banged up for the rest of his life.'

Nick calls. 'How are you doing?'

My throat tightens at the question. 'Been better. I just can't believe this is all happening.'

'Do you need me to come round?' he asks. 'No strings.'

'I'm not exactly great company right now,' I say with a broken voice.

'I'm a good listener and hugger,' he replies.

'Thank you.'

Twenty minutes later, he's at my front door. He doesn't say a word, just takes me in his arms and holds me.

'I'm so sorry,' he whispers in my ear eventually.

'I just don't know what's happened to my life. In one week it's gone completely up shit creek. You were right about Stuart Porter. Do you think he knew I'd withdrawn my testimony?'

'You know he's out, right? He had to have known.'

'Out?'

Nick has broken the hug and is looking at me now.

'He was let out on bail yesterday afternoon. I thought you'd know.'

'Oh my god,' I say, collapsing backwards onto the sofa. 'So he could have easily done this? Why was he let out?'

'The case against him for murder wasn't strong enough without your witness statement. His lawyer is arguing that the scene could have been tampered with. It's just your word against his and without your version of events, things can look a lot different. It means that the investigation has a lot more work to do and his solicitor argued they didn't have enough to hold him for murder. The judge agreed.'

'What do I do?' I say, looking up at Nick. He comes and sits beside me on the sofa, taking my hands in his.

'I'm not going to tell you what to do Abbie. You must do what's right for you and Ben. That's what matters.'

'What would you do then if you were in my shoes?'

He pauses and then shakes his head. 'I won't let what happened to my family influence yours. You've got to make the right decisions for you.'

'You mean your dad?'

Nick nods. 'What it does mean is that you know I can understand some of what you're going through right now.'

'Does DI Roberts know that Stuart Porter killed your father?'

Nick looks away and gives a shuddering sigh before turning back to me. He studies my face for a moment and then looks down.

'Conor Roberts was my dad's partner.'

I'm searching his face now, looking for more meaning in his words.

'There's something you're not telling me,' I say to him.

He looks away again before turning and studying our hands, clasped together on our legs. 'Look I don't want to create any issues between you and Roberts. This is my problem, not yours.'

'But it's not, is it? Do you suspect him of something?'

I can see Nick battling with what to say next.

'Nick?' I say, tugging on his hands.

'When my dad was killed, Roberts was unharmed. They were supposed to be investigating together. Yes, I suspect him of something. I think he's somehow mixed up with Stuart Porter. There was a suspicion that it was someone in the police who was helping run this corruption racket.'

'Oh my god, and he's supposed to be protecting us. No wonder that police car disappeared when the rat was delivered.'

'I've purposely not told you any of this because I don't want you to be scared. Roberts has bosses and they're keeping an eye on him. There's a whole team looking into Jordan Christie's murder. He might be in charge of the investigation, but there are some good cops working with him.'

Nick wraps his arms around me, hugging me in tight. 'And that's why I'm here. That's why I'm keeping an extra eye out. I won't let him hurt you or Ben. I promise. He's not going to take away anyone else who's important in my life. I'll take him down first.'

'*We'll* take him down,' I say, a fire rising in my belly. I pull my head up from where it's been buried into his chest. 'I'm going to testify against Stuart Porter and make damned sure he's locked away for good.'

16

———

Knowing the truth about DI Roberts suddenly explains a lot. I never felt any warmth from him. I thought that was simply because he thought I was lying and he believed I was investigating Stuart Porter before the murder. I know Nick felt bad about telling me, but I'm so glad he has. I'd had a feeling before that he was holding something back and I can understand why he was reluctant to tell me, but forewarned is forearmed.

Nick only stayed for a couple of hours as it still didn't feel right if I woke up next to a different man on the day I went to give permission for my husband's life support machine to be turned off. Today my focus and priority has to be Dylan. Tomorrow, I am going to deal with Stuart Porter and DI Roberts.

Cheryl and Joe come and pick up Ben and I to take us to the hospital. I see Cheryl's eyes scan the rooms and I don't miss the disappointment in them. There's nothing in the house that reflects Dylan anymore. He took all his stuff and I got rid of anything that reminded me of his betrayal. The last time they were here, Dylan and I had been together.

Now, he's been eradicated from our home and later this morning he'll be eradicated from our lives totally. I feel her pain and I see it in the way she clings to Ben. Whatever happens, I wouldn't cut them off from him.

We travel to the hospital in silence, the only voice in the car is Ben's as he babbles away about nothing in particular. He's no concept of what's going on – it's better this way. In years to come I can tell him about what happened to his father. Maybe I will even skip the part about how he walked out on us three months before. The photographs I have of Dylan, me, and Ben, all hidden away in the attic for now, will come out and there will be happy images for the adolescent or adult Ben to look at. Today is for us adults.

When we get to the hospital, Harper is already there. I suspect she may have actually been there all night. The grief on her face makes me feel like the interloper. I'm his wife in the eyes of the law, but not in love. Her love for my husband is conspicuous, an open wound, that weeps her devotion. I feel detached and cold in her presence. I've cried, but there are no more tears left to spill.

Harper has attached herself to Dylan's left hand. She cradles it, rubs her cheek against it, kisses it. I let go of that hand three months ago.

Cheryl and Joe sit on the other side of Dylan's bed, and his right hand finds its home in his mother's. I stand holding Ben.

'Abbie do you want to…?' Joe asks me, nodding towards Dylan and quickly glancing at Harper.

Harper looks up at me through tear-filled eyes. I could easily get back at her for taking my husband away from me by asking her to leave his bedside and taking her place. I can be the woman who is with him as he slips from this world, not her. But I don't. That fissure of grief opened but was replaced by anger, followed by the realisation that despite my financial circumstances, I was better off on my own than with a man who didn't love me. As he breaths his last on this earth, it's not me he'd choose to be beside.

'It's OK. I'll stay here with Ben,' I say to Joe and glance over at Harper, who is already head bent, forehead on the back of his hand.

The doctors have prepared Dylan, and explained what will happen when they turn off the machine. What they don't say again is that he's effectively already died. His brain has all but stopped functioning and what we see is just a shell of a man being kept alive. The illusion of life created by the respirator inflating and deflating his lungs, is just that. An illusion.

It's as if the whole room stops breathing when the switches are turned off. At first you imagine his chest is still rising and falling, but it's not. Without the mechanical respirator, there is silence, until Cheryl's sob signals the end.

AFTERWARDS, Cheryl and Joe take Ben and I home, and come in for a drink.

'Did he make a will?' Joe asks me when we're on our own in the kitchen.

I hadn't even thought about that.

'We both did when Ben was born.'

'And I presume he hasn't changed it since...' Joe leaves the obvious unasked.

'I don't know. I don't think so,' I reply.

'Good.' Joe nods. 'It's right that you and Ben should be the beneficiaries. You need to get that checked out tomorrow.'

Our wills had been simple. We'd left everything to each

other, or in the event of both of our deaths, to be put in trust for Ben. I feel immediately guilty at the relief that trickles through me at that thought. I might not have to sell the house now. It's all mine. I tell myself that I'm a total bitch for even considering that at this time, but it's there in my head and I can't help it. He left us. He hurt me, badly. I would never have wished this on him. I might have thought it, and even said it a few times to Julia, but I never actually meant it.

When I take Cheryl her cup of tea, I can't look her in the face. It's as if my guilt is there for all to see, written across my forehead like a burning tattoo. *I wished your son dead, and now it's happened and I'm going to benefit.*

Instead, we sit and talk funerals. Dylan had never expressed any preference and I don't have any strong feelings either way, so when Cheryl asks if he can be buried in their home church where her parents' graves are and they've reserved a plot, I agree. I want to help ease her grief, and if that will go towards it then I have no objections. They should take Dylan home. It's the right thing.

They say they'll handle arrangements with a local undertaker. I'm relieved that they're sorting it all out if I'm honest. I feel like a fraud discussing plans, going through the motions of being the grieving wife when we all know that he'd left me.

It's a relief when Cheryl and Joe go. I'm emotionally exhausted and spend the rest of the day vegging-out with Ben. I'm all he has now, the possibility of Dylan ever being a part of his life, is no more. I'm his world, and he is mine. Every time I look at him, I feel Cheryl's loss. I can't let anything happen to my son.

The police car outside changes every now and then along with the officers inside, but it's always there. I text Nick to say I'm exhausted and going to bed early. I'd love to see him but it still doesn't feel right lying in bed with my lover on the day my husband has officially died in front of me. Instead, before I head to my room, I stand in Ben's watching him sleep, feeling the overpowering love I have for him. We're going to be alright. I'm going to make sure of it. I will keep him safe.

Stuart Porter and DI Roberts are not going to hurt my son.

I wake up early and for a few seconds I'm confused by the red and black nightmares that have been swirling around my head. Then it all comes flooding back to me. My week of hell. This time last week I'd woken up focusing on a meeting at work and making sure I got there on time. In just one short week, my life has completely changed. Now, I don't even care whether I go back to my job or not. Everything has been put into perspective. I also now know what matters in my life, and getting that promotion was not going to make things better. It would have put a temporary sticking plaster on my finances, but at what cost? Pete and Mason were right about that. I couldn't and wouldn't want to spend irregular hours away from Ben.

I'm awake so early that Ben still hasn't even stirred. I check on him and he's still fast asleep, his little fist curled around the blanket rabbit which has been his constant bed companion since he was born. For a few moments I'm steeped in sorrow as flashes of Dylan cradling our newborn son come back to me. But they're just that, memories.

Memories which were already put away in boxes before Dylan died. I go and take a shower.

I'm all set up and ready for the day by the time Ben wakes and I enjoy being able to go and pick him up and have breakfast with him. I have some big decisions to make. With Stuart Porter out on the streets, I can't be sure that he's not going to try and hurt Ben and I again. I've been working through the dilemma for the past forty-eight hours. I need to get Ben somewhere where he's not in danger. I'm the threat, the target, so if he isn't close to me then he should be safe. I don't want to let him out of my sight, but that's being selfish. I need to get him away from here to a place of safety, and then I can be free to ensure that Stuart Porter gets locked away.

As soon as 9 a.m. comes around, I'm on the phone to our solicitor. I need to find out if Dylan has changed his will or not. I suspect he hasn't. It was, after all, me who insisted we made wills in the first place. The minute I'd had Ben I began to think of all the things that could make his future better. If something had happened to either one of us, or even both of us, I wanted Ben's future to be as secure as it could be.

The conversation is brief. Paul Adisa tells me that Dylan hasn't requested any changes. He gives his condolences and explains what we need to do next. I need to register the death certificate for one thing. I've got a copy of the will in my desk drawers so once I've finished on the phone, I go and read through to check what we'd said. Everything goes to me. I'm not entirely sure what other assets Dylan still has, but I know there were shares and we'd both taken out small life insurance policies. I log in online and check to see if he's made any changes to those. He hasn't. I know I'd been paying the joint premium because it was one monthly bill I'd been considering cutting. Thankfully I hadn't. Dylan's death will give me a £250,000 payout. I'm grateful to my husband for the first time in months, and once again feel guilty. For a few moments I think about the price of a life. If it hadn't been for me witnessing that murder, Dylan would still be alive.

It does help me make my mind up though. I type a resignation email to Pete and send it before I can change my mind. I have got to change my lifestyle to make sure it works better for Ben, and that includes the hours I work and my pay. Dylan's life insurance is going to take away our immediate financial problems, but £250,000 will only last so long. I've got to think about the longer term.

Pete is on the phone almost immediately after I've sent the email.

'Abbie,' he says to me, 'I anticipated this, but you shouldn't make rushed decisions. You've had a tremendous shock and you're grieving. I acknowledge receipt of your email but why don't you just take a few weeks off, compassionate leave, get away for a bit, and then let's talk again after.'

'I don't think I'll change my mind Pete, but thanks.'

I've not got the emotional energy to argue with him. I've not got the emotional energy for anything right now.

Ben and I read some books, or at least I read them and he looks at the pictures. We choose some of our favourites, *Stick Man* and *Giraffes Can't Dance*, before I'm distracted by a car pulling up outside our house. As it's the working day, lots of my neighbour's vehicles have gone so the stationary police car is more obvious, as too is this new one. I watch as DI Roberts gets out of it and walks over to the squad car. He chats for a few minutes, looking towards the house.

I don't have long to wait before he knocks on my front door.

'Mrs Murphy,' he says, 'I'm terribly sorry for your loss. Would it be possible to come in?'

I open the door wider and he follows me through it.

'We have now upgraded your husband's accident inquiry into a murder investigation,' he tells me. 'I'm sorry to have to ask you questions at this time, but it's important we get as much information as possible.'

I know that my voice comes out accusatory and my body language is definitely not welcoming, but I can't help it. 'Why didn't you tell me that Stuart Porter had been released? It was probably him who cut my brake lines.' I want to ask the questions first.

'It's not quite that simple, I'm afraid,' he says to me. He's got that look on his face again, studying me and judging me. 'I don't think he could have had enough time to get out and come here and then to tamper with your car without being seen. It's more likely that it happened earlier that day, or possibly overnight.'

'You're saying more likely, but it's still possible right?'

'We're keeping an open mind,' was all he'd say. 'Is there anyone else who knew that Dylan was going to be driving your car that day?'

'I don't know, maybe Harper, his girlfriend.'

'That's Miss Rodriguez?'

I nod.

'Is she the beneficiary of your husband's will?'

'No. I am.'

'Right, and how long had the two of you been separated?'

'Three months, but why are you asking me this? What are you insinuating DI Roberts?'

'I'm not insinuating anything Mrs Murphy, but as you know, you'd made several comments about wanting to kill your husband, or at least injure him, in your emails and messages to friends and so I have to ask these questions.'

'Really! So you've read all my personal messages from my phone and now you think that I've murdered my husband? Great.' I fold my arms and glare at him. 'Next thing you'll be blaming me for killing Jordan Christie too. I'm the one who has been threatened by that man, my son's life threatened when you said you'd protect us. If that patrol car had been outside when it was supposed to be, then maybe he wouldn't have had the chance to cut my brake lines and Dylan would still be alive. So perhaps it's me who should be asking you what your agenda is, DI Roberts.'

He looks taken aback by my outburst and goes to say something, then doesn't. 'Mrs Murphy,' he says, in a calm conciliatory tone. 'You've been through a lot in the last week. I'm just trying to do my job and do right by your husband. You withdrew your statement so I don't understand why Stuart Porter would feel the need to kill you.'

'Because of what I'm about to do, which is to request that my statement is still taken into consideration. I want that man put away for what he's done to my husband and what he did to Jordan Christie.'

'Are you sure?' he asks me, studying my face.

'Are you asking me if I'm sure because of the danger to me, or because you don't want me changing my mind again?' I don't give him the chance to answer. 'I'm not going to change my mind again and I'm not going to let that man get away with it.'

'Would you feel better if we relocated you to a safe house?'

It's my turn to study his face.

'Whatever you seem to think about me, Mrs Murphy, I do have your and your son's best interests at heart and perhaps it would be good for you to be isolated under police protection for a while?'

'I'll think about it,' I reply, 'but first I have to bury my husband.'

THERE IS one other thing I have to do first, but I don't tell him that. I need to get Ben out of here, to somewhere really safe. With someone I can trust. I don't know if Roberts is on my side or not right now, and so I need to protect my son.

I WhatsApp Julia. *Hi, you going to be in later this afternoon for a chat?*

Sure, Mum's picking George up from school, I'll be here with my nipple attached to a small human being all afternoon. Call anytime.

I pack two bags full of Ben's things: clothes, favourite toys, a couple of his books and a couple of days of nappies. I shove them under the pushchair and hang them off the handles, trying not to make it obvious what they are, then I take Ben to the bus stop. I don't have a car now, so that's my first challenge.

I'm nervous. What if I'm followed? I raise a hand to the police officer in the car outside my house and he smiles at me. I wonder if he has to report what I'm doing and where I'm going.

At the bus, I watch to see if anyone else gets on. Nobody does. What about someone following me in a car? I have to sit towards the front because of the pushchair, but I keep a watch through the back window to see if there are any cars tailing us. Nothing.

We get out a bus stop after the one I want, just so that I can double check I'm not being followed. We then walk back towards the car hire place and with one final check, I go in and book a car.

I know you're supposed to use cash if you want to evade anyone knowing what you're doing, but that's impossible with hire cars as you need to give a credit card to secure the vehicle. They're not going to know where I'm going and it's quite reasonable that I've hired a car seeing as mine was written off. First thing I do though is turn off my mobile phone so it can't be tracked. I'm turning into some kind of fugitive, but until I know who I can trust, that's the way it's going to have to be.

I'm glad to be driving out of this city. Part of me wishes I could just carry on driving and never come back, but I've never been a quitter. Stuart Porter has put my life through hell in the last week. He's killed my husband and he's threatened my son, plus he probably had Nick's dad murdered. I want to make sure he goes to jail and never gets out.

18

———

I knew Julia would welcome Ben and I with open arms. She's surprised, but she's so happy to see us.

'Of course he can stay. Lucy is going to be so delighted.' She ushers us into the house. 'Sorry about the doorstep, it's the only part of the house that the decorators have still got to sort out.'

'It looks amazing,' I say as we go inside, looking at her impeccable home.

'Yeah, I'm quite pleased with it, now that it's done.' She smiles back. 'You know you're welcome to stay too. The spare bedroom is big enough for both of you.'

'Thanks,' I say, 'but it's me he wants to silence. I don't want to put you at risk and it's safer for Ben if he's not around me for a bit.'

Julia turns round and gives me a huge hug. 'I'm so sorry this has happened to you. Please stay safe.'

'It was my fault. If I'd stayed in that traffic jam instead of going up that road, none of this would have happened.'

'You can't blame yourself. You didn't murder that man, that Stuart guy did. He's the one at fault.'

'Yeah…' I know she's right but I still can't help feeling that this is my mess to clear up. 'You sure it's not going to be too much trouble having Ben?'

'Trouble?' Julia laughs and nods over to where Lucy has already kidnapped Ben and is playing with some kind of doctor's kit with him. My little boy is sitting happily smiling at her with a fake plaster attached to his arm and having his heart listened to. For a moment it brings back the hospital and Dylan.

'I feel so guilty about Dylan,' I say to my best friend. 'He was a shit but he didn't deserve to die. And the detective in charge of the inquiry was asking me if I'd basically cut my own brake pipes to claim Dylan's life insurance and assets because the will is still in my name.'

'What? You are kidding me! Is that the Nick guy?'

'No. Nick's been wonderful, he has put in some security cameras for me and been keeping a close eye on us, in fact—'

'Oh my God, you've fucked him, haven't you?' Julia is studying my face.

I can't help it, but I smile.

'Yay, was he any good?'

I smile again.

'Hallelujah! Well hang out the flags and ring the bells, you've finally had a good fuck!'

For a few moments my life feels normal, being with my best friend, talking about Nick, joking, and watching the kids playing. But I can't stay here. This little bubble isn't my reality. Waiting for me at home is the hell that I left behind and I've got to go deal with it.

It's heart-breaking leaving Ben behind, but I know that I'm doing it for the right reasons and that he's going to be with someone I trust. I ask Julia not to mention him in any of our messages, just in case someone gets hold of my phone. We've decided that she'll refer to him as Charlie, cousin to their kids. She chose Charlie after Bonnie Prince Charlie who went into hiding.

I CRY as I drive home, quickly brushing away the tears welling up in my eyes so that I can see clearly. I cry for Ben, for Dylan, and for me. I just want our lives back to the way they were.

When I get home, the police car is still outside. I park my hire car behind it and opposite the house. Perhaps that might dissuade anyone from trying the brake line trick again. The police officer gets out of his car and asks me if everything is alright because they'd not been able to get hold of me. I tell him everything's fine, I just had to get a hire car and then went for a drive. He looks in the car and I realise that he's probably wondering where Ben is.

'Your son?'

'He's fine. He's on holiday for a bit.'

'Mrs Murphy, are you sure everything is OK?' he asks again and while I appreciate that he's looking out for us, I don't give him any more information. I just tell him everything is OK.

My phone is still off until I get into the house and then I get a stream of messages and missed calls from Cheryl, Nick, and my mum. All of them are worried about me because they haven't been able to get in touch with me. I realise that turning off my phone would have been worrying for them, but it had to be done. I didn't want anyone tracing where I've just been. I quickly reassure them all.

The house is silent and empty without Ben. I have the urge to text Julia to say I'm home and ask how he is, but I don't. I have to protect my son and that means not giving away where he is, just in case the wrong person gets hold of my phone again, or is able to intercept my messages. Instead I call Cheryl back and talk through her plans for Dylan's funeral. An hour later, there's a knock on my door.

DI Roberts is standing on the doorstep.

'Mrs Murphy,' he begins as usual, 'may I come in?'

I look out onto the road and see the officer in the car looking over at us.

'Sure,' I say and walk through into the sitting room.

'I just wanted to be sure that everything is alright with you.'

'It's fine,' I say, trying not to sound defensive.

'And your son?' He asks. I saw him scan around the room as he came in.

'He's fine.'

'Please, if anyone is trying to coerce you or threaten you, it's important that you talk to us.'

'I did. And you didn't prevent my husband from being killed, although you seem to think that might have been my doing.'

'I didn't say that, Mrs Murphy. I have to ask questions and sometimes those questions are not comfortable ones. Where is your son now?'

'He's safe.'

'We can't protect you both if I don't know where he is.'

'He's fine. If anything changes I'll let you know.'

He studies me for a moment and I can feel the tension between us. I don't trust him and he doesn't trust me.

'Mr Porter has received a warning that neither he or his associates are to approach you or try to contact you. If you receive any more calls please report them to me immediately.'

'So it was him who called me?'

'I didn't say that. We cannot determine who the caller was at present.'

'No, of course you can't.'

'But likewise, you should not approach Mr Porter or his family either, whether as part of this inquiry or through your work.'

So Roberts is saying he doesn't want me investigating him myself.

'Fine,' I say, but I've no intention of not doing that. If Stuart Porter is threatening my family then I'm going to go after him – and DI Roberts isn't going to stand in my way.

He gets up to go, but just as he opens the door, he hesitates and turns round.

'Please Mrs Murphy, be careful.'

'What do you mean?' I ask.

He looks uncomfortable and steps outside. 'Just take care and please trust us to do our jobs.'

With that, he's gone. I watch his back as he heads down the path and back to his car.

What was that about? Was it a threat or a genuine plea to stay safe?

The truth is, I don't trust him to do his job. The track record so far is not great. He didn't save Nick's dad, and he didn't save Dylan. I'm certainly not entrusting my son's life to the protection of a man whose loyalties might well be on the wrong side of the law.

19

Nick has been an absolute star. After DI Roberts left I cried for about two hours solid, missing Ben, missing my old life. Nick turns up at about seven o'clock to find me most of the way through a bottle of wine with eyes like pink, puffy dough balls.

'Are you upset about Dylan?' he asks me, enveloping me in a muscular hug. I breath in his musky scent and a little shiver runs through me.

'Not really, it's just all of it...' I tell him.

'Is Ben already in bed?'

'No. He's somewhere safe.'

Nick holds me away from him and studies my face. 'Somewhere safe? You are being honest with me aren't you?'

'Yes. Absolutely.' I realise that the state of me, and no Ben to be seen, might be giving him the wrong impression. 'He's safer away from me right now. I'm the one that Stuart Porter has the issue with. If Ben's not around me, then he'll be much better off for now.'

Nick considers me for a moment longer and then squeezes me into a tight hug.

'I know how hard it must have been for you to make that decision,' he says. 'You don't need to tell me where Ben is. Keep his location as secret as possible, and I'll help look after his mummy until we can sort this all out and put Stuart Porter where he belongs. You're such a great mum to him Abs.'

'Thank you,' I reply, looking up at him, 'that means a lot. It must have been hard on you when you lost your mum so young.'

Nick clenches his jaw, I see his muscles tighten and he looks away.

'I didn't have a great childhood. My dad was always working and we had no money. I guess he did his best but I missed my mum being around.'

'I can't imagine how difficult it must have been.'

'Yeah, I kind of went off the rails for a short while, angry at the world for taking mum. It's hard to rationalise these things as kids. It's good that Ben is that bit younger and so doesn't understand what's going on.'

'Ben is fine, he really hasn't noticed any change because Dylan had already gone.'

'That's good. I was about fourteen, tough enough being that age without losing your mum.'

'What made you want to become a cop then?'

'My dad I guess, it's all he talked about when he was at home. A couple of his buddies gave me a good talking to which made me realise that I couldn't carry on like I was, and I replaced the hurt and anger with a new drive.'

THAT NIGHT, after we make love, I sob again. Quietly, so as not to wake Nick. Tears, soaking into the pillow. I missed kissing my little boy goodnight, and I lay awake imagining him fast asleep at Julia's house. His little hand clutching his rabbit blanket and the static of his baby monitor playing out in Julia and Oscar's room. I know that he's oblivious to all that's going on, thankfully, but he must wonder where I am. This situation can't go on for weeks or months – I couldn't expect Julia to look after him for that length of time for one thing.

As the sobs subside, I start to formulate a plan. This week I'll get in touch with Mason and see if we can team up to investigate Stuart Porter. I'm not bothered about having the byline in the paper anymore, he can take the credit. I just want that man off my back.

MOST OF THE next week is taken up with funeral arrangements and the other legal stuff that comes with dealing with death. I get constant messages from Harper asking what's going on. I've told the solicitors, who are acting as executors of his will, that Dylan's stuff is all at hers and so she needs to be contacted to ask her to box it all up. I'm not bothered about the sentimental stuff – she can keep that. Everything that Ben might want to look at in later years is already here. I just need his paperwork, bank information and so on, so that I can finalise everything.

Julia is an absolute star, she carries on sending me her usual cheery messages of domestic bliss, and includes little mentions of 'Charlie' for me.

FROM: Julia
   Subject: Shouting mummy
   Took George to school this morning and Mum watched baby James, Lucy, and their cousin Charlie. Couldn't drag Lucy and

Charlie away from the game they were playing. She's so happy having him to play with and it's actually taking pressure off me.

Went into school with George and the teacher was putting some of their work up on the wall. It's a kind of mini biog about your family. George had put, 'My daddy plays with computers'. Which isn't far off really, then for James he'd said, 'My little brother cries and eats a lot.' Again not far off the truth. For me he'd written, 'My mum's favourite hobby is shouting at me.' I nearly died. What kind of mother must his teacher think I am? His teacher was ever so good, said that's nothing compared to some of the things the children say about their parents. She showed me what one little girl had written about her mother. 'My mummy smokes, drinks, and she doesn't work.' That kind of made me feel a bit better.

Hope you and Ben are doing OK. You know where we are if you need us.

Love Julia

I'VE SPENT most of my time in the house. I took the hire car back, paranoid after what they did to Dylan. I'll hire another one when it's time to drive to his funeral. Trips to the solicitor and registrar have been via bus. I got in touch with Mason and asked him how the investigation into corruption was going. He was a little evasive at first, but when I told him I'd resigned but was happy to help him with the story, he became more forthcoming.

Nick has been round most evenings, but tonight he couldn't make it because he had work on. It's the eve of Dylan's funeral anyway, and so I think it's probably for the best. Nevertheless, the house is empty and I feel alone.

I can't be bothered to cook for myself and instead finish up the cold custard that's in the fridge and manage to polish off an entire family-size pack of Doritos while staring at some movie which I can't even remember the name of, but involves lots of humping and car chases. The one problem with having had the financial pressure taken off me, along with my parental responsibilities, is that I've been buying more wine. I sit and just drink a whole bottle tonight before at some point realising I need to go to bed. I send a text to Nick telling him I'm missing him and then bounce off the walls as I lollop up the stairs, stopping briefly in Ben's room where I sniff his blankets and promptly begin to cry.

I go to bed via the bathroom, but something makes me look out of my bedroom window before I get into bed. I think I see a light flash outside. Nothing like fear to sober you up fast. I creep to the window and peer around the curtains. There's a black shadow climbing back over the garden wall. I crane to see them. I could swear it's DI Roberts – with his height he's quite distinctive. The figure stops and takes one last look in the garden and at the house, panning their flashlight around. It is him. I can see his face. He disappears and I rush to the front window in Ben's room to look out onto the street. My heart is thumping in my chest. I'm not thinking totally straight because of the wine, but I'm certainly compos mentis enough to be scared.

There he is, coming out down the side of the house and crossing to the squad car. It's definitely DI Roberts. He bends and speaks to the driver through the window before looking around and then walking off down the street. It's 2 a.m. in the morning. Why would DI Roberts be creeping around my garden at 2 a.m.?

I look on my phone for the SeeCam app. The cameras have briefly picked up movement at the patio doors but nothing else. I'm so relieved that I didn't tell him where Ben is. I go downstairs and look out the patio doors, straining to see outside into the garden in case he left something out there. There's nothing. My mind races. He had to have some reason to be here, sneaking around. Did he try to get in to hurt me? Was he testing the doors to see if he could get in and nose around the house? He has no reason to do that legally so maybe he's trying to break in.

The wine makes everything bigger and more threatening. My head is throbbing with the increase in blood pressure. I'm so grateful for these little security cameras. If I hadn't got it recorded, I might have thought I'd imagined it, just like I did a week ago. Was DI Roberts the shadow in the garden and then the black gloved hand through the window?

I pace around and check all the windows and doors again, pour myself a glass of water and go back upstairs. I miss Ben, but I'm so grateful that he's somewhere away from all this, and safe. I can't wallow in self-pity, I need to work out what DI Roberts' agenda is and how I can send Stuart Porter away for life.

20

I had a crap sleep. I kept waking up with a fright at the slightest noise and by the time my alarm goes off, my head feels as though it has been bumped down the stairs of a twenty floor tower block. I take some paracetamol and then go out into the back garden and look again at what DI Roberts could have been doing. I can't see anything. I text Nick and tell him. He calls me straight back.

'That's just strange, and he didn't contact you about it?' he says. 'And you can't see anything that he could have done?'

'No. There's nothing, and the cameras didn't show anything other than that he came up to the patio doors.'

'OK, he might just have been acting on information, perhaps the surveillance officer saw something. I can double check later, but I know you need to focus on Dylan's funeral today. I'll be thinking about you.'

'Thanks,' I reply.

I would love for him to be there to support me, but that's just not an option. The grieving widow taking her new boyfriend to her husband's funeral would not go down well

– and would be especially cruel for Cheryl and Joe. I have to face this alone.

I half expect a phone call or message from DI Roberts to explain his nocturnal visit. I get neither. Maybe I'm getting paranoid – it wouldn't be a surprise – and not having Ben around has left me without purpose. Tomorrow, I'm due to go into the station and talk through my statement again. I'll see if there's any mention of it then.

I HAVEN'T TOLD anyone that Ben isn't with me. As soon as I turn up for Dylan's funeral, Cheryl asks me where he is.

'I didn't think it was right to put him through this,' I say to her. 'I'll bring him another time when he can understand it all better.'

She nods and I see the fragile honeycomb of her motherhood.

It's a small group of mourners. There are a couple of Dylan's work colleagues, Jim and Harvey his two best friends along with their wives, Harper, and Dylan's sister Rachel who has flown over from America to be here. I sit with the family at the front but I don't feel as though I belong here. We were going to get divorced. My actions caused his death and every tear that they shed feels like a splash of vinegar on an open wound.

I listen to the eulogies and prayers. Rachel, Dylan's sister, shares stories of when they were children, and how he's always been a big brother to her. It's strange but I don't remember him having all that much to do with her when we were together. She used to call him and they'd chat, but he rarely called her, and I can count on one hand the number of times that we've seen her.

We only ever say the good things about the dead. The

disappointments, the frustrations, and anger, they all get buried with them in silence. I force myself to stop thinking about the negatives – Dylan is in that coffin because of me. Instead, I focus on our early years together. The happiness, our wedding. Most importantly, he gave me the most precious gift of all, Ben, so I have to thank him for that.

It is only at the end, as we file out to the graveside to bury him after the service, that I see DI Roberts and DS Fuller at the back. They've kept a low profile, but they're there. Watching. Cheryl, Joe, Rachel, and I walk towards the family plot. One of the undertakers is chaperoning us, and he stops to speak to somebody behind.

'The family have requested a private burial,' he says gently to somebody.

'He loved me, not her.'

I hear Harper's voice and it makes us all turn round.

'She killed him. She knew he was leaving her and was going to change his will. She killed him to get his life insurance before he could. Persuaded him to borrow her car to do an errand and fixed it so he'd have an accident.'

Her words might not be true, but they still hit me in the guts as if she's let loose with a barrage of punches.

'Harper,' I say, 'that's not true. You know that's not true.'

Her face is pure hatred and she steps towards me now, stiff with anger. Her voice filled with dense growling vitriol fuelled by grief. 'So why are the police investigating you then? The detective told me about the life insurance. You paid the premiums, Dylan probably didn't even know you still had him insured.' She looks at Cheryl and Joe who have stopped and are watching in horror.

'That's not true,' I say to them as much as her, 'Dylan and I had a joint policy to protect Ben, we just hadn't got round to changing anything after he left.'

'Really! Convenient, wasn't it? The police don't even believe your story about the so-called murder. You're a liar and you didn't love Dylan. You haven't even brought his son to say goodbye to him. That's how much you care.'

I'm rooted to the ground, speechless. Is that what she really thinks? Do other people believe that too? Do Cheryl and Joe think that? I turn to them and see their faces. Amid the pain and the distress, I see doubt.

'None of that's true,' I say to them again.

'Come on Miss, let's get you somewhere quiet,' the undertaker is saying to her.

She shrugs him off.

'Admit it!' she screams at me. 'You murdered Dylan. You couldn't stand that he was in love with me and had left you. Admit it!'

'No,' is all I can respond.

From behind her I see DI Roberts and DS Fuller approaching. It's Roberts's fault. How did he even know I was paying the premium on the life insurance? He must have contacted the company. And why did he tell her? Does he really believe it too?

'Miss Rodriguez, come with us. Dylan's parents are upset as it is, this isn't the time or place.' DI Roberts puts his hands on her shoulder and firmly guides her away. I hear her break into sobbing as she goes. DS Fuller gives me a stare which is anything but friendly.

Not the time or place? So it's OK to attack me another time then, is that what he's saying?

I turn around and Cheryl, Joe, and Rachel turn too, but now I'm walking a few steps behind them and they don't say a word. Do they believe what Harper has just said?

I'm at a loss and don't know what to do. But DI Roberts was right about one thing: now is not the time or place, so I don't attempt to defend myself further. This is about saying goodbye to Dylan. The stark sight of his coffin being lowered into the ground, makes me focus on what we're here for.

I try to imagine my husband in there, his swollen broken head, the man he had once been. But I don't feel any connection to the wooden casket. Joe and Rachel are supporting Cheryl on either side, a trio of unity. I stand like a lone cactus in the desert, indignant from the attack I've just suffered, but unable to be a part of the oasis of love that comes from Dylan's family.

I might be his wife, but I feel like an outsider standing with them on the edge of their private grief. All I can think about is DI Roberts and how he's doing whatever he can to discredit me. Is this his plan? To ensure that when I give my evidence against Stuart Porter, that the defence will be able to put doubt in the mind of the jurors about my character? He certainly hadn't spent too much time persuading me not to retract my statement and he wasn't overjoyed when I told him I would testify after all.

I leave the wake afterwards as quickly as I can, making the excuse that I need to go and pick up Ben from the childminder. Cheryl and Joe hug me, but there's a thin film of separation between us that hadn't been there before. I know they'll want to keep in touch – not for me, but for Ben. He's all they have left of Dylan. Yet I wonder what doubts have been planted in their minds. I can almost see the seeds growing there behind their eyes. *Our son left her, maybe he had his reasons. Why did she continue paying his life insurance? Why was it that when he borrowed her car the brake lines were cut?*

While I've been at the wake, Nick has messaged me to ask how it's gone and am I ok?

I tell him it was awful and he immediately messages back to see if I need him to come round. I say yes.

Knowing he's watching my back is the only source of strength that I have right now. I long to hold Ben but I am not going to give in to my own selfish needs and endanger him. If DI Roberts is watching me, then he'll find out that Julia has him and I don't want that man knowing anything more about us – especially not where my son is.

Driving back home, I feel a chapter has been closed and now I can move on. There's going to be the police inquiry into how Dylan died, but something tells me they're not going to find anything conclusive that can pin it on Stuart Porter. I got myself into this mess and I need to get myself out. If Ben and I are going to live our lives without constantly looking behind in fear, then I need to get on with my own enquiries.

21

———

Nick is shocked when I tell him what Harper said.

'That's so unprofessional. Roberts should never have told a member of the public about what line of inquiry he is following. No wonder she reacted like she did – and that's just so bloody awful for you. I don't know why he was even there in the first place.' He said this as he poured us each a glass of wine to go with the takeaway he brought round.

I can see he's angry.

'Should I report him?'

Nick thinks. 'I'm not sure that will do any good at this stage. He'll just argue that it's his word against yours and alert him to the fact you're on to him. I think we need to keep a record of all this and build a case.'

'Well you can't do anything, you might get into trouble,' I say to him.

'It's not easy, agreed. But I've got friends in the force. I can try to keep an eye on what he's doing.'

'I'd still like to know why he was in my garden the other

night in the early hours of the morning. He hasn't mentioned it since and I haven't asked him.'

'Maybe I should stay with you every night. Make sure he doesn't try anything.'

'You think it was him who cut the brake line?'

'I really don't know anymore. I don't know how deeply involved he is with Porter. I had thought maybe he just turned a blind eye to things, but now... Now I wonder if he's been playing a bigger role.'

'HOW LONG DO you think it'll be until the trial?' I ask him as we eat.

He sighs. 'These things can take months.'

'I can't be separated from Ben for months.' Just the thought wrings my heart and brings the tears to my eyes again.

'Abbie I'm so so sorry you've been caught up in this. Maybe you should get away with Ben somewhere for a bit, wait it out. You've got money now and you're leaving your job. I'll miss you, but I'd rather know you're both safe and then you can just come back for the trial.'

'I can't leave until I'm sure that Stuart Porter is going down.'

Nick reaches across the table and takes my hand. 'I'll do whatever I can to protect you, and to help you. That man has to pay for what he's done to your life, but you have to think about what's best for you and Ben.'

'What's best is ensuring he doesn't get let out to hurt us,' I tell him. 'He might be out on bail now, but I want to ensure that when this goes to trial, he is locked away for life.'

· · ·

IN THE MORNING, I get up with renewed energy. The first thing I do is text Mason and ask to meet him for a coffee. I feel a buzz when he agrees and suggests this morning at 10 a.m. It's time to start my fight back.

I've taken the hire car back again, but I don't need a car this morning. It's not that I'm paranoid after what happened to Dylan, but the parking situation in town can be a nightmare. I also want to make sure I'm not followed. The last thing I want is for DI Roberts to know that I'm talking to Mason. It won't go down well if he thinks we're running our own investigation.

Part of me can't believe that Roberts is going to have me under surveillance – even after seeing him in my garden. Surely I'm being overly paranoid, this isn't a movie? But when I get on the bus and I catch a glimpse of a man in a baseball cap getting on behind me, I'm not so sure. It's just something about the guy – he doesn't look as though he's on the bus for a purpose and he seems to be ensuring that I can't see his face.

I get off two stops earlier than I need to. As I walk past him, he turns away, dipping his head, and I can't see his reflection in the bus window.

I walk along the main road and watch the bus drive on past me. I know where the man had been sitting and that seat is now empty.

I make a snap decision and take a left down a residential street. A hundred yards on, I turn around. He's there, behind me.

I'm getting a little scared now. I get my phone out and take a photo over my shoulder while still walking, as though I'm looking at my screen. I can see his face better in the photograph. I'm not one hundred per cent sure, but it looks like it could be DS Fuller.

I keep walking and come to the end of the residential street, where it meets another road. One way goes back up to the high street, the other heads away.

I turn right. If he follows me this way, then he's definitely on my tail.

For a moment I think I've lost him. Perhaps I was mistaken, he was just an innocent member of the public after all. I keep on walking and fifty yards along I realise my move had probably just got him wondering if I'd clocked him. He hasn't given up, just hung back a little further. As I walk up the road, I see him turn the corner, still on my tail.

I run.

I run across the road and down the high street, and the second I turn the corner out of his sight, I dive into the nearest shop.

He comes running past a few seconds later, scanning the street, looking for me. I stand, hiding from sight, watching him go past. It is DS Fuller. Why is he watching me?

I step back away from the window and the door. When he realises he's lost me, he might start checking out the various shops. I'm panting and trying to catch my breath after the run.

'You alright love?'

I've walked into a key cutting shop and the guy behind the counter is looking at me.

'Yes, sorry. There was a man following me, I just needed to lose him.'

'You want me to call the police?'

'No, thanks, it's fine. I've lost him now.'

'You sure?'

I nod and smile at the man. He looks worried about me and I appreciate his concern, but calling the police is certainly not going to help me.

A few moments later I say thanks and slip out.

The café where I've arranged to meet Mason is just off the high street. I head across the road and down the side streets to keep out of view. I don't see DS Fuller again. I just hope he hasn't learned to be less conspicuous.

By the time I get to the coffee shop, Mason is sitting at a table in the corner with an empty cup which had until recently contained a double espresso.

'I'm sorry I'm late. I was followed from home.'

'Followed? By who?'

'I think it's DS Fuller who works with DI Roberts. I've got a photo. I lost him.'

I pull my phone out and show Mason the image of the man walking behind me.

'Have the police got you under protection?'

'Not like that. Let me get us coffees and I'll fill you in.'

It takes fifteen minutes to recount all that's happened over the past couple of weeks. From the murder on the dead-end road, to the threatening phone calls and the rat, to Dylan's murder. Mason listens and scribbles notes.

'Before Stuart killed Jordan Christie, I'd heard rumours that there was a police officer involved,' he whispers.

'You were investigating it?'

'Yeah. I've been looking into all the corruption stuff quietly for the last six months.'

'So that explains why DI Roberts kept asking me if I was investigating Stuart. He must have got wind that a journalist was looking into it but just didn't know who.'

'Makes sense.'

'So how far did you get?'

'Well obviously nowhere near far enough because I hadn't connected the dots to Stuart Porter. I'd even suspected Jordan Christie.'

'Well, Stuart may possibly have killed him to silence him. We don't know that he was a complete innocent.'

'No, we don't. People are really scared to talk. There are a lot of businesses and individuals who have benefitted from what appears to be a pretty sophisticated network of public office employees awarding fake contracts or some with over-inflated costs. It's quite ingenious the way that it's set up. Nobody knows who else is on the take besides the king pin, and so sometimes one deal could involve several layers of fraud. Each layer is protected from the other because of the anonymity. That's why this has got so big and gone on for so long. I think it started with security contracts and went on from there. There was a fraud trial about a year ago and I reckon that was someone in the network, but because of the way the deals are set up, nobody else could be implicated. The guy who got convicted had much bigger charges against him, but the evidence wasn't there, there was too much doubt and he only ended up with a suspended sentence and a fine. That appears to have been paid, probably by the network to keep his silence. Someone very clever and very manipulative is masterminding this. From what I can find out, nobody ever meets them, it's all done through third parties and phone conversations. I think that people have been killed before, but it's been cleverly covered up to look like accidents, so fear must also be one of the tactics used to keep the network tight. Stuart Porter made a huge mistake killing Christie – it completely blew his cover. He must have been desperate to have done that, although no doubt didn't expect you to be there watching.'

'Wow Mason, you must have been looking at this for ages.'

'Yeah, it's become a bit of an obsession. I've been trying to trace the money, but Pete doesn't want me investigating.'

'What? Why not? This is a huge story and he doesn't want his crime correspondent digging around?'

'No. Told me to leave it, that it's too dangerous at the moment. I got the impression he was being fed some intel by somebody, but he's not sharing.'

'I don't get it. What are we here for if not to investigate issues like this that are in the public interest? You don't think...'

'I don't think so, but I'm also not letting him put me off. I'll do some sniffing around, even if it's in my spare time. I've been waiting to speak to someone, a guy who I think was involved on the periphery. He's been too scared to talk, but I'm working on him.'

'Be careful. Stuart Porter has already killed twice,' I say, genuinely concerned.

'Yeah, I know. I will. I've got some pretty reliable informants now.'

'So do you think that DI Roberts could be involved?'

'Maybe. I need to do some trawling and see if I can spot any connections between him and Stuart. There has to be some links or clues somewhere.'

'What can I do?'

'Well you're pretty compromised because you're part of two murder investigations now. You can't go digging around like I can. What would be useful is if you can keep pushing the police to tell you what the latest is on their enquiries. It will keep the pressure up on DI Roberts. He has to make headway or his bosses will start asking questions. Besides, you've a right to know what's happening with your husband's murder case. Report everything back to me. Even the tiniest thing.'

I nod, the memory of Dylan in the hospital bed coming back to me.

'Sorry,' Mason apologises. 'How are you doing? I was really sorry about your husband. I mean I know you'd split up and all, but it must have still been a real shock.' He looks embarrassed.

'Thanks, I'm getting there,' I say and give a small smile.

'So DS Barnes reckons his dad was also killed over all this?' Mason changes the subject.

'Yeah. He reckons his dad was close to working out that Stuart Porter was behind it all. He wants to see him put away as much as I do.'

'And DI Roberts? How did Barnes figure that he fitted in?'

'He was his dad's partner. Nick reckons that he would have known what his dad was investigating.'

'Nick is it?'

Frustratingly I blush, realising I've just given away my relationship.

'Yeah, well, he's been really good to me.'

Mason smiles and raises his eyebrows but doesn't say anything more.

'I'll send you the photographs that I took on the day Stuart Porter killed Christie.'

'Photos? You didn't share them with the paper?'

'No,' I look down feeling a little embarrassed. 'I forgot in all the stress.'

Mason looks at me but doesn't say anything else.

'I'm due at the police station later. They want to clarify a couple of things now that I've agreed for my statement to be included as evidence again.'

'OK, well we need to be careful how we communicate if you think that Roberts and Fuller are tracking you, and we don't want Pete knowing what we're up to. Wait here and I'll go buy us a couple of burner phones. Only talk to me on that, OK?'

I nod. I feel much better knowing that Mason is now also in my corner. The more he knows and can find, then the harder it's going to be for Roberts and Porter to silence me.

22

I have a mixture of dread and expectation as I walk into the police station. I know that I'm spoiling for a fight with DI Roberts and his sidekick, and I also know that I need to be careful and try to get as much information as I can out of this session. I want to get my son home with me where he belongs and that's sending me into full mummy-protector mode.

As it is, when I get there the reception woman has an apology to relay to me. He's going to be half an hour late, and please can I wait. Is this some kind of ploy to make me feel nervous?

Most of the seats are taken with a nefarious group of individuals from a woman who looks remarkably like she might be a sex worker, to a guy who has the ruddy, rough skin of a drunk. I take the safest option and go and sit next to the sex worker.

She smiles at me as I sit down and I smile back. There's not exactly much room on these chairs and so I feel as though the two of us are sharing each other's space. I'm wondering what her story is, but then I see the scars of needle marks on her arms. Bloody drugs are responsible for ruining so many lives.

Any time that I'm not doing something, my thoughts turn to Ben. I miss him terribly. I take out my phone and start scrolling through my photographs, looking at his little smiling face, wishing that he was here and I could hold him.

'That your boy?' the woman next to me asks.

'Yeah,' I reply looking up at her sadly.

'He not with you no more?' she asks again.

I sigh. 'He can't be with me at the moment.'

She shoves an old mobile phone under my nose with a photograph of a little girl. 'That's my Maisy. They took 'er away from me too. I'm gonna get her back though.'

'She's so pretty,' I say to her smiling, but the pain in her eyes forces me to look away. 'They haven't taken my boy away from me, I've just had to send him somewhere to be safe.'

'Safe? You got an abusive man?'

'No. Someone killed my husband. I think they were aiming to kill me, cut the brake line on my car, but he was driving.'

There's silence from my companion and I turn back from looking at Ben's face to study hers.

She's watching me. Her attitude has suddenly changed. She looks nervous.

'What is it?' I ask her.

'You saying your little boy could have been killed?'

'Yes. It was my car. I use it every day to take him to the childminder and it was only because my husband's car was in the garage, that he borrowed it.'

She turns away and scans the room.

'Another girl,' she whispers, looking around her again, 'my flatmate, she 'ad a bloke in a few nights ago. Saw the newspaper on 'er table and was boastin' bout having caused the crash. Paper only said it were an accident. 'e said 'e cut the brake line.'

'Who was it?' My heart is racing.

She shakes her head.

'Dunno. She said 'e was nasty. Had a vicious streak to 'im. Said she'd never go with 'im again.'

'He's the man who has been threatening my son's life. Said he'd kill him. I need to know. Can you give me your flatmate's name so I can ask her?'

She gives a nervous shake of her head.

'I'll talk to 'er. You call me later today, I'll see if she'll meet ya. I don't want no part of this mind. I'm doin' it to help ya cos of your boy, nobody should risk a kid's life like that, but I've gotta keep out of it. I don't want nuffin wrecking my chances of getting my little girl back.'

'I totally understand,' I say, putting her number into my phone. 'I really do appreciate this. Thank you.'

It is all just in the nick of time because a minute later, DI Roberts walks out and calls me in. I see him look at the woman next to me. I don't say goodbye to her in case he realises we've been talking. She looks down at her lap, not making eye contact.

'I'm really sorry about the delay, Mrs Murphy' DI Roberts says to me as we go through the security door. 'We had an urgent meeting and I couldn't get out of it. How are you doing?' He turns and looks at me.

'Fine,' is all I can bring myself to say, and I remind myself to keep a neutral face and be polite. I don't want to let on that I suspect him.

'DS Fuller is joining us,' he's telling me as I walk into the interview room.

I stare at the man sitting in the room waiting for me.

There's no doubt that DS Fuller is the man who was following me, he hasn't even bothered to change his clothes.

'I believe you and the DS saw each other this morning...' DI Roberts says to me. I can feel his eyes watching my every move. Trying to bore under my skin and get into my skull to read my thoughts. I try not to show anything on my face, keeping my muscles rigid.

'Why were you following me?' I come out with it.

'Please take a seat,' DI Roberts says. He indicates the other side of the table, that puts him and DS Fuller with their backs to the door, and ensures they're both between me and the exit.

DI Roberts seems to sense my hesitation. I'm not about to let him think he's intimidating me, so I go and sit down.

'I asked DS Fuller to keep an eye on you as I'm concerned about Ben and you. Where is your son, Mrs Murphy?'

'He's safe.'

'You do understand that as a minor, we have a particular duty of care to ensure his welfare is being looked after. I understand that you've been through a frightening and traumatic time but we need to know that Ben is safe and you're not being coerced.'

They're both looking at me as though I'm somehow a bad mother. I don't believe this. He's twisting it to make it out as though Ben needs their help. That I'm not capable of keeping him out of danger. I am absolutely not going to tell him where he is.

'He is safe, with someone I can trust.'

DI Roberts and DS Fuller exchange a glance.

'You do understand that we are bound by law to report any concerns there are for a minor's welfare.'

'Are you threatening me DI Roberts?'

His shoulders slump and he lets out a big sigh. I'm sure that it's for effect in front of his colleague.

'No, Mrs Murphy. I want to ensure that you and your son are safe. Have you received any more death threats? Do you have reason to think you or your son are in danger?'

'Yes. I do have reason to think our lives are in danger. In case you've forgotten, my husband was recently murdered in a car crash that was clearly meant to be for me. Ben and I could have been in that car.'

'I haven't forgotten, it's why we are trying to provide you with some police surveillance. Why did you run away this morning? Did you know that it was DS Fuller or did you think it was someone sent by Stuart Porter?'

'I didn't know what to think,' I lie slightly. 'I'm a woman on her own and a man was following me.' I glare at DS Fuller again. He is watching me impassively, his face giving nothing away, so I change the subject. 'So how is the inquiry going? Have you re-arrested Stuart Porter yet or are you spending all your time watching me instead? And as we're on that subject, why were you in my back garden in the early hours of the morning?'

DI Roberts sits up and leans forward on the table. 'Right, let's get something absolutely clear. I am concerned for your safety and that of your son. The surveillance officer last night said he thought he'd heard something and I went round to check. We would like to offer you police protection – that can come in various forms, right up to going into witness protection which is where we hand you over to a specialist team. Even we won't know where you are. If that is something you would feel safer with, then I can get that ball rolling, but it does mean you have to cut ties with everybody that you know. It's not a decision to be taken lightly.'

He pauses a moment to see if I'm going to respond. 'Our

investigation is progressing, and now that you have agreed for your witness testimony to be included in evidence, we are pursuing further lines of enquiry. His solicitor is arguing self-defence but seeing as Mr Christie didn't have a weapon on him, I think we can discount that. Our only issue is that the crime scene was left unattended for a period of time after you left and before you and the traffic officers arrived back. However, your statement seems to be clear. Are you absolutely sure that Mr Christie did not attempt to attack Mr Porter first?'

'Yes, I'm absolutely sure.'

'And you could one hundred per cent testify to that?'

'Yes.'

'I'm pressing you on this Mrs Murphy, because his defence team will certainly focus on this in court. Mr Porter is saying that Jordan Christie pulled a gun out.'

'Did you find a gun?'

DI Robertson slowly shakes his head.

I shrug my shoulders and raise my eyebrows at him. 'All I saw was a phone.'

'We have a phone but it's not consistent with having been knocked out of someone's hand and hitting the concrete floor of a barn.'

'But there were two phones,' I try, not sure if he's testing me.

'No. Just one.'

Why is he not admitting to seeing the second phone? I saw Nick hand over the evidence bags to Fuller, and he says that there were two phones.

'Will you tell us where Ben is, Mrs Murphy?'

That's what all this is about. He's trying to get me to disclose where my son is by talking about the case and protecting us.

'He's safe. What's happening about finding the person who killed Dylan?'

'We are awaiting the full forensics report on your vehicle.'

'I see.'

'Mrs Murphy, we are doing our best to bring the killer – or killers – of Jordan Christie and your husband to trial for their murders. Please work with us and trust us to do our jobs. I'm sorry that we were unable to prevent Dylan's death, but evading our team when they're trying to ensure you are safe is not going to help you or us.'

I look at DS Fuller. He's watching me, like I'm the problem here.

'Is there something you want to share with us?' DI Roberts tries again.

'No.' I'm not going to tell them that Mason and I are doing our own investigation and I'm definitely not going to repeat what the woman in the waiting room just said to me.

'OK. Thank you for coming in today, but I am going to have to warn you that we will need to have evidence that Ben is safe. Can I ask you to think about that please – or it will be taken out of our hands.'

'He is safe,' I reiterate, but I'm beginning to feel like that woman I just met in reception. If they find out where Ben is, they could take him away from me – and then I won't be able to protect him at all.

23

———

I'm like a caged lion when I get home. How dare that man insinuate that I don't know how to protect my own child. I want to call Nick to rant, but I don't. He'll be at work and it also puts him in a difficult position.

I've literally not told anyone where Ben is. The only people who know are me, Julia and Oscar. That way nobody can feel compromised. If something did happen to me, I know that Julia would do the right thing.

What I am excited about is the fact I may find out the identity of whoever it was that cut my brake line and murdered Dylan. I know I'm taking a risk believing that woman, but something tells me she was being genuine. I think she told me out of empathy, mother-to-mother. Our lives might be totally different but we have that connection.

I dial the number she's given me.

'Yeah?'

'Hi, we met earlier in the police station and you said you would be able to put me in touch with your flatmate who knows who killed my husband.'

'Yeah, right. I spoke to 'er. She says she'll meet you but

she won't go to court or nothing. She don't want to be dragged into no police inquiry.'

I think quickly. It's going to be hard to prove anything without her testimony, but at least if I know for sure who it is, maybe Mason and I could do something. Maybe it wasn't Stuart or DI Roberts who cut the line – they could just as likely have hired someone.

'OK, that's fine. I just need to know. What's your friend's name?'

'Inga.'

'Inga, Inga what?'

'Just Inga.'

'OK, where do I find her?'

'We'll be at the Blue Note Bar tonight. Nine onwards. She wants fifty quid.'

I had half expected something like this. I have no problem paying her, my only fear is that she's leading me on, but my gut tells me not. I don't think she had time to think up the con sitting next to me in the police station. I just hope I'm not being naive.

'No problem. I didn't get your name.'

'Dee.'

'OK, thanks Dee, I'm Abbie. I'll see you both later.'

I'm buzzing when I get off the phone. At last I'm making some headway. If this woman can give me a name, then that's going to be a huge leap forward in finding Dylan's killer and hopefully linking Stuart Porter to another murder. The more evidence we can find against him, the longer sentence he's likely to face.

I text Nick to say that I'm going out this evening and so not to worry about coming round. He messages me back and asks me to check in with him.

I'll be worried if I don't hear from you all evening, just message to let me know you're home safe x

I promise that I will.

THE BLUE NOTE Bar is an old jazz bar in a basement down some stone steps in town. It used to be one of those places filled with smoke and the smell of spilt beer. The stains of the nicotine are still on the walls, but now it's just alcohol, and no doubt under-the-table drug deals, that fuel the atmosphere. It's been a long time since I've been here and I notice that a new handrail has been put up on either side on the way down to the entrance, no doubt a modern concession to health and safety regulations and the desire not to be sued by anyone who takes a dive down the steps.

The handrail appears to be the only evidence of modern upgrades, because when I go inside, it doesn't look as though the place has been redecorated since it opened. Old posters of jazz musicians who have played the Blue Note line the walls, some layered on top of others. They haven't faded thanks to the lack of sunlight in the bar, and they give the place its authentic bluesy feel. The small stage area, with its worn wooden floor where so many have stood and sat, tapping their feet, lungs pumped full of smoky air as they played their saxophones and trumpets, is empty for now. The soulful jazz that is playing comes from speakers placed around the walls and no doubt the old CD player I can see behind the bar.

I stand and scan the whole room. It's not busy – only about a quarter full, but I don't immediately see Dee, the woman from the police station, or another single woman. I walk around in case there are hidden nooks that I can't see. Nothing.

A few lone men are watching me and I hope they don't think I'm here for the same reason Dee and Inga might be. There's an older woman and a young guy behind the bar. I decide my safest option is to sit at the bar and order a drink until they arrive.

I'd been careful coming here, making sure no one was following me again. I left via the back gate, being careful to lock it again after me. The memory of DI Roberts and the previous intruder scaling the brick wall, still indelibly marked in my head.

I arrived five minutes early at the Blue Note, but by the time half past nine comes round and they've still not arrived, I'm getting jittery. I haven't taken my eyes off the door, apart from to rebuff three hopeful men who wanted to 'buy me a drink'. I've bought a white wine spritzer, a little alcohol to give me dutch courage and a long drink to last me. My glass is now empty.

I beckon the woman behind the bar.

'Do you know Dee and Inga?' I ask her. 'I'm supposed to meet them here and I wondered if they have already been in?'

The thought that maybe they'd arrived earlier and then got a client each, which would have meant turning down money, crossed my mind. I wasn't sure how long these things took.

'Not seen 'em,' the woman replies, eyeing me suspiciously. 'You want another?'

The thought is tempting, but I need my wits about me.

'Just a soda water and lime please,' I reply, and don't miss her *not impressed with that order* look.

Five minutes later, the glass of soda and lime is plonked in front of me and I return to watching the door.

.   .   .

IT's ten o'clock by the time I decide they're not coming. I've tried Dee's mobile several times but it's going to voicemail. I go to the loo and then leave. Perhaps she changed her mind and is out working. I know where the girls hang out touting for business – they could be there, or maybe someone has seen them and can tell me where they live.

Not surprisingly, the area of town known for its red-light district is not the most salubrious of locations. I keep my phone in an inside pocket and hold the rape alarm I carry with me in my hand. I think of Nick and know that he'd be cross at me for walking around here on my own, but needs must. I've been in worse places.

I spot two women standing chatting and smoking under a lamppost. I'm mindful of the fact that I could get my face slapped if I insinuate that someone is a sex worker and they're not, but as I approach them, I'm pretty sure that I'm on target. They are looking down the road, behind me, and I realise that a car is cruising slowly up. With horror, I hear the electric window wind down next to me.

'You working?' a male voice asks.

'No. Piss off,' I hiss back at him.

The engine revs up and the car speeds away up the street. That probably wasn't my smartest move – I may have just lost these two girls some work. They're staring at me now as I walk up to them.

'Hi,' I say smiling, 'have either of you seen Dee or Inga?'

'You a rozzer? Why you wanting them?' the older woman of the two asks me. Underneath the bright red lipstick and heavy blue eye make-up is an attractive woman.

'We were supposed to meet at the Blue Note,' I say to her. 'I'm not with the police.'

'Well if they ain't there then they don't wanna meet with ya after all,' she replies, looking me up and down.

I can understand the reticence and mistrust, but I don't give up. She definitely knew who I was talking about. I say thanks and walk on to see if anyone else will help me.

Down the next street I can see a couple more girls hanging out. One of them has just got into the car from earlier. She looks younger than Dee, but I'm hoping it wasn't Olga. One girl is left, kicking her feet on her own.

'Hi,' I say.

She looks up at me, hope in her eyes. She looks so young but I can tell from the desperation in her eyes that she needs to score her next hit.

'Hi,' she says looking me up and down. 'You after a little fun?'

'No. Sorry. I was looking for Dee and Inga, don't suppose you've seen them have you?'

'Where you from? That church lot again?' she asks, her tone becoming defensive.

'No, I'd just arranged to meet them and they didn't show. I'm checking they're ok, that's all.'

She shrugs. 'Try Esther on the corner over there, she's been round here forever and might know.'

I look over to where she's pointing and see a woman in her forties leaning against the wall. She's on her phone.

'Thanks,' I say to her and walk off. I was sorely tempted to give her some money, tell her to go and get a decent meal, get off the streets, get some help before it's too late, but I know she'd only go and turn whatever cash I gave her into something to inject. She needs more constructive help than just cash.

'Hi Esther,' I say approaching the older woman. She's staring at her phone looking upset.

She looks up and her face hardens.

'Have you seen Dee and Inga round here tonight?'

She stares at me. 'What are you, press?'

I'm shocked at her observation skills. I lie. After all, it's not why I'm here tonight. 'No. We were supposed to meet up earlier and they didn't show. I'm worried about them. Don't suppose you know where they live do you?'

She doesn't say anything for a few moments, just stares at me, her face rigid. Then I see a wave of something else go across her features. Something of the upset from earlier.

'Not hard. Turn the corner and follow the blue lights,' she says to me and walks off.

I'm pretty sure she's joking with me. I know they call this the blue light district, but we're not in Amsterdam; prostitution isn't legal and people don't put blue or red lights outside their apartments. But, I go round the corner anyway.

What I see makes me stop dead.

The street is filled with police cars, forensics, and an ambulance. People are milling around staring up at a building.

I suddenly feel sick. Very sick. The acidic bile of white wine and lime at the back of my throat.

I walk towards the police cordon, but it's like I'm having an out-of-body experience. I can't believe what I might possibly be seeing. I don't want to believe it.

I ask the first person I come to. 'What's happened?'

'Two women murdered,' she says. 'Bloody awful.'

'Do you know who they are?' I ask, dread filling my insides with black, writhing poisonous snakes.

'Not sure.' She nods over at another woman. 'She lives in the same block. She might know.'

I look over to another woman, middle aged, clutching a small dog which is shivering.

'Hi,' I say walking over. 'He's gorgeous,' I add, my

journalist training starting to return. 'He must be scared with all this noise.'

She looks down at her little dog and kisses his head. 'They won't let us back in. Still searching the place.'

'I've got friends who live here,' I add. 'I'm worried about them. Do you know who was attacked?'

'I didn't hear nothing. They reckon it was about seven o'clock, but I didn't hear a thing. The bloke in number four called the cops. Said he heard screaming and a struggle. Blood everywhere apparently.'

'Who is it?' I ask again. The woman is staring transfixed at the building in front of us.

'They were nice you know. I think maybe they were an item, do you know what I mean? Street workers, but that don't mean you're not a good person.'

'Dee and Inga?' I ask her.

Finally she turns and fully registers me, looking at my face.

'Yeah. Dee and Inga. Friends of yours are they? I'm sorry love.'

I don't hear anything else she says to me. I have backed away, panic rising up through me like a volcano.

This cannot be a coincidence. How did he find out? How did he know that they were going to talk to me? This is my fault. I as good as murdered those women myself.

For a moment I step out of the crowd and lean against a wall trying to catch my breath. I think I'm having a panic attack. My breathing is shallow, I am struggling to get in enough oxygen; and my heart has accelerated so fast that I'm beginning to feel slightly giddy and faint.

This can't be happening. This just cannot be happening.

'Mrs Murphy! Mrs Murphy, are you alright?'

I look up. In front of me is the detective who'd followed

me that morning, DS Fuller. He's staring at me with his dark eyes. 'Why are you here, Mrs Murphy?' he's asking me, but I don't reply. Beyond his shoulder, across the road, I see DI Roberts standing watching. DS Fuller takes a step closer. 'Mrs Murphy?'

I catch what little breath I have – and run.

24

—————

I run down the road, away from there, away from DS Roberts and DS Fuller. I literally pushed DS Fuller out of my way. Absolute panic taken over.

How...? How did they know?

I run from the murder scene and back towards the centre of town. It's nearly eleven o'clock; most pubs would be shut. For a few moments I think about going back to the Blue Note, but then I'd already asked them about Dee and Inga. When they see the headlines tomorrow, they might report me. I head to the bus station instead, scanning the timetables. The last bus home is in twenty minutes.

I slump down onto one of the metal benches and try to calm myself down.

Blood everywhere, the woman said.

It's my fault. My fault that two women are dead.

I feel my phone vibrating in my pocket and pull it out. It's DI Roberts. I ignore it, letting it go to voicemail. Instead, I phone Nick.

'Hi, you home now? Did you have a good evening?' his cheerful voice comes to me from a totally different world.

'He's murdered them,' I say, my voice shaky.

'What? Who? Are you OK? Is Ben OK?'

'Yes, fine. I was going to meet a woman who said her flatmate had spoken to the man who cut my brake line. They're both dead. How did he know? How did he know I was going to meet them?'

'*Shit,*' is all Nick says and then there's silence. I know he's thinking. 'Where are you?'

'At the bus station, my bus is in ten minutes.'

'Were you followed?'

'No, but DI Roberts and DS Fuller were there at the flats where the women were murdered.'

'Did the women tell you anything?'

'No. They didn't get the chance.' I watch as my bus pulls into the station. 'My bus is here...'

'OK, I'll meet you at your bus stop. I'm not having you walk home alone.'

HE'S THERE WAITING for me as the bus pulls up to the stop. It's only a five or ten minute walk from my house, but I do appreciate him being by my side. I am taking steps but I don't feel my legs. I have a feeling of being untethered in a world that's gone crazy, filled with dark evil in every corner, and he is my anchor, my light.

'There's a company you need to call first thing tomorrow morning,' he says to me. 'I've used them once before, they're good. They have equipment that can test for monitoring devices, on your phone, bugs in your home, that kind of stuff.'

'You think they could be listening in on my phone calls?' I say, feeling my throat constrict even more.

'I don't know Abs, I'm really sorry. I don't know. But I do

know you need to get everywhere swept, especially after you saw Roberts in the garden the other night. Where did you have the conversations with the two women?'

I think back to earlier in the day.

'Oh god, he saw me sitting next to her.'

'Who?'

'DI Roberts, when I was in the police station going over things, he saw me sitting next to Dee.'

'But how would he have known she was giving you information?'

'I rang her. Called her from home on my mobile. I can't remember exactly what I said, but I think I said something about her knowing who had cut the brake line.'

'And how did she know that? Why did this woman know who it was?'

'She's a sex worker. Her friend had a client and he said he did it. Boasted about it apparently.'

'Shit. You should have told me Abbie. If you ever get another lead like this, you need to tell me first. You could have walked into an incredibly dangerous situation. As it is, they're dead and you're thankfully alive, but next time...'

'I'm sorry,' I say and feel the tears welling up inside me.

'It's ok, sorry I didn't mean to sound so harsh.'

'No, you're right. I should have told you.'

'Did you tell anyone else?'

'No. Nobody.'

'Then I suspect we've lost the opportunity. He's beaten us again.'

'Yes,' I say in a small voice. The image of my son in my head. 'Maybe I should get away with Ben. Roberts was asking where he was earlier, saying it was a safeguarding issue. He's using the law against us.'

'That's exactly why they get away with so much, they use the law to their own advantage.'

WHEN I GET HOME and Nick has gone to the toilet, I get out the burner phone that Mason gave me and tell him what's happened. He sends shocked emojis back and says he can't talk right now but will call me tomorrow. I wonder if he's working or just out on a date.

Thinking that DI Roberts could have bugged my house has left a sick feeling in my stomach. It no longer feels safe in my own home. Even with Nick here, I feel self-conscious, as though some peeping Tom is watching our every move.

Nick gets his phone out and goes online, then shows me the website of the company he'd been talking about. I write it down. I'm now becoming totally and utterly paranoid about anything digital. If they have bugged my phone, can they see everything on it?

'I've got tomorrow morning off, do you want me to stay?' Nick asks. 'I'm worried about you. You've got to stop trying to investigate this, it's going to get you killed.'

'Thanks for offering,' I reply, burrowing my face into his chest. Then another thought comes into my mind. What if something happens to Nick? What if Stuart Porter or DI Roberts start thinking that he's an obstacle? That he knows too much. 'Maybe you shouldn't be around so much. They might target you.'

He holds the top of both my arms and gently pushes me off his chest so that he can look in my face.

'Abigail Murphy, I am not afraid of either of them. Policing is my job, I swore to protect the innocent and while I may have got a little more involved with you than I should have, that is exactly what I'm going to do. I believe that

Stuart Porter had my father killed – whether he did it, or Roberts did, they're obviously both in this together. I am not going to let anything bad happen to you. We have to keep fighting them until Porter is in jail.'

'But what about DI Roberts? We've got nothing on him.'

'We'll find something, there has to be a way to expose him.'

'*Shhh*,' I say to him, looking around the house as though I'm going to see the bug that's been listening in to my conversations. 'Maybe we shouldn't say things like that,' I whisper.

'Fuck you Conor Roberts. Fuck you Stuart Porter,' Nick says loudly. Then he whispers in my ear, 'They're not going to win Abbie. We are. I promise.'

25

———

I listen to DI Robert's voicemail before I go to bed.

'Mrs Murphy, is everything alright? Why were you in Liston Street this evening? Were you reporting or were you there for something else? Could you please call me. You looked upset – I want to know that you're OK.'

Needless to say, I don't ring him. The second I get up in the morning, it's to the security company that I put in a call. I ring from the garden on the burner phone that Mason gave me, keen to not alert whoever might have bugged my phone that I am on to them. I'm impressed when they say they can come round immediately.

The man arrives with his equipment and immediately sets about scanning the whole house. I trail him around, a nervous shadow, waiting to see if he finds anything.

He does.

He points toward the air vent near to the patio doors. That's where I was standing yesterday when I made the phone call to Dee. I remember looking out over the garden as I spoke to her.

The man doesn't say a word, just starts to unscrew the

vent. Seconds later, he produces a small electronic device which he places into a box.

'Standard listening device,' he says to me once it's in the box.

'How did it get in there?'

'That I can't tell you, but could have been slipped in through the vent from outside. Didn't even need to be inside the house to do it.'

The image of DI Roberts in my back garden near the patio doors in the early hours of the morning comes back to my mind.

'I'll carry on checking for you,' the man says.

'How's it going?' Nick was in the kitchen taking a phone call and missed the find.

'He's just found a listening device in the air vent,' I say nodding towards it.

'Well that explains a lot. Has Roberts been on his own in here at all? Did he ever come round and you left him alone?'

I think back over the times he's been round the house. 'Yes. The day of Dylan's accident. I left him on his own while I got ready to go to the hospital. But he could also have just put it in through the vent from outside... that must have been what he was doing in the back garden.'

Nick shakes his head, not because he's saying no but because he can't believe what he's hearing.

We don't say anything more because the doorbell goes. I head to the window to see who it might be.

My heart jumps. It's DI Roberts. He must know we've found the bug. I mouth to Nick, who raises his eyebrows and indicates that he's going to go upstairs out of the way.

Once he's gone, I open the door to Roberts. I have no intention of letting him in so he can plant another device.

'Mrs Murphy,' he says, 'Did you get my message? I was concerned about you after last night.'

'I'm fine, thank you,' I reply.

I can see him trying to peer behind me into the house.

'Is Ben with you?' he asks now.

'No.'

'Can I ask you again why you were in Liston street last night? Did you know the two women who were murdered?'

I think quickly; I need some kind of excuse. 'No. Why would I? I was out in town, someone told me there'd been an incident and I thought I'd go along and see if I could write a story.'

'So what happened?'

'I beg your pardon?'

'Well, did you write the story? I've not seen anything online or in the paper yet?'

'No. I felt ill. I think I'd eaten something dodgy, that's why I had to leave.'

DI Roberts sighs and stares at me. 'Mrs Murphy I want to help you but you need to let me help. Please.'

'I'm fine,' I reply and meet his stare.

'OK. I am going to have to ask you to let us know where Ben is and to show us that he's safe. I can only give you another twenty-four hours before this will get taken out of my hands. Do you understand Mrs Murphy?'

'Oh yes, I understand,' I reply. 'Is that all?'

He sighs again. 'Yes. Please remember I am trying to help you.'

WHEN I SHUT the door on him, I realise that I'm shaking. The past few weeks have hit me emotionally and physically. My head feels as if it will explode and my body is rigid, my neck and shoulders painful. Behind me, Nick and the security guy come down the stairs.

'You OK?' Nick asks me.

I nod, momentarily leaning on the bottom stair rail for support and comfort.

'All clear upstairs,' the security guy says. 'Do you want me to check your phone?'

'Yes please,' I reply and pull it out my pocket and give it to him.

He swipes and clicks, and then runs it over with some sensor. 'It's clear, you're ok.' He replies and hands it back. 'Any other phones?'

'No that's it,' I reply. I know I'm lying but Mason's phone is just between me and him and I'm going to keep it that way.

What's worrying me the most right now is DI Roberts' warning that I've only got twenty-four hours to prove that Ben is safe before he says it's out of his hands. What do I do to keep my son safe? Am I going to have to go to jail to protect him?

Nick's face says it all when I tell him. 'This is what they do. They wreck lives. Ruin families. They have to be stopped.'

I'm one hundred per-cent in agreement, but how?

26

Do you ever sit and look at your life and compare it to how it was you'd imagined it would be when you were growing up? I blame American family sitcoms for a generation of missed expectations. They were always so perfect. Even if your family life as a kid wasn't like that, it didn't matter because when you became a grown up you were going to make sure your kids had the perfect dream home life. When Ben was born I wanted a house with a big garden and a little wood at the bottom so that he could run around building dens and climbing trees. I imagined us in our big family kitchen, laughing and chatting at breakfast and dinner, then at night, tucking him in all smiles and going back down to snuggle on the sofa with Dylan. But Dylan is dead, having walked out on me. We're not only on our own – I'm having to keep Ben far away, and I don't know when we'll be together again. Safe. My life has become a horror movie and I don't know how to get that family sitcom dream back.

When Dylan and I first split up I would phone his mobile, making sure he couldn't see my number and know it was me. As soon as he answered, I would end the call. I didn't do it to irritate or scare him, but just to hear his voice. To remember him... know he was still there. I haven't done that in a long time. I also used to Facebook-stalk him, searching for signs of what he was doing, who he was with, checking out all his Facebook friends (which aren't that many) to see if he'd commented about any of their posts. I tried to spy on 'her' too, googled her, saw her perfect gym body and all her sickly selfies on Instagram. Now she's an emotional wreck as well and thinks that I murdered her boyfriend. I wouldn't have had Dylan back, but I also wouldn't have wished him dead. Nick has started to show me just what I was missing in a relationship. It's amazing how we settle with what we've got because we think that's our only choice.

Nick has to leave shortly after the security expert and I'm suddenly alone, in a house of silence again, my fears about Ben and his safety, my only company. When my phone rings it makes me jump. My boss's name comes up.

'Abbie, how are you?' he says.

'Surviving, thanks Pete,' I say. I'm not about to tell him all my woes.

'Abbie, I've had the police on the phone. They're concerned for your welfare and asked me to make sure that you're OK.'

An icy grip clutches at my insides. 'Police? Any particular police officer?'

'DI Roberts. He's worried about threats you received and the fact he hasn't seen Ben for a while. Was asking me if I knew anything and if I could see if you were alright? He's concerned that you are either being threatened or coerced in some way.'

'I was threatened, in fact someone tried to kill me,

although unfortunately for them and Dylan, they killed my husband instead. So yes, I'm very concerned about Ben, so he's somewhere safe and I won't tell anyone where he is in order to keep him safe.' I stop, realising that my voice has turned aggressive and defensive.

There is silence from Pete. 'OK. But you know Abbie, if you need help we are all here. You've been through something terrible, you're still going through a stressful time. You can't do it all on your own. Sometimes you need to ask for help.'

'I will, thanks Pete. I appreciate the offer.' I let out a sigh and soften my voice. He is only looking out for me. He isn't the enemy.

BEING without Ben is hurting me. I'm desperate to see his little face and to hold him to me. Every cell in my body is telling me to go to him and protect him, but I know Julia is keeping him safe. The further away he is from all this, the better. I have to stay strong for him.

I scour the local news reports about the murders of Dee and Olga, devouring every meagre scrap. There's so little detail. I've asked Nick if he can find out anything about it without getting into any trouble, but the truth of it is that it's all too late. Too late for me to find anything out about who murdered Dylan, and tragically too late for Dee and Olga. If I hadn't asked to speak to her, then they would still be alive today. If I'd known that DI Roberts, or Stuart Porter – whichever one of them was listening – had a bug in my house, then I would never have been so careless. One wrong turn, and I've caused so much devastation. I know I'm not the killer, I know I never meant for any harm to come to

Dylan, Dee, or Olga, but it's because of me. I'm the common denominator.

I read the short interviews with people who knew Dee and Olga.

They were such a lovely couple, always ready to help out even though they didn't have much themselves.

Dee had been through a tough time and Olga helped get her life back together.

There was a suggestion that the attack might have been related to their line of work, but the police detective in charge, Detective Inspector Lisa Rubin, said she has an open mind and doesn't want people speculating. She's appealed to the community for information and for any witnesses to come forward.

I think about Dee sitting next to me in that police station reception and her hope that one day she'd get her daughter back. That will never happen now. Her daughter will spend the rest of her life without her mother.

If Stuart or Roberts killed Dee and Olga, then why not just kill me instead? I'm the fly in the ointment, the one who will testify against him in court. It has to be only a matter of time before they come after me again.

I've lost weight these last few days. Most of the time I feel sick, my intestines like a pit of snakes twisting and writhing. At times I struggle to drink, let alone eat. Julia has been amazing. Every day she's sending me her humorous updates on their family life. I know she's making sure she doesn't forget so that I can hear news about Ben. They're the only thing keeping me going.

FROM: Julia

Subject: Feline Freak-out

Hi, hope all's good with you. The decorators have officially left the building, although not without one final stress yesterday. The inside is all done, but the painter was putting the finishing touches to the outside, which included painting the doorstep in black gloss. He then knocked on the front door to let me know he'd finished.

Of course, Ziggy cat decided to choose that moment to return home and came racing into the house, seemingly from nowhere. He managed to put all four paws, that's eighteen cat toes, onto the freshly-painted doorstep and then shot into the hall and tried to turn left into our sitting room. That's where we have the new, two-weeks-old, carpet, which is about as far away as you can get on a colour chart from black. The English rugby squad would have been proud of me. It took a matter of seconds, but I saw it all unfold in slow motion. I managed to leap and grab Ziggy by the tail as his front foot was literally inches from the new carpet. He screamed and yowled and ran straight back out again, where he sat under the hedge looking mortified, while Lucy and Charlie thought the whole game was highly amusing and the painter just stood with his mouth open and said, 'Oh!'. I mean WTF, 'oh!' Was that the best he could do?

Mum was luckily due to come and take Lucy and Charlie out to the park so I also got James ready in his pram, because I could see Ziggy trying to lick black gloss paint off his paws which meant I was going to have to take him to the vet. He wasn't impressed with me after I'd pulled his tail so trying to catch him to shove him in his travel basket was another entire episode of Gladiators. He's even less impressed with me now that I have to keep him in with one of those lampshade collars around his neck for three days so he can't lick his paws, and he has to take some horrible medicine, which I've no idea how I'm going to persuade him to eat. All I know is I felt sick after I got the vet bill!

Hope life is easier your end now the funeral is over. Give Ben a big hug and a kiss from me.
Julia x

I AM SO grateful for great friends like Julia, and for the support that Nick is giving me, but I'm terrified about what's going to happen tomorrow when I don't tell DI Roberts where Ben is.

I'm working myself up into a frenzy of worry, running various scenarios through my head, including buying tickets to Mexico for Ben and I, when my phone goes. Not my usual phone, but my burner phone that Mason gave me. I hope he's not ringing because Pete's put him up to it.

'Hi Mason, you're not calling me to ask about my welfare too are you?'

'Abs, we need to talk,' he says. His voice sounds different. Anxious, urgent. 'I've found out some information.'

'What information?' I reply.

'You need to hear this, but not on the phone. I've spoken to that contact. Meet me in town?'

'At The Coffee Pot?'

'Yes. In one hour. Make sure no one follows you, and Abbie, don't tell anyone.'

I AM SO grateful for the fact my house has been de-bugged. I'm confident we won't get a repeat of last night. All I've got to do is make sure nobody follows me. I look out the sitting room window and see the police car outside. It's been there for days now, with just the occupant changing. I feel a little guilty that they're there, trying to keep me safe. Surely not every police officer on the force is on Stuart Porter's payroll?

I hope they haven't sussed out my back garden exit. I sneak out through the back gate again and disappear through the side streets, watching my back as I go.

How has my life ended up like this? I feel like I'm the fugitive, the one on the run from the law. How much longer will I have to live like this? How much longer do I have to be apart from my son? And will we ever get our lives back?

27

———

I'm absolutely sure that I make it to town without being followed. I've even turned off my usual phone even though I know the security guy said it was clean, and just brought the one that Mason gave me. This way, I can be sure that as only Mason and I know about this phone, it's not likely to be traced to me.

I stick to back roads, taking lots of turns to ensure I'm not being tailed. As I'm making my way there, I hear sirens not far away and it makes my heart race again. Now, I think every emergency service siren is related to me. But it's no wonder I'm paranoid.

At The Coffee Pot, I order both of our usuals, expecting Mason to turn up while I'm still waiting for them. He doesn't. I take them over to the table we sat at before and hope that he hasn't been caught up in traffic, as otherwise his coffee is going to get cold. I cover it with the saucer to keep the warmth in.

Ten minutes later and most of my coffee has been drunk but there's no sign of Mason. I'll give him another five minutes and then ring.

Five minutes later, I call him.

Nothing.

A vine of dread is starting to grow inside of me, and I can't stop its tendrils from entwining themselves around my guts.

I wait another ten minutes and then call again.

No answer.

I text him.

No reply.

Someone comes into The Coffee Pot and starts chatting to the girl behind the counter about something that's happened in the high street.

'Some bloke got mowed down by a hit and run. Horrible,' she says.

Every molecule in my body turns to ice.

No. It can't be Mason. Nobody could know we're meeting. He's probably just late because the High Street has been blocked off, or maybe he's stopped to cover the story for the paper. That's the most likely explanation. It's hard to resist a story.

I call his mobile again. Still no reply.

I wait a few more minutes and the tendrils of dread turn into a forest.

I have to find out for myself.

I get up and leave, heading straight for the high street. The area has been cordoned off and lots of police in uniform are corralling people away from the area.

'What's happened?' I ask a man who is walking out from under the cordon.

'Some woman got run over I think,' he says.

A woman. That means it can't be Mason. I'm so sorry for the woman but relief floods through me.

I'm not far from where the accident took place and can

see that they're trying to preserve evidence. How can someone run somebody over like that and then just drive off? I hope that there's plenty of CCTV around so the police can catch them.

I bet Mason is covering this for the paper and that's why he's late.

I take out our burner phone and try him again. As it rings in my ear, I hear a ringing nearby. That has to be his phone, so he's here somewhere close by. Probably in the crowd on the scent of a story and having totally forgotten our coffee appointment.

I push along to where I can hear the phone ring, looking for him.

I can't see him.

The phone rings off and I hear the other phone stop.

I call him again, and again I hear his phone ringing. Why isn't he answering it?

It's then that I realise it's not coming from anywhere in the crowd, but is instead coming from inside the cordon.

It rings off again.

I press the call button once more, trying to track the sound.

Then I see it.

A police officer is standing by the back of the ambulance with an evidence bag in his hand.

No!

No! No! No!

I almost faint. This cannot be happening.

'Excuse me, excuse me...' I push past the officer at the boundary and head towards the police officer holding Mason's phone. 'Who is it that's been run over? I think it's my friend.'

'Madam you need to move away please, this is a crime scene.'

'No. I've been waiting for him and he's not turned up. That phone you're holding rings when I call him.' To prove my point I dial his number again, my hands trembling. The phone in the police officer's hand rings.

He looks at me. His face has gone from annoyance to sympathy.

'Is it Mason in the ambulance? Mason! Mason!' I call out.

'I'm sorry I have to ask you to leave this area,' the officer tries again. 'Your friend has been taken to hospital,' he says.

'Isn't he in that ambulance?'

'No. Two women were also struck but they've only got minor injuries and are also being treated for shock.'

'What about Mason?'

'His injuries are more serious, but you'll need to call the hospital, I'm afraid.'

'Have you caught them? The person who did this?'

'The driver failed to stop.'

I can't stand this anymore. It feels like everyone is pressing in on me. Watching me. Listening to me. The whole world is against me. Whatever way I turn people are being killed, the investigation stopped.

I panic.

I start to run.

I push at people to get past them. Fear is fuelling my legs, adrenaline pumping around me.

How did Stuart Porter or DI Roberts, or whoever it is, how did they know that I was meeting Mason? I told nobody. Our phones are burner phones. Did Mason make a mistake somehow? Did he ask the wrong person the wrong question? Where did he call me from? The office? Is his house or the office bugged too?

The bus home is just about to leave and I jump on board. The driver looks at me as though I might be on drugs, or about to rob him. I pay my fare and go and sit at the back where I can see everybody getting on and off the bus.

All I can think is thank god Ben is somewhere safe.

I text Julia.

How you all doing?

She replies straight away. *I'm attached to a baby. Lucy and her cousin are playing happily building a nest for Ziggy cat. Not sure he's going to appreciate it though, he's still grumpy. How are you?*

I feel the longing for that life. For the days when all I had to worry about was getting Ben and I up in the morning so I could go to work and then come home to him. Four people are dead, all murdered, and now I don't know if Mason is just hurt or dead too. All of them, apart from Jordan Christie, connected to me.

Fine, is all I reply. *Speak soon.*

I call Pete at the paper. He doesn't answer his office phone, so I try his mobile. It rings for a bit and then he picks up.

'Pete, it's Abbie,'

'I can't talk right now Abbie,' he sounds distracted, as though he's with someone.

'Have you heard about Mason?' I ask.

Silence.

'Yes. What do you know about it?'

'We were supposed to meet, he didn't turn up and then I found out he's been involved in a hit and run. Is he OK?'

'He's in a critical condition. What were you meeting about?'

'He was looking into Stuart Porter and the corruption, he said he'd found something out... Pete, those two women murdered yesterday, they were also connected to all this.'

More silence. I think I hear a whisper.

'Abbie you need to stay out of it. You've got Ben to think about. Go home and stay there. Leave it to the police.'

He's got no idea. No idea that the police – or at least some of them – are involved in this. How can I just leave it alone? They won't leave me alone. I am not going to let Stuart Porter hurt my son. I'm also not going to let Stuart Porter make Ben an orphan. I'm going to fight this.

'OK,' I say and end the phone call.

It's my stop and I get off the bus, but I feel like a rabbit on open ground near to a nest of eagles. As I walk, I'm constantly scanning the street, listening out for any danger. I've been so careful. How could Porter have known about Mason unless the leak wasn't from my end?

I glance at the police officer in the car outside my house and see him write something down. They're keeping tabs on me, logging my movements.

I push the key in the lock and let myself in. I've already scanned the cameras on my phone app to make sure nobody has got in while I've been out. The house is silent, just the whirr of the fridge. I collapse onto the sofa and I start to sob. I don't know what is going on anymore. Who I can trust. I'm afraid to ask anyone for help or information because they just wind up dead. What if they go after Nick next? I feel totally and utterly alone and helpless.

28

————

I start writing a letter to Ben. If something happens to me now, I want him to know just how much I love him and that everything I did was to protect him. Whatever happens next, I have to make sure that he's provided for. I've dealt with the financial side of things, but now I need to address the emotional.

I start by describing how I felt the moment he was born. How my world changed overnight; that when I first laid eyes on him I knew that nothing else mattered more than him. I tell him how amazing I know he is going to be, that he should seize every opportunity that life gives him and run with it. That I hope his days are filled with laughter and his life made richer with friendships. That he should never be afraid to love, and that I will always be looking over him, no matter what.

I'm crying by the time I finish the letter. I'm tired and I'm scared. Whatever way I turn, I don't seem to be able to get myself out of this situation I've found myself in. If I withdraw my testimony, he's still going to come after me. If I try to find out information that can convict him, then more people die. I can't trust the police to secure a conviction, and I don't know what is going to happen next about Ben. I'm going to have to be prepared to break the law to protect him if I have to. I can't trust anyone else but Julia, and if they figure out he's there then that could get her into trouble. We're going to have to run.

I've just finished the letter when my mobile rings. It's Nick.

'Abbie, I've just got into the office. Have you heard about Mason?'

'Yes. We were supposed to meet but someone got to him before he reached me.'

'Are you OK?'

'I'm scared, Nick.'

'What were you meeting about?'

'Mason said he'd found something out. He sounded worried.'

'What was it? Did he tell you?'

'No. He wouldn't talk over the phone.'

'I'm worried about you Abbie.'

'What about you?'

'I'll be fine. We need to get you away from here until the trial. Somewhere safe where they can't reach you or Ben. You've got to keep clear of everything.'

Perhaps Nick's right. Perhaps that is the best option. At least Ben and I can be together somewhere, but my fear is that if they can know my every move here, if they can follow me and anticipate what and who I'm talking to, then they can find out where we've gone.

'I'm not sure that's enough,' I say.

In the background I hear voices.

'I've got to go Abbie. Stay home and stay safe.'

Nick ends the call. I hope he's OK. Right now I don't

think anyone who knows me is safe. Stuart Porter is clearly trying to eradicate anybody who is a threat – and I'm well aware of the fact that one of the biggest threats is me. I witnessed him murdering someone.

I pace around the sitting room for a few minutes, trying to work through the options in my head. The safest thing to do is just run. Go and get Ben and get away from here. The issue with that is that the authorities might come after me if they think Ben could be in danger. Then there's the problem of what I do when I come back to testify. He's going to be waiting for me.

I'm just checking my phone for news of Mason, when there's a frantic knocking on the front door. I look through the sitting room window and see it's Nick. He looks agitated.

He doesn't say anything until he's inside. As soon as the door is closed he hugs me, holding me tightly.

'I've just found out that social services have been called in about Ben. They're going to be coming round here. I didn't want to tell you over the phone in case... well you know.'

'Can they just come in? Will they break down the door?'

'Not this time, no. But it will come to that eventually if you don't co-operate.'

Nick hugs me as the tears start.

'Did you find out anything about what's happened to Mason?' I ask. There's nothing online and no emails from work about his condition.

'Just that they still haven't found the driver. The car was found abandoned and burned-out a few miles away. Stolen of course. That's it. They're trawling CCTV, but you can bet he – or she – was wearing a balaclava or something. The only hope is if they can trace it back to when they stole the car, or they left some DNA that survives the fire, but the latter is very unlikely.'

He breaks away from me and paces the living room.

'How did they find out about your meeting with Mason, did you tell anyone?'

'No, Mason told me not to. I've no idea how they knew, but Mason was investigating the corruption, he has been for a while, and he'd just found something important out.'

'And he didn't tell you anything about what he'd found? Not even a hint?'

I shake my head.

'Porter must have found out Mason was onto him. I just can't see how else he could have known. We've cleaned this place and your phone.'

'Mason gave me another phone, just for us to talk.'

Nick stops and looks at me. 'I asked if you had any other phones and you said no.'

'I know, I'm sorry. Mason told me to keep it just between us. It's a burner phone, I saw him get it out the packet, there's no way that they could have got to it.'

'Abbie you've got to be totally honest with me. Stuart Porter is a very dangerous man. I know what he's like. I understand how people like him work. You have to trust me to help you but I need you to be honest.'

'I'm sorry,' I say again and I feel the tears welling up in my eyes.

He walks across to me, his arms open. 'I'm sorry I don't mean to be harsh. I just don't want to lose you and Ben. If that man takes you from me then I just don't know what I'll do.'

Just then, there's a knock on my front door. We both freeze.

I move across to the window and carefully peer out. It's

two women I've never seen before. One of them has a briefcase. She knocks again.

I mouth to Nick that I think it's social services. We keep well out of sight.

They knock again. 'Mrs Murphy it's social services. We're from child protection and we need to speak to you about Ben. Could you open the door please?'

My heart goes cold and my hand shoots to my mouth. They're coming to take my son away from me. Even the law is going to work against me. I need it to protect us, but Porter and DI Roberts are using it to get at me.

Nick gives me an encouraging look and motions for me to stay calm.

'Mrs Murphy, we know you are in. Please open the door.'

The house phone rings. I ignore it and the answerphone clicks into action. 'Mrs Murphy it's Cassandra Fleming from Social Services. We have to speak to you please about your son Ben. We're not here to cause an issue, we just need to know that Ben is safe. If you don't open the door then we'll have to come back tomorrow with a warrant.'

Nick grabs my hand and squeezes it. The feel of his touch is the only thing stopping me from screaming out. We stand like this, him giving me reassuring looks, until they finally leave.

'They're going to take him away from me,' I say to him the minute we can talk again.

'They won't, they just need to know he's safe.'

'Yes, but if I tell them where he is, then he's at risk. How is that a good decision?'

I look into his eyes and I know that he doesn't have the answer. I can't expect Nick to solve this problem for us, I've got to do it myself and I don't have long.

29

I don't tell Nick that I'm planning to see if I can find the evidence that Mason dug up, because I know he's going to try to stop me. He's been amazing – I couldn't have done any of this without his support – but I started this chain of events, and so I need to end it. I'm also worried that the more I involve him, the more likely he could become a target too. Dealing with this is the only way Ben and I are going to be able to lead a normal life again together. I have to work out who is trying to hurt us.

I wait until I know that most people will have gone home for the day, before I head over to the newspaper office. I'd taken the hire car back, but the solicitor had reminded me about Dylan's car which was still at the garage waiting to be collected. Dylan's car insurance company is the same as mine and so I log on to his policy online to see if he'd taken me off his insurance yet. He hasn't. Dylan's lack of action always irritated me when we were together, but it's been a big help to me since he died. He's not changed any passwords or insurance and bank information. That has been a positive at least.

I head out the back again, knowing full well that they're going to be keeping an eye on me coming and going. It's easy to get to the garage on the bus. I pay the service bill and drive away in Dylan's BMW. It takes a bit of getting used to because it's turbo, quite a step up from my Fiesta, but by the time I'm on the dual carriageway, I'm feeling more confident.

I'm glad to see that Pete's car isn't in the *Editor* parking space. I don't want him seeing me nosing around Mason's desk. I'm also relieved that my pass still works to open the door. The thought that perhaps Pete might have cancelled it after I'd resigned had only dawned on me when I was on my way. I'd have got round it somehow though; people know me there and someone would have let me in. I could have just said I'd forgotten my pass and needed to get something.

The only person working in the editorial section is one of the subs, who has his back to the door and is focused on the screen in front of him. I'm hoping that if I'm really quiet, he won't turn round and see me.

We used to have to change our passwords every three months and Mason was forever forgetting his, so I know that he'd come up with a method whereby he just changed the number at the end. Yellow5 was the last one he'd shown me when I was moaning about having to change my password yet again. That was about four months ago, so he'd be on Yellow6 or possibly Yellow7 by now.

I sit at his desk and hunker down so that I'm as small as possible in the seat. If the sub does turn around, he may not see me above the screens.

I turn on his computer and type in his email and password. It judders at me and tells me the password is wrong. I try Yellow7, but I get the same result. *Shit*, has he suddenly changed his password routine? It can't be Yellow8, but I try it anyway. The judder and wrong password pop-up comes up again.

I think.

Maybe he's changed it completely because of working on the corruption case. He said that Pete didn't want him investigating – perhaps he wanted to make sure nobody knew what he was doing.

Quietly, I open his drawers where he keeps his notebooks.

It's empty.

This drawer is always full of his old notebooks – we have to keep them in case there's ever any come-back on a story. Mason always liked pen and paper. He didn't go digital like some reporters. I open all the drawers but there's no sign of any of his notebooks. Shit. Did Mason move them, or has somebody else come in after the hit and run and taken them?

I can't see that Pete would have been happy if the police took them. We need to protect sources and so to just hand over all Mason's notebooks when he's on the crime beat would go against the freedom of the press. Maybe Pete has moved them to prevent such a request.

There's nothing in his drawers except old press passes, pens, a couple of printed press releases and a yellow Post-it note with a drawing of a cactus and the number 1.

I close them quietly and I'm just about to turn off his computer again, when that Post-it note comes into my mind. Cactus1. It's worth a try.

Bingo. I'm in.

I'm not sure what I'm looking for, or where I might find it, but I start to look through his emails, see who he's been talking to. If they're an informant then they're not exactly going to have had an email conversation, but there could be something that gives me a clue.

I look at his recent documents. Most of them are related to the stories that have been published in the last week. I can't see anything that in any way links to Stuart Porter and the corruption at the council. I scan through the list of folders that he's got in his user area. Nothing. Perhaps he has given it a code name. I click on any that I don't recognise, but they're all other stories.

I'm wasting my time here. There is literally nothing that I can find. Frustrated, I log out and turn the computer off, and slip back out without the sub having even noticed I was there.

If there's nothing at work, then there may be something at his home address. I realise at this point that I'm about to do something illegal. I'm planning on going to Mason's house and rooting around his belongings without his permission. If I'm caught then I'm definitely going to be in trouble, but if I don't look, I may never know what it was that Mason had found. I have to do this.

I DON'T WANT to have to break any windows or force anything, and so I'm hoping that Mason is still a creature of habit. When I was pregnant, there were a few drunken nights out with the office crowd. As I wasn't drinking, I became designated driver, depositing various drunk colleagues back home. I remember that Mason was particularly inebriated one night and I'd been concerned about him, so I'd walked him to his door to make sure he got in. He'd told me that he'd lost his keys a couple of times when he'd been on benders and so when he went out for a night, he always had a spare hidden under some stones in the front garden.

'Never keep it near your front door,' he'd lectured me that night, 'too obvious.' I mentally cross my fingers and hope that he still keeps a spare under the stones.

I park a couple of streets away from his house. The last thing I want to do is have some nosey neighbour report the registration of Dylan's car if it comes to light that somebody has been in Mason's house. I search through Dylan's glove locker for the torch we used to have. It's still there. For a moment I get the flash of a memory, the two of us holding hands and laughing, walking by torchlight to the abandoned house on the edge of the park, which is supposed to be haunted. We'd been watching too many ghost programmes on Discovery+ and decided to have a real adventure of our own. As we walked, we'd made up stories of who might haunt the house, taking it in turns to use the torch to light up our faces as we told the spooky stories. In the end, when we got there, we just found a urine-smelling, run-down heap, and when Dylan spotted a used needle in the hallway, we'd left quickly.

I keep to the shadows, looking out for anyone who might be watching Mason's house. I can't see anybody, so I cross over and into his front garden, to where the stones were the last time I was here.

They're gone. There's a big plant pot with some kind of fern in it instead. Perhaps it's under the plant pot.

I heave the pot off its spot and peer underneath. Nothing but mud and worms.

Shit.

I scan around the rest of the garden. He's planted a few more shrubs since I was last here. I methodically walk around, looking underneath the branches, and then I see them. The same pile of stones, only this time they're in the corner under the window, partially hidden by some African daisies.

The key is still there. I go to pick it up and then stop myself. Forensics. If the police start investigating Mason's 'accident' or if he dies and it becomes a murder inquiry, then they're possibly going to look at every aspect of his life. I cover my hand with my sleeve before I pick up the keys. I should have thought to bring some gloves.

I slip the key into the lock and turn it, hoping that Mason hasn't got an alarm system. I can't see a box advertising any security. The door opens to silence.

Before I go inside, I replace the keys. I want to leave everything as it was.

I close the front door quietly so as not to alert any neighbours. The house is as silent as you'd expect it to be.

I need to find where he has his office. I start searching, careful to make sure that nobody can see the torch light moving around. I scan the sitting room in the half-light from the window. I see the stamp of Mason's personality on the place and feel a great sadness. There's a photograph of him with his brothers when they went travelling round Europe together. Three smiling faces with no idea of what was to come. I still don't know if he's going to survive. Dylan's swollen, battered face comes to mind. There's nothing much in here besides Mason's Xbox, TV and some books, I head off further into the house.

At the back is his kitchen and I see his desk in the corner. I am about to go and start searching when I think about fingerprints again. There was a coat rack in the hallway with some hats and gloves on it. I put on a pair of Mason's leather gloves. They're too big and a bit cumbersome, but at least I won't leave any trace of myself behind. I'll have to take them with me.

The first thing I see is Mason's cactus. On a shelf at the back of his desk, its prickly arms outstretched as though asking for a hug that it will never get. It looks somehow forlorn, human-like in its loneliness. I hope Mason will be able to come home to it. The other thing I notice is that there's a sort of mind map on an opened notebook on his desk with initials and dates. I can't immediately make sense of it, but I take a photograph so I can look at it again later. I'm wondering if he's got the other notebooks from work here, but I can't find any others besides this one. I flick through the pages, taking photos. He's used shorthand in some places, and some weird kind of code in others. It's not making any sense to me at the moment, but if I have the images, I can try to decipher it.

I've almost finished going through the notebook when I hear a key go into the front door lock.

My blood freezes. Who the hell could that be? I turn my torch off.

Whoever it is, has already got the door open.

I scan the kitchen quickly looking for a hiding place. I don't have time for anywhere clever – a torch light is heading into the hallway and towards me. I duck down behind the kitchen island and try to squeeze into the space where a pedal bin sits. Any idiot is going to be able to see me here if they look properly, but I've no choice.

I strain to listen for what's happening. The person has gone to Mason's desk and I can hear them opening drawers and shutting them again. I'm itching to try to see who it is but that would be suicide. I have to keep hidden.

I hear a cough. I recognise that cough, but I can't quite place who it is. Definitely male.

I see the torch light leave the kitchen and hear footsteps go up the stairs. Damn. I didn't have the chance to look up there yet. If Mason has anything hidden up there, then they will probably get to it first.

Footsteps on the floorboards above my head. More sounds of drawers and cupboards opening. Then into another room and finally they come back down the stairs again.

I hear the latch on the front door being opened, that cough again, and then the door shutting behind them.

I have to know who it is. I creep out on my hands and knees and peer around the kitchen island to make sure they're definitely gone. The hallway is empty so I race to the sitting room window and hope I'm not too late.

I'm not. Outside, under the street lamplight, I see the unmistakable silhouette of our editor, Pete Webber, and he's handing a notebook over to Roberts' sidekick, DS Tony Fuller. They exchange words and then walk in separate directions. I'm in shock. Is Pete somehow involved in all this? Why would he be handing over Mason's notebooks?

My heart is pounding. I know what he's taken, but I go back to check anyway. The notebook with Mason's mind map is gone.

Our own editor is wrapped up in this whole corruption scandal! Do they have something on him? Or is he a willing participant? No wonder he didn't want me or Mason investigating. That also explains why all Mason's notebooks are missing at work. Shit, shit, shit. A whole new range of possibilities open up in front of me. How big is this and how long has Pete been playing us?

Mason's cactus catches my eye again. I pray that he'll be home to look after it soon. The blipping machines and smell of antibacterial and cleaning products under white strip lighting fill my memory. Dylan never stood a chance, but maybe Mason will be OK. I swing my torch away, ready to leave, when I notice something. A glint in the gravel of the cactus.

I take it down from the desk shelf and carefully scrape away some of the surface gravel. There is something metallic there. It's a USB memory stick. Mason is such a creature of habit, he hides his keys under rocks in the garden, and now I'm hoping that he's hidden the key to what's going on in the investigation, under the gravel of his beloved cactus.

30

———

I drive home, but I don't park Dylan's car outside my house. I leave it several streets away in the hope that nobody connects it to me. I'm still terrified about having the car tampered with after what happened to Dylan.

As usual, I double check the security cameras to make sure there hasn't been anyone in my house. It's all clear. What I need to do now is to look at what's on this memory stick and also to see if the photographs of Mason's mind map make any sense. Somewhere in those notes could be the clue that he'd wanted to tell me. Had he found out that Pete was involved? That would have panicked him. Is there any chance that Nick and I are wrong and that DS Fuller is the one pulling the strings, not DI Roberts? Or is he just his errand boy? He was the one who followed me that day, and the one who approached me outside Dee and Olga's house. I can also tell that he doesn't like Nick. There's a kind of simmering hatred that emanates from him.

I've got a headache and I realise that apart from the stress, I've not drunk anything in hours. I down two full glasses of water. Then I sit down with a third at my breakfast bar and open my laptop. I take a deep breath as I push the memory stick in. It instantly appears on my home screen. That's the first hurdle. It doesn't have a name and I suddenly panic that it might be something personal, like porn or something that Mason doesn't want found. I'm relieved when I click on it and a spread sheet and various documents appear. This will be what Pete and DS Fuller were looking for.

It's obvious that Mason was trying to solve it by tracking the money, and he's really put the work into this. Credit where credit's due, he'd done a pretty good job. Despite the circumstances, I'm impressed. This must have taken him months not just weeks.

He seems to think there's twenty-one million pounds missing. That's a big sum, clearly worth protecting and for Stuart Porter, obviously worth killing for. Mason has tried to trace the money to a shell company in the Cayman Islands which has a similar name to the council's bank account, but with one slight difference. There's no indication as to who is the ultimate owner of that bank account. I recognise some of the contractor company names that he's written down, but I don't have the full list. The rest of the names were on the last couple of pages that I didn't get the chance to photograph. Could one of these hold the key?

If only I could find out who Mason's mystery source is, the one he was waiting to speak to. Surely, somewhere in all this I should be able to retrace his steps.

I stare again at Mason's mind map trying to understand what it means. From what I can see, he had originally been looking at the money trail to see if he could work out who was responsible, and then the focus had turned to the murders, i.e. who had alibis and could be eliminated, and who had opportunity.

The other notes on the USB are more about the corruption itself and the way that it worked. It's ingenious. Several procurement managers within the council have been recruited and will either negotiate additional fees for services and goods, accept inflated bids for supplying them, or a fake supplier will be created for fake work. The proceeds from this are then split between the procurement manager and presumably Stuart. There are also suppliers who are in on the game.

From what Mason seems to be implying, none of them knew each other, so if one got caught, the whole network was still intact, but different sections of it seemed able to support another if there looked like trouble on the horizon. The only person who knows everything is the big question mark in the centre. Clearly, a persuasive man who is good at manipulating people and persuading them to do things they might otherwise not. Mason also suggests that a couple of deaths could be linked to the network, long before Stuart killed Christie. One man who took an overdose of insulin, and another who had a car accident. His brake lines were cut. That sends a shiver down my spine. Is Stuart acting alone in this? Does he have some kind of enforcer who does his dirty work for him? Is it just one person, or are there more working together?

I get the mind map up on my phone. It's all initials and code names which I don't immediately recognise, and a series of dates, which I do. The dates are when people were murdered and go back further than Jordan Christie's death. So, who are the names? There's SW13, Highlander, Bonhams, Little, Bob, and Tiger.

I know the date of John Christie's murder, that's

indelibly marked on my brain and next to it is Bonhams and Little. Bonhams is an auction house. I google it and instantly Christie's pops out at me in the section, 'People also searched for'. Bonhams could mean Jordan Christie. So Little might be Stuart Porter. Of course: Stuart Little. I have to smile at the way Mason's mind works.

The trouble is, that's as far as I get. I can't work out who the others are. I guess at people but none of it makes sense. They could be anybody. People who work in the council who were involved in the corruption or a supplier.

Where does Pete fit into this? Could he be one of the remaining code names? I can't seem to make him fit into any of the codes Mason has written.

I carry on looking through the notes, trying to replace real names with the code ones. It's not making any sense and the back of my eyes are hurting, my vision blurring with tiredness. My headache is also pounding still and so I resort to taking a couple of paracetamol. I go and sit on the sofa and lean back, closing my eyes while the pills can take effect. The key to all this must be there in Mason's notes. Who was it that he was waiting to see and who gave him such important information that he had to see me urgently and was run down for? I'm right in the middle of all this and yet I can't see the picture clearly. The only thing I do know for sure is what happened that day on the dead-end road. I saw Porter kill Christie. I need to start with that again.

I go back to that morning, keeping my eyes closed, trying to remember and re-live every second of that moment. Sitting in my car, watching them argue, Christie lifting his arm and then Porter knocking it away and pulling out a knife. The slash to the throat. The blood.

I'm deep in thought when my doorbell goes and my whole body jumps what feels like two feet off the sofa.

My heart instantly goes into the fast beats of panic. Please don't say that it's the social workers back already with a warrant? I need more time. I carefully go to peer out of the sitting room window and see the bleached blond hair of Harper on my doorstep. She has a box in her arms. It's probably Dylan's paperwork.

I nearly don't open the door, and then the thought of all that's happened in the past couple of weeks, encourages me. I need to wrap up Dylan's affairs as quickly as possible so that Ben and I can leave.

'I brought all the paperwork the solicitor told me to bring,' Harper says, thrusting the box at me.

'Thanks. Did he tell you that you can keep everything else?'

'Yeah.'

'Harper, I would never have wanted to hurt Dylan, you do know that don't you?'

She looks at me, studying my face, and shrugs.

'The police aren't investigating me you know. Which detective said that to you, was it DI Roberts?'

She shakes her head. 'No, the younger guy.'

So, it was DS Fuller again.

'I've gotta go,' Harper says to me and turns, walking down the path.

I'm left standing on my doorstep as she leaves. Across the road, I see the police officer in the squad car watching. Who is he reporting back to? And, who is DS Fuller and how does he fit into all this?

31

I don't even make it to bed. I fell asleep on the sofa still trying to figure out Mason's notes, my brain too tired to think. Sleep is unsurprisingly fitful, and I awake to not only a stiff neck but burned traces of traumatic dreams, seared through my mind like vapour trails of dragon's breath. I need to see my son. Social Services could come back round with the police and a warrant at any time today. I might be forced to reveal where Ben is or I'll end up in jail and then I'll be no use to anyone, especially Ben. My only option is to bring him back home and keep him safe. I can't put this on Julia. If needs be, Ben and I can stay in the house until I've figured out what to do next. Once I've had some proper rest then I might be able to decipher Mason's notes. I text Julia to let her know I'm coming to visit, I still don't let on about Ben, not until he's in my arms – just in case.

Before I go for my shower, I need to hide the memory stick. I can't lose this, it's months of Mason's work and Stuart Porter would no doubt be very keen to get hold of it. The saving grace is that nobody knows I've got it. Even so, I'm not taking any chances. First, I make a duplicate. Two copies is better than one. The first I tuck behind a picture that hangs near my patio doors. It is canvas stretched over a crude wooden frame and so there's space behind to balance a memory stick. The other, I hide under a small corner of carpet which is coming up just behind the sofa at the other end of the room. I put the USB into a plastic bag and tuck it under there and stand back to look. Nobody would possibly know either of them are there, not unless they ransacked the place and I'd see it on the SeeCam security camera app. Even if they did find the one behind the picture, I'm pretty sure that the other one would be safe.

I'm running on adrenaline. I barely ate all day yesterday, just drank coffee and water. As I stand in the shower, relishing the hot water on my skin, the faces of those who have died float around me in the steam. All this because of one stupid mistake. If only I hadn't driven up that dead-end road, then Jordan Christie's murder would just be another story we'd be covering in the paper and I'd be getting divorced from Dylan and getting a new job in PR. I'd still be taking Ben to the park at the weekends, dropping him off to Jo for childminding, and maybe I'd have met Nick some other way. Maybe our paths would have crossed in different circumstances, and we'd still be lovers but in a happier world. I hope that one day that world will still be possible.

I get out the shower to the sound of the house phone ringing. I throw a towel around me and run down the stairs but I'm too late and the answerphone picks it up.

'Mrs Murphy it's DI Roberts, we need to speak with you today so could you please call me back at your earliest convenience and we can arrange a time that's convenient for you. Thank you.'

As I dry myself and put on my make-up, I look at the reflection which stares back at me. It's of a woman who has aged about ten years in just a few weeks. Dark circles under my eyes accentuate the haggard, paleness of my complexion. Putting on my jeans, I realise I've also lost weight. For a moment I allow myself a few thoughts of self-pity and then I am reminded of those who have suffered far worse than me. Dylan, who thought he was starting a new life with Harper, Dee who will never get to bring her daughter home, and I wonder how Mason is doing. I can't bring myself to email Pete to ask him. For all I know, he might have helped put him in hospital. When I get back from retrieving Ben I'll call up one of the subs at work, they'll know.

I leave via the front door. I've got nothing to hide today. They're going to know soon enough that Ben is back with me. There is a uniformed officer sitting in the patrol car and he gives me a smile as I walk past. I smile back.

I turn the corner to where I parked Dylan's car and immediately my hackles are raised. Someone is watching me. There is a man sitting in a black BMW on the other side of the street. I'm hyper alert to anything and everyone at the moment but even I'm shocked when I realise it's DS Fuller. I hope I haven't shown the shock on my face, I don't want to show any weakness. He's obviously sussed out that I'm using Dylan's car. When he sees me, he gets out of his and crosses the road to intercept me.

'Mrs Murphy I was hoping to catch you. We really need to talk to you. There's been some new developments we want to discuss.'

I look at him. New developments, I wonder whether that has anything to do with Mason.

'I can't stop right now,' I say, walking around him and unlocking the car with the fob.

'Are you going to see Ben?' he asks, eyes narrowing as he studies me.

I stop and turn, looking him directly in the eyes. 'Yes,' and then I turn quickly and get in the car. I want to drive away before he has the chance to ask me anything else or follow me. I know that the number plate recognition software can track the car, but I don't want him tailing me all the way to Julia's.

'Mrs Murphy it's really important that we talk,' he has come up to the side window and is tapping. 'It's for your own safety and that of your son's.'

'I'll call you,' I say, putting the car into gear and driving away. I see him in my rear view mirror. He stands and watches me and then takes his phone out of his pocket and makes a call. Who is he reporting to? Was that a threat, *for your own safety and that of your son's*?

IT'S SO good to see Julia again. Oscar is there too with a welcoming hug and his concern. I can see they're both really worried about me, but they don't even know the half of it. Ben is so excited to see me and I hug him for ages, pulling him into me, soaking myself in his innocence. He soon gets over the joy of seeing me again and squirms to get away and go play with Lucy.

'Will you stay for lunch? I'm just pulling together a pasta salad,' Julia asks me, her eyes hopeful.

'I'm sorry I really can't. Not this time. I am so grateful for you having taken care of Ben for me, but I've got to get back.'

'You know, it's a lot you've been through, no surprise if you're struggling,' Oscar says to me now. He and Julia share a glance.

I look at him, not allowing myself to get annoyed by the

impression his words have just conveyed. I'm not struggling with being a mother. I'm just trying to do the best for my son. I know Oscar wouldn't have meant to criticise. He's just concerned. They both are.

'I'm fine. Really. I'd love to stay longer, but it will have to be next time. I really owe you both, I'll make it up to you, I promise,' I say to them.

'You don't owe us anything Abs, it was a pleasure having him, we're just worried about you. Please remember, we are here for you if you need us anytime, OK?'

'OK. Thank you,' I say, feeling blessed to have such good friends because I know they're true to their words. They would always help me out if I needed it.

It's hard, but I have to tear us away from Julia and their home, which feels like a haven compared to what I know waits for me. I have to take Ben back, make sure that social services can see he's safe, and then I need to work out what to do next.

32

———

I can feel the tension in my neck and shoulders as I drive home. Ben is happily babbling away to himself in the back, he has a little train which he's playing with and keeps pressing a button so that the various catchphrases from Thomas the Tank engine and Friends squawk out. They jar on my nerves but I don't tell him to stop. He's so happy in his imaginary world, if only I could subvert reality and join him there. Instead, I am bringing him home to a life where the truth is distorted not by imagination, but by greed and murder. It makes me angry and sad at the same time.

We are still about an hour away from home when I get an alert on my phone. It's the SeeCam app, the security cameras have detected movement in the house. I pick up my mobile and my blood runs cold. It's him. The man in the yellow frog hat. The man who tried to break into my house weeks ago. He's there now and he's taking the picture off the wall by the patio doors and is stealing the memory stick from Mason.

I'm so glad we're not on the motorway, I pull over into a

bus stop, screeching to a halt, and shout at my phone, turning on the microphone on the cameras.

'Get out of my house. I'm calling the police!'

He doesn't even flinch. Instead, he calmly turns to where the camera is and waves a gloved hand at me, a gloved hand containing the metallic memory stick I'd taken from Mason's house. Then he calmly leaves via the patio doors and I see him heading off down the garden and vaulting the wall.

How did he know that the memory stick was there? He walked straight up to it. I feel totally violated. He must have some kind of surveillance in the house, or perhaps he was watching through the patio doors earlier this morning as I hid them. Has he found the second one? I can't call the police because then I will have to explain what it is that he came to steal. Perhaps the yellow frog man knows that. Perhaps that's because he knows exactly what it is that he's just taken.

I'm shaking with anger and I want to cry. I'm also scared. If he can just walk into and out of my house that easily, then what's stopping him doing it again when Ben and I are there? Why didn't the squad car out the front notice him? Or perhaps it's because the man in the yellow frog hat was already parked around the back and knew he was out of sight. Parked near to where I'd left Dylan's car last night. Could DS Fuller be yellow frog man?

I look in my rear-view mirror and Ben is watching me. He stopped playing when I shouted at my phone and he can tell I'm upset. I reassure him.

'It's OK sweetheart, mummy was shouting at her phone, not you baby.' I twist in my seat and turn round to smile at him. 'I love you,' I say to him. I doubt the words have much meaning to him yet but I hope that one day he'll come to understand just how much I really mean them.

I wait for about ten minutes as I feel shaky and don't want to drive. I message Nick instead.

Just had an intruder in my house. I'm out getting Ben. Saw him on the cameras. Don't suppose you can come round can you? We'll be home in about an hour.

Nick replies with a string of expletives and then, *Of course, I'll be there when you get back. I'm not letting you out of my sight!*

It brings on my first smile of the afternoon and I thank my lucky stars that he's there for us.

33

———

The joy of bringing Ben home is ruined by the intruder. I park outside the house in full view of the police car and consider walking over and asking what they were doing when someone broke into my house. I don't. I'm just getting Ben out of his car seat when Nick pulls up.

'You OK?' he asks me, while giving a smile and wave to Ben.

'Yeah. No thanks to them,' I nod over at the police car.

The second the words are out of my mouth, Nick is off, marching across to the car. I can't hear what he's saying but I can see he's angry. I want to go inside but I'd rather not go in alone. Just in case.

A few moments later Nick comes storming back.

'Bloody ridiculous. What the hell point is there of him sitting outside supposedly watching if Porter still gets in?'

'Did he see anything?'

'Nothing.'

'He must have come in the back way anyway, that's how

he left,' I tell Nick. I can look at the recording later, see if there's anything that I didn't see earlier. It was all so rushed.

'I'm so sorry Abs. Let's get you inside. I've got shopping. I'm going to cook you my famous lasagne tonight, washed down with a glass of Malbec.'

I sigh with relief.

'First, I'm going to make sure he's gone and that it's safe in there. Give me your key and you wait on the doorstep until I'm sure. OK? We don't know what he was doing in there. Did you see him take anything?'

I nod meekly, suddenly becoming aware that I haven't told Nick anything about my visit to Mason's house and finding the memory stick. 'I'll tell you once we're inside,' I reply.

Nick heads in, leaving his bags in the hall and sprints up the stairs. I can hear his footsteps go from room to room checking. When he comes back down again he goes straight into the kitchen and then the sitting room/diner.

'All clear,' I hear him shout. I'm relieved. Ben has been wriggling in my arms, the prospect of getting inside and playing with the toys he's missed, too much for his infant will power. He's no clue of the danger that I fear. I'm still wary though, and step inside with him rather than allowing him to run free into the house.

Once I'm inside the exhaustion hits me. The emotional energy that the last few weeks have drained from me, has left me fragile and wrung-out.

'I'll put the kettle on,' Nick says taking one look at me, 'and then you can tell me what you think he took and why.'

While Nick heads into the kitchen, I go straight to behind the sofa where the carpet looks untouched in the corner. Relief floods through me as I feel a lump underneath and I pull it back to see the copied memory stick, still there. So how did he know I'd put one behind the picture? I stand up and look around. Here at the other end of the room from the patio doors, it's shadowed. I've taken to keeping the curtains closed at the front, street side, to keep the surveillance police from peering in. What I clearly hadn't thought about were the patio doors at the other end of the room. Someone could have been watching through those glass doors and seen me put the memory stick behind the picture, but they would have struggled to see me at the back of the room where I hid the copy. I'm just so glad I thought to make a duplicate. I put it in my jeans pocket. Once I've had a cup of tea and given Ben something to eat, I'm going to sit back down at my laptop and see if I can figure out what on the memory stick is so important.

I head into the kitchen, pausing at the patio doors and looking out.

'I think he's watching me,' I say to Nick.

'What did you say?' he asks, as the boiling kettle flicks off.

'I think that the intruder, was watching me through these doors. How else would he have known my hiding place. He went straight to it.'

'What hiding place?' Nick walks through to stand next to me holding two mugs of tea.

'Behind this picture, I'd hidden a memory stick that I found at Mason's house.'

'Mason's house? When did you go there?'

'Yesterday. I went looking for Mason's notes. Porter must have thought he was getting too close and I wanted to see what he'd dug up.'

'What did this memory stick have on it? Did you get a chance to look?'

'He'd been following the money, there's so much work

gone into it, he must have been investigating for months. No wonder Roberts thought I had been following Porter. He must have got wind that a journalist was investigating the corruption and assumed that was me.'

'So, could you work out who's involved?'

'Not yet,' I shake my head. 'The names are all in Mason's unique code so I still haven't figured it out, but I will.'

'But you can't now surely if the intruder stole the memory stick?'

'I made a copy. He didn't find that.'

'A copy?' Nick says to me, 'that was clever.'

I sigh again, 'Well, let's just see if I can work it all out first, otherwise it's useless.'

'And you didn't recognise the intruder at all?'

'I recognised him as the same man who'd tried to break in that first night.' I pull my phone out of my pocket and pull up the SeeCam camera app, winding back to when I saw the man.

Nick leans over my shoulder and watches the pixelated video.

'It's not Porter. Looks like a younger man,' I say to him.

'Yes, you're right, I wonder...' Nick tails off thinking.

'Wonder what?' I ask him, sipping some tea which has the effect of instantly making me feel a little better.

'Well, the officer outside said that DS Fuller was parked round the back for a while. It looks like his build.'

I play the clip again.

'It's crossed my mind. He told Harper that I was under investigation and that they suspected me because I was still set to benefit from Dylan's life insurance. He's also tailed me, was at the murder of the two women, and I saw Pete handing over Mason's notebook to him outside Mason's house last night.'

'The guy hates my guts too. He's definitely got some axe to grind. Maybe that's because he's working with Porter and knows I'd like to see him sent down.'

'But he's on the investigation with Roberts,' I put to Nick.

'Yup, slight conflict of interest which is just what Porter needs. That's why it's so important that you testify and don't take reckless risks with your life by sneaking around where you might get caught. If Fuller is destroying any evidence that could implicate Porter, then we don't want him finding out that you've got another copy of that memory stick.'

I feel chaste.

'You have to think of Ben. Perhaps you should give it to me for safe keeping?'

'Maybe,' I concede.

Nick holds out his hand like a school teacher asking a pupil for a stolen pencil.

'Later. I want to have another look at it first and see if I can figure anything out.'

I'm about to take Mason's memory stick out of my pocket, when the doorbell goes. Nick and I exchange a wary look and I cross to the window to see who it is. The big bulk of DI Roberts standing on my doorstep is unmistakable.

'It's Roberts,' I whisper to Nick.

He nods, 'tell him you're about to have dinner. We don't want him in here now.'

I agree and do just that.

'Mrs Murphy I just wanted to see if everything is alright? The Sergeant on lookout tells me that you had an intruder earlier?'

'Yes,' I say, holding onto the door to keep it half closed so that DI Roberts gets the message that he's not welcome inside. 'This afternoon while I was out getting Ben.'

'Was anything stolen? Or damage done?'

'He stole some computer files.'

'Anything to do with the investigation?' Roberts asks, his left eyebrow raising. I can see he's trying to peer around the door to see what's going on inside.

'It's fine,' is all I say in return. 'I'm just surprised that he managed to get in when you've got somebody watching my house.'

'Yes. I've told them to do regular patrols around the perimeter. That should have been happening anyway but it seems the intruder must have got in round the back. So, Ben's home with you?'

'Yes.'

'And DS Barnes?'

'I don't think that's really relevant is it Detective?'

'We still need to talk to you Mrs Murphy. Sooner rather than later, so if you don't mind I'd like to come round in the morning. I presume it will just be yourself home then?'

'Yes,' I say but I'm not really sure. Nick said he didn't want to leave us on our own, he wants to protect us, but I know he also has a job to do.

DI Roberts nods and turns to leave. 'You do still have my number. If you're at all worried about anything, call me.' Then he says goodnight before heading off down the path.

'Nosy sod,' Nick says as soon as I've shut the door. 'Probably jealous,' he adds.

'I wonder if he's twigged that I found Mason's memory stick and have seen his notes.'

'Maybe.'

I collapse down onto the sofa and watch Ben playing with his toys.

'I'm not sure I can take much more of this. I don't feel comfortable here anymore, not knowing that someone has been watching me. I feel totally violated and with Roberts or

Fuller accosting me every five minutes it also feels like harassment.'

'Why don't we get away?' Nick suddenly says. 'I was going to suggest it later, but why don't we just go now. Get away from all this and go somewhere that Porter and his network can't reach us.'

'Where?' I ask. The idea is certainly appealing.

'There's a cottage in the Lake District that my granddad owned. It's nothing luxurious, but it's child friendly and it's secluded. We could get away there for a bit, let things calm down here and hope that the investigation progresses and you can come back and testify against Porter.'

The thought of being somewhere away from here with Ben and Nick fills me with hope. That other world I'd been dreaming of where we can just be together without all the stress and fear. I can take my laptop and work on Mason's notes.

'It sounds perfect,' I say to Nick, smiling.

'Great. Go chuck a few things into a bag and we'll leave immediately. I'll cook dinner in the Lake District. It's only a couple of hours drive.'

I feel like a huge weight is being lifted off me as I pack. The kind of excitement I haven't felt since I was a kid going away on a family holiday. I hadn't realised just how much I've been feeling like a prisoner in my own home and the realisation that somehow I was being watched has been the last straw.

We go in Nick's car, chucking our bags in the boot and settling Ben into his travel seat with a bowl of food to keep him from being hungry and bored.

'Are you sure you're OK with him eating?' I ask Nick. 'He's not the neatest of eaters and your upholstery might get a bit crumby.'

Nick kisses me on the forehead and smiles. 'I think that's the least of our problems, don't you?'

I notice that the officer in the car is on the phone as we leave and it feels so good to be driving away from their constant surveillance and all the lies and mistrust. I put my hand on Nick's thigh as he drives and he gives it a squeeze. Not long after that I fall asleep, the exhaustion finally getting the better of me.

'Abbie, Abbie, we're here,' Nick's voice pulls me from a deep sleep and I wake up with a gasp. It's dark. We seem to be in the middle of nowhere. There's no street lights or the halo glow of light pollution from a big town, and there's no prying eyes.

'I'll go get the lights on,' Nick says and I watch as he disappears off into the darkness. A minute later, a door and windows are illuminated and the façade of a small stone cottage comes into view.

Ben is stirring in the back and so I carefully unclip him and carry him into the cottage.

'We have two bedrooms,' Nick explains, leading me up the stairs. 'This one is perfect for Ben.'

He shows me into a little room, decorated for a young boy, faded blue wallpaper depicting action scenes, and a single bed that's made up and ready. I look to Nick.

'Yeah, this was my room when I was little. My grandparents owned this place. It came to dad after they died and now to me.'

He fits the bed guard rail underneath the mattress so that it forms a barrier on the side of the bed that isn't against the wall. I'd brought it with us so that Ben wouldn't fall out of bed as he's still used to sleeping in a cot.

'I'll get the bags and get started on dinner while you settle him down,' he says to me. 'The bathroom is on the left if you want to bath him. I'll have that wine opened and ready for when you come down.'

I smile at him. For a few seconds all the horror that my life has become is forgotten. This caring, handsome man is all I want to focus on. He leans in to kiss me tenderly and then turns and heads back down the stairs.

Once Ben's bed is organised, I take him through to find our bags. I'd brought his towel and baby bath soap with us, along with a clean pair of PJs for him. Nick has already deposited all our bags in the room and I can hear him downstairs banging around in the kitchen.

While Ben chats away to one of his teddies, I go and run the bath. I love bath time with him, it's always fun and relaxing for both of us. A time when I can focus on him after a day at work, or now after several days apart. I pour in some of the baby bubble bath that is gentle on his skin but great for making bubbles. It froths under the taps, a big mound of bubbles growing. I keep checking the water to make sure it's not too hot as it runs. Now all I need is a little boy to put in it.

My heart lurches as I walk back into the bedroom. The first thing I register is that my son has been raiding Nick's bag, the second thing is the most shocking but because it was so incongruous, it just didn't hit me at first. Ben is holding a gun. A black hand gun. I am across the room and taking it off him before I even have time to take a breath. *Holy shit! What's Nick doing with a gun?*

My initial thoughts of embarrassment that Ben has been into his bag, are instantly overtaken by the question of why Nick's brought a gun with us. I quickly scoop up his belongings and put them back into the bag as neatly as I can, but there's no way I can put the gun back in there. Ben might get hold of it again. Instead, I look around for a safe place. There's an old stand-alone wooden wardrobe near the door so I reach up and put it on top, well out of Ben's reach.

Bath time isn't the relaxing play that I'd expected, I can't get my thoughts away from that gun and how Ben could have been injured. It's my fault. I should have been watching him, but why has Nick got it and is it legal? I'm busting to ask him but first I want to get Ben to bed. He's tired and I don't want him getting over-tired because then it will be harder to get him to sleep.

I carry Ben to his bed, holding his head against my cheek and sighing gratefully that I have him with me again. He chatters away in his own toddler language and gives me one of his kisses back where he presses his lips onto my cheek. He hasn't quite worked out yet how to do the lip movement.

I'm eager to get back downstairs to Nick but I pause a few moments just to look at my son as he settles into the bed. Then I turn on the star mobile I'd brought with us, which plays a gentle lullaby and projects little golden stars onto the ceiling that slowly turn in a circle above his head. Once the monitor is turned on, I slip out of his room and take the listening handset downstairs with me, the tinkling melody of his star mobile cutting across the static.

NICK IS STANDING by the stove, stirring a bubbling pan of ragu. Two glasses of red wine sitting on the side ready.

I don't know how to ask him about the gun, so I just come straight out with it.

'Nick, I'm really sorry but Ben got into your bag. I couldn't help but see—'

'The gun,' Nick says before I can finish my sentence. 'I'm sorry I should have told you before. I'm seriously concerned about your safety Abbie. Things seem to be escalating and I'm not going to forgive myself if something happens to you. It's for your protection.'

'Is it, is it legal?' I ask, not sure if I actually want to know.

'It is. I have a licence, but I shouldn't be carrying it around in my bag, it should be locked up. All you need to know is that I've got it for the right reasons.'

'But what if you get caught? I don't want you getting into trouble.'

'Abbie, what's more important? Your and Ben's safety, or me having to explain why my gun isn't in the safe?'

I don't know what to say to that question. Instead Nick reaches over and hands me a glass of wine. The thought of the gun upstairs makes one half of me feel more secure and the other half very afraid.

34

While the lasagne is cooking, I sit down with my laptop in the little sitting room. It's a quaint traditional cottage with an open fireplace and traditional furniture with faded upholstery. I suspect that as Nick's dad didn't have much money, this place has stayed pretty much the same as when his grandparents had it. There's that slight dusty damp smell which you always seem to get in old buildings like this, and I can imagine in the winter it's very cosy in front of the fire.

I allow myself to imagine the three of us coming here for holidays when things are back to normal. I've no idea where we are or what's around us, but I'm looking forward to exploring tomorrow. Nick's right, getting away is already helping me to relax.

I look at the laptop in front of me and force myself to focus. I've got to think logically about all this. The clues are all here, I'm sure of it. I've just got to work out if Roberts and Fuller are both in on the fraud with Porter, and find enough evidence that will convict the lot of them for the rest of their lives.

'Why don't you just chill for tonight,' Nick says, coming up behind me and massaging my shoulders.

I groan with pleasure at his touch. My neck and shoulders are so stiff that just the slightest pressure and rub, sends them into ecstasy, reminding my body that this state of perpetual stress is not good.

'I will,' I smile up at him. 'I just want to find out what it was that Mason wanted to tell me. I'm sure that's going to be the final nail in Porter's coffin.'

'OK,' he says sitting down opposite me, watching, as though he expects me to magic up some incredible answer in a flash.

The first thing I want to look at isn't Mason's memory stick, it's the photographs I took on the day this all began. I'd sent the ones the police didn't see to Mason, but with all that's been going on, I haven't really looked at them myself. I'm not expecting them to help me much as the crime had been committed by then but maybe it will spark a memory.

There are nine photographs. The first couple are just the traffic cops, and I see the crumpled body of Jordan Christie on the floor, lying in his own blood. It makes me shiver.

Then the next one is when Nick has arrived and he is with the traffic guys looking at the scene. Then, it's Nick approaching the body and putting on forensic gloves, followed by him pulling something out of Christie's pocket. I'd thought it was a wallet at the time, but now in the photo, I see a glint, the sunlight coming through the roof on a glass screen. It's definitely a mobile. Christie must have had two mobiles. I open up the next photograph and Nick is looking around the area. This was when he saw the other phone. I move on to the next one – there he is bending down and picking it up. The next photo is the item going into an evidence bag. It's not clear enough to see what it is from the angle and distance, and Nick's back is to the camera, mostly blocking it, but it's black and shiny just like a mobile. I move on. This photo shows Nick slipping it into his pocket, and then the final one is him starting to walk back towards me.

As far as I can see, the photographs back up what I've said, it's just that Christie had two phones not just the one. It was shortly after this that both DI Roberts and DS Fuller turned up.

'Why do you think that Christie had two mobiles? Do you reckon he was involved and Porter wanted to silence him?'

'Christie? I don't think so. I think it's more likely he had some evidence and was going to blow Porter's cover. But I didn't find two mobiles, just the one which he'd pulled out his pocket.'

'Did you know of him before that day?' I ask.

'Not really, no.'

'So how did you know who he was, from the wallet?'

'What wallet? I didn't see one. No, I'd heard of him, knew of him, just didn't know him well, that's all. What's with the fifty questions about Christie? He's not our problem, Porter is.'

'I know, sorry, I'm just trying to get it all straight in my head.'

Nicks stands up and comes over to me. 'What are you looking at? Mason's notes?'

Something makes me click off the photographs and all he sees is my home screen. He looks at me suspiciously.

'No. I was just thinking through it all.' I look at him and wonder if he'd just forgotten what he found that day. It was a few weeks ago and he's not investigating the case so it's quite feasible that it's all a blur to him. He frowns at me. I don't want to ruin the evening. I've been asking him a million questions. The guy is here to protect us and is even cooking our dinner and I'm treating him like he's a suspect.

'Sorry, I didn't mean to sound like an interrogator. You're right, I don't need to do this now.' I close down my laptop and shut the lid. 'I was just trying to work out the sequence of events. Porter claims it was self-defence, that Christie was going to attack him. I have to be sure.'

'Abbie you were sure. Don't you remember, you told us all that you saw Christie pull a mobile phone from his pocket, Porter knocked it away and stabbed him. It's in your statement. I even found the mobile and gave it to Fuller. Porter is bound to try and claim self-defence because he's facing a murder trial.'

I nod. He's right. I just need to take a chill pill.

DINNER IS WONDERFUL. We sit at a little wooden table on the far side of the living room from the fire, chatting about normal everyday things as though we're an ordinary couple. It's so refreshing. The lasagne is good, I'd forgotten that I'd missed lunch again and my slack waist band on my jeans reminds me that I need to look after myself too.

When we're finished, Nick reaches across the table and holds my hand in his.

'This is nice isn't it?' he says to me, smiling.

I smile back, real pleasure curving my lips and warming my heart. 'Yes.'

For the first time in weeks, I can feel myself physically relaxing. The edge of danger that has been a constant presence in my life, appears to be melting away. We cross to the sofa and Nick sits down holding his right arm up for me to snuggle in next to him. I do. Burrowing into him and wishing I could just stay here like this forever.

'I wish this was all over. Porter in jail and whoever is working with him sent away too,' I say into his chest.

'I know,' Nick kisses my head. 'It will be. But we don't need to think about it all now. Tomorrow we can go for a lovely walk. The landscape around here is just amazing. I'll show you some photos from my last trip here.'

Nick pulls his phone out and starts to scroll through his photographs. I sit up and pick up my wine from the side table to finish it off. It has hit the spot and I allow my head to fall back against the sofa.

'Here you go,' Nick says, holding his phone up to me. Now tell me that's not beautiful.'

'Wow,' there's no doubting the beauty of the landscape.

'I'll top your wine up while you take a look, there's loads of pics,' he says, offering me his phone and getting up.

I swap my wine glass for his phone and sit scrolling through photograph after photograph of stunning views. Sunsets over a lake, trees in the early morning light, a deer silhouetted against the sky. Then my whole body turns to solid ice and I am unable to breathe. I can't believe what I'm seeing.

I stare at the photograph for what feels like forever, suddenly aware of Nick in the kitchen looking for a corkscrew.

My heart is banging, making my ears throb with its beat.

A thought flashes into my mind and I quickly flick away from the photographs, checking over my shoulder that he's not coming, and look for the icon of the SeeCam app on Nick's phone. It's there. I'm praying that I'll see the inside of his flat, but a part of me already knows that isn't what I'm going to find. As I click on it, the familiar grid view of my patio doors and the front and back door, come into view. Then I hear Nick returning. Quickly, I flick off the app and go back to his photographs, scrolling away from the selfie of him in the yellow frog hat, and back to the silhouetted deer. I feel frozen and vulnerable, just like the animal in the image.

A million different thoughts are rushing into my brain but none of it makes sense. If Nick is working for Porter why is he seemingly so hell bent on getting him convicted? Has Nick been lying to me right from the start? He was the first detective at the murder scene on the dead-end road.

I think back to that morning. Christie took his phone out of his pocket and Porter knocked it away. That's what I told the police. But Porter says that's not true, that Christie was going to kill him. Could I really have got it so wrong? What if it wasn't a phone? Why was I so sure that it was? It was quite far away. Too far really to be sure. So why was I so adamant? Nick said he'd found a phone a few feet away, he suggested that must have been what happened.

My breathing is shallow and ragged as Nick returns holding the glass of wine out to me and sitting down next to me on the sofa again.

'You OK?' he asks me, studying my face. 'You don't look well.'

'I'm fine,' I manage to say, but my voice sounds choked to me. I have to pull myself together. Think this through. I can't give myself away.

'So, what did you think of the Lake District?' he asks, taking his phone off me. The screen has thankfully locked and gone to black and so he just places it on the sofa next to him.

'It's beautiful,' I try hard to smile, but I can barely bring myself to look at him and my mouth trembles as I attempt to hide my emotion.

Flashes of the events in the past few weeks are crashing

into my brain. I told Nick that Dylan was borrowing my car. He was the only other person who knew that. Did he cut the brake line? I'm miles away from anywhere, I don't even know where we are and now I'm thinking this!

I feel sick. He holds his glass up to say cheers and I go through the motions of clinking and putting it to my lips but there's no way I can bring myself to drink any. The wine suddenly smells acidic, making the bile in my stomach rise even more.

Am I going totally crazy? I don't know what to do. Nick wouldn't do this to me. There's a rational explanation for why he's got my security camera feed on his phone, he wants to protect us and there's bound to be more than one person with the same hat. Only it's all too much of a coincidence. The intruder with the yellow frog hat was the reason I rang Nick and this whole relationship began. He would have heard the phone conversation I had with Dee, setting up the meeting with her and Olga and why. He'd also have been able to see where I hid Mason's memory stick, but the cameras don't point down the other end of the room, so that's why the second one was missed. My mind is in overdrive.

No, no, no. This just can't be true. I am going mad. I'm accusing the man who has been so good to me, of being a murderer. Why? What reason could he have? Why implicate Porter at the Christie murder scene if he is working for him?

'I'm just going to get a glass of water,' I say, rising up from the sofa.

'You sure you're OK?' he asks again. 'You're very quiet.'

I can't raise his suspicions. I have to figure out what I'm going to do next.

'Yeah fine, I think the shock of everything has just hit me,' I say and head into the kitchen, opening the cupboard and pulling out a glass to get some water. All the time my head is still whirring, still working through all the possibilities.

What about Roberts and DS Fuller? Where do they fit into all this? Then another thought comes crashing in. Was it definitely DS Fuller who told Harper that I was being investigated? I quickly text Harper with the image of DS Fuller that I'd taken the day he was following me. *Is this the cop who told you I was being investigated for Dylan's murder?* I press send and then pray that she's not still so annoyed with me that she doesn't reply.

I still cannot believe that I'm even thinking this. Mason's last words come back to me. He needed to talk to me urgently. Made me promise not to tell anyone. Did he think Nick was involved too? I'd told him about our relationship when we'd last met. Mason had SW13 at the centre of his mind map, who is that?

'You OK in there?' Nick calls through.

'Yes, coming,' I reply. Quickly I bring up Google and search SW13. Of course, it's a London postcode. How did I not think of that. I scroll down to see where it relates to, perhaps it's a location clue.

I nearly pass out when I see the suburb of Barnes is linked to it. SW13 is Nick Barnes. How did I not see that?

I have to get Ben away from here. I take a few deep breaths and force myself to go back into the sitting room.

'You know, I'm really not feeling well. I think everything has just caught up with me and I need to sleep.'

'That's OK,' Nick says, watching me as I go and sit on the armchair opposite him. It's closest to the door. Closest to Ben. 'We've got plenty of time, it's not surprising that you're tired and country air can knock you out. I'm here and I'm going to look after you and Ben, so you can head up to bed if you want.'

My phone vibrates in my hand. It's Harper. *No. Not him.* I quickly send her a photograph I have of Nick. No time for words or explanation, he's watching me.

I'm waiting for signs that she's typing. Praying that she answers me straight away.

'Who's that?' Nick asks.

'Just Julie,' I give him a wonky smile. 'Problems with George again,' I add.

My phone vibrates, it's messenger. I'm praying that Harper tells me it's not him either, but I get the reply. A thumbs up emoji.

All my muscles are quivering now with the natural instinct to run. I want to ask him outright. Perhaps there's a rational explanation to all this. Perhaps I'm reading far too much into it. It's easy to get over reactive in situations like this.

'I'm going to go and check on Ben,' I say. I'm trying so hard not to show the fear in my voice and on my face, but it feels as though my whole body is betraying me.

'OK' Nick says, but his face has grown serious and his eyes turned darker. I'm sure he suspects something.

I virtually run up the stairs, and into Ben's room. What can I do? We are in the middle of nowhere with a man who isn't who I thought he was and who might very well kill us both. I go to text DI Roberts. *At Nick's cottage in Lake District. Need help* but I don't press send. What if I'm wrong? What if Roberts is the enemy like I'd thought? I'm so confused. So scared. I've no idea where I'm going to go but I know I have to get out of here. I have to get Ben away from Nick. I pick him up out of bed and run.

By the time I'm at the bottom of the stairs, Ben has

started to cry at being so rudely woken. He's frightened. I know Nick will have heard him. He's going to come out and see what's going on any second.

I race to the front door. It's double locked. My hands are shaking and I'm trying to get the locks undone while also constantly trying to watch behind me.

'Abbie!' Nick is in the hall. 'What are you doing?' I freeze and turn to look at him. He's frowning, but he still hasn't realised what's going on. He has his phone in his hand and swipes it on, I know he's going to see what I've seen within seconds. I scrabble at the locks and start to open the door.

'Abbie,' he says looking back up at me. 'This isn't what it seems. You're making a big mistake.'

I'd been hoping he was going to say that. I'm desperate for him to tell me I'm just being paranoid. I pause, clutching Ben to me, trying to soothe him and waiting for Nick to explain. I don't want this man who I've been falling in love with, to be a murderer and liar.

'You understand that Stuart Porter needs to be sent down right? I thought maybe you had evidence that could convict him, that you were investigating him,' Nick begins.

He's only seen the yellow frog hat photo, he doesn't know that I've seen the SeeCam security app. I say nothing, letting him continue and opening the door a little further, ready to run.

'That man is evil Abs, We can't allow him to keep on ruining peoples' lives. My father was a good man, trying to do the right thing. He killed him in cold blood. He's murdered your husband, Ben's father.'

He stops now, considering me, trying to see if his words are having an effect.

'So why have you got my security cameras on your phone. You've been listening in and watching me.'

'I was trying to keep you safe, you know that. It's all I've done since I met you. I have been there for you Abbie, right from the start of this.' He has a look of pain on his face as though I've taken a huge knife and stabbed him in the guts.

I hold Ben to me, tighter. I have to be sure. I can't be wrong about this, even if it's hurting Nick.

'Keep us safe or spy on me? You were the only person I'd told about Dylan borrowing my car. You would have heard my conversation with Dee—'

I stop, I'm watching him now, my turn to see what impact my questions are having. Is he going to have a good reason to deny my suspicions?

He sighs and bows his head. When he looks up again, his expression has changed. His face is hard and threatening.

In that moment I realise my fears are true.

I pull the door open and run.

It's pitch dark outside. The sky must be cloudy because there's not even a moon to light the way. I'm running for our lives, but I've no idea where I'm running to.

I know I'm at a disadvantage. Nick is strong and fit and no doubt faster than me, and I'm carrying Ben. But, I find strength in my legs and lungs that I'd never known I had. I'm running to save our lives. There's a dirt track and woodland running alongside. I run into the trees hoping that the darkness will save us.

My phone is still in my hand and I press send on the text to DI Roberts. He's two hours away but maybe, just maybe he can get help here. If he knows where Nick's cottage is. It's a long shot but it's our only chance.

I don't even get twenty metres into the tree line before I feel Nick's hand grab my hair and yank me back, unbalancing me so that I fall backwards, still clutching Ben, trying to protect him from the fall. I land on my elbows and back, banging my head on a tree trunk. I go to scream but Nick's hand is over my mouth, clamping down. Hard. I can smell him. The familiar scent of Nick which I'd longed for, but there's a stranger here instead.

'I guess it's time we have a chat,' he says with a growl. 'Don't even think about screaming because there's no one here to hear you and if you think about trying anything then just think about your little boy.'

He grabs Ben out of my arms and turns with him to head back to the cottage. I scan the ground looking for a branch or something to hit him with, but what if I hurt Ben as I do it? Nick could fall onto him; or if I don't succeed in knocking him out, he might take out his anger on Ben. I scramble to get up, the smell of pine sap and needles filling my nostrils. Nick doesn't even look back at me. He knows I'm going to have to follow him because he has my son.

'Upstairs,' he growls at me when we get back into the cottage. He virtually drags me up by one arm. It feels like my shoulder is being ripped out of its socket but all I can think about is my little boy who is now screaming and crying in Nick's arms. I catch a glimpse of his face, red and wet with tears.

He takes us into the main bedroom, almost throwing Ben at me.

'Shut him up.'

'He's scared,' I say, 'please don't hurt him.'

I'm shaking, breathless. I'm vaguely aware of everything hurting, but I know the situation is far more serious than that. Nick is pacing back and forth in front of us. I try to console Ben, hugging him to me.

'Put him back in bed,' Nick barks at me again. 'I can't stand that noise.'

I don't want to leave Ben alone in that room, but at least it means he's away from Nick so I do as he tells me.

'I'm sorry baby,' I whisper to Ben as I walk away from his outstretched arms and crying face. 'Stay here. Mummy will be back.'

I close the door. Nick's standing right outside.

'Give me your mobile,' he says to me.

I hesitate, but hand it over. I don't have a choice.

'Why?' I manage to get out.

Nick shakes his head. 'Pete chose the right man for the crime correspondent's job. He was a far better investigative reporter than you'll ever be. Unfortunately for him, that's why he had to die. He worked it out. Do you still not have a clue?'

I feel hot tears pricking the corner of my eyes. I don't want to cry in front of him, but I'm not in control of my body. Fear is the ring master.

'Jordan Christie worked for me. He was my money man but unfortunately Porter got too close to working out what was going on. He knew Christie was involved, although he still hadn't guessed my role. When he told my dad all this, he figured the whole thing out.'

'Your dad? You didn't...'

'It was him or me,' Nick barks back, as though my question is a stupid one. 'I still had to deal with Porter and so Christie was going to kill him; only Porter was too quick and killed him first. You shouldn't have been there. But, once I knew that you'd seen the attack, I realised you could be useful. If we played things right then Porter could be sent down as a murderer, trashing his reputation. Nobody would believe him then, and I've been working hard to make it look as though he was behind the missing money at the council. That way I don't need to keep looking over my shoulder for the rest of my life. It's just you kept throwing spanners in the works. Porter's youngest son scared you off with the threatening phone calls and so you pulled your statement because you were so worried about Ben. An eighteen-year-old kid had you too terrified to testify. Pathetic. Porter would have walked. I had to make you hate him enough to agree to go back to court and so I used your fears over Ben's safety to persuade you. Quite ingenious I thought. It worked.'

A little whimper escapes me now. I can't believe all I'm hearing and the knowledge that Dylan died purposely, hits me right in the solar plexus.

Nick frowns angrily. 'What are you whining for? I saw all your messages to that friend of yours. You wanted him dead. Well, I gave you what you wanted and you made a nice tidy sum as well. All you had to do was keep quiet and testify against Porter and you'd have been fine, but you kept trying to be the investigative journalist. It's your fault those women had to die.'

I am crying full flow. I feel the warm tears cascading down my cheeks. What's Nick going to do now he's told me all this? I can think of only one option. He's going to kill us. I'm completely alone.

'Mmhh I can see you're wondering what I'm going to do next. Well, I can't obviously let you wander around knowing all this so I'm going to have to alter my plans a little. I have my escape sorted, I just need to tie up a few loose ends and you're not going to stop me. Being here should give me a bit of leeway on timing even if things haven't quite worked out as I'd hoped. So, I'm afraid Abbie dear, your usefulness has come to an end and you're going to have to be silenced.'

The gun.

In the split second that I've remembered the gun, he does too. He turns and heads back to the main bedroom.

I run after him. I'm close behind but not close enough to stop him getting to his bag and picking it up, tipping its contents onto the bed. He starts searching through his things.

Only, I know that the gun isn't in there. I reach up to the top of the wooden wardrobe behind him and find the cold barrel of the pistol.

I've just got hold of it and backed towards the doorway as Nick turns around. His face is puce with anger.

'What have you—' but he doesn't finish.

He sees me standing there, pointing his gun at him.

He stops and his face relaxes. Then he smiles and softens his eyes.

'You won't shoot me Abbie. You can't. I know that. You know that. It's not in your nature.' He takes a step towards me.

I back up a step. 'Keep away from me,' I say. My voice doesn't come out the strong, commanding way that I wished it would. But I'm holding the gun, he has to do as I say.

Nick steps towards me again. 'Don't be silly Abbie. We can sort this out between us.'

I back to the middle of the landing, leaving him with a clear exit down the stairs and ensuring that I'm in between him and Ben's room.

'Give me the car keys Nick and let us leave,' I say again and this time it's with more conviction.

He smiles again at me. 'Really? And what if I don't, are you going to shoot me? Come on Abbie. Give me the gun.'

'I will shoot you if you take one more step Nick.'

He steps towards me, one foot forward, not taking his eyes from mine. I'm looking into the eyes which I've loved. I reverse one more step. I'm just a couple of feet away from Ben's door now. Inside I can hear his desperate crying and I'm angry that he's so upset.

'Don't do this,' I say to Nick.

But Nick just smiles again, his face back to the man I recognise, and he takes another step towards me. I can't go much further back without being against Ben's door.

Nick still stands there smiling at me, and then his face changes. He lurches towards me.

I think of only one thing. He is not going to get to my son.

I squeeze the trigger of the gun.

One. Two. Three. Four. Five. Six. Until there are no more bullets, and it clicks at me. Empty.

Nick slumps against me, his hands reaching out for something to stop him crumpling to the floor. His eyes still looking at mine, only this time there is complete shock.

'Abbie' I hear Nick gasp out. 'How could you...'

'You were right Nick. I'll do anything to protect my son, you should have remembered that.'

He makes another sound but it isn't words, blood comes from his lips and his eyes roll. He falls to the floor and doesn't move.

When I look at my hands, they're covered in blood. I smell it too, the rich, iron-laden narrative of death slowly pooling on the ground beside me. I glance down at myself: my clothes are damp and crimson; my cheek sticky in the breeze from the open front door, bringing the sounds of faraway police sirens to my ears.

Six bullets to the chest and abdomen. No one can survive that.

My vision blurs and I feel myself slipping into unconsciousness.

Perhaps that's a good thing. An escape from this reality.

My eyelids flutter.

If I let them close, then I won't have to face up to what's next.

But I have to.

Hasn't this been all about justice?

Justice and revenge – and one terrible mistake.

I just never thought it would end this way.

Then I hear Ben's crying through the swirling fog. I go to my son and I hold him and I tell him that nobody is ever going to hurt him. Mummy won't let them.

35

—————

A MONTH LATER

I was arrested after the shooting. DI Roberts knew where the cottage was and had local police come to help me. Of course, they were too late to help Nick Barnes.

Conor Roberts turned out to be a nice man. I'd just not given him the chance before, and he'd been unsure of what part I was playing in everything. Roberts didn't know if I was telling the truth about why I ended up at the Christie murder scene and when I got together with Nick, his suspicions had only increased. He was convinced that Nick was not who he said he was, especially after his partner, Nick's dad, was killed, but he'd never been able to prove anything. In the last 24 hours, the information they'd managed to glean from Mason's notebooks had heightened his suspicions and they were close to moving on Nick. That's why they wanted to talk to me. His concern for Ben and me had been genuine. I can see that now and I'm grateful.

'I feel such an idiot,' I say to DI Roberts when I'm finally allowed to go back home.

'He manipulated you. Used your fears over Ben's safety

to cloud your judgement. He was very persuasive, that's why he got away with it all for so long.'

I realise that DI Roberts is right. All my animosity towards him and DS Fuller had come from things which Nick had said. He'd told me that Porter was the one behind the fraud, that he suspected DI Roberts was working with him and all the doubts and suspicions had grown from there. DS Fuller despised Nick. The Nick that I'd seen was not the man that Fuller and most others recognised. That Nick was arrogant and ruthless. I'd only seen a flash of that at the end.

I had photographic evidence that Nick had picked up two items, one from Christie's body, which was his phone, and it turns out that the second was the gun. The same gun that I shot Nick with weeks later. Straight after the Christie murder I hadn't been sure what I'd seen. Turns out that's common when you've witnessed something traumatic. You're a less reliable witness and when Nick planted that story about Christie having pulled out a mobile, not a gun because that's what he'd found, I'd come to believe it.

DI Roberts had taken Pete into his confidence and told him to tell me and Mason not to dig around as it was too dangerous. When Mason was mown down in the street, Pete had given him everything he could find to help track his attacker. Mason will be in recovery for a long time, but they're confident that he'll make a full recovery eventually. I've been to see him and took his cactus in to him.

My mum and dad came to stay with Ben while I was kept in for a few days to be questioned. In the end, it was Nick's own method of keeping tabs on me that was his downfall. The security camera in the sitting room had recorded so many of his lies. The rest of his web of deceit unravelled when I gave the police Mason's memory stick.

SW13 had been at the centre of it all but I'd just not been able to see it.

The investigation still has a long way to go. Stuart Porter and I are now both pleading self-defence, but he no longer has to worry about my testimony. My solicitor says he's confident things will get sorted for both of us.

I sent Harper a cheque for £10,000, out of the insurance money from Dylan. I know I didn't have to, but I think it's what Dylan would have wanted. I owe him that much at least. In the meantime, Ben and I are spending quality time together, including visiting Julia and Oscar, before I start applying for a new job with flexible hours so I can be home for when he needs me. I'm still driving Dylan's car as it's comfortable and easy to drive, but most of all because it has a built-in sat nav. I am never going to risk trying a short cut on a dead-end road ever again.

IF YOU WOULD LIKE to receive an epilogue chapter that tells you what happened to Abbie and Ben after this book finished, you can sign up to my free Readers' Club and I'll send it to you along with some other reading goodies: subscribepage.io/DeadEnd

I HOPE YOU ENJOYED DEAD END

I hope you've enjoyed reading *Dead End* thank you so much for choosing my book. This was an idea and characters who have been kicking around in my head for quite some time. I first came up with the concept after I'd had my first son and that's over twenty years ago, so it was about time that Abbie told her story.

I have certainly enjoyed writing Dead End, this is my first stand-alone book in a while as I've been focusing on the three series I've written. I'm going to be writing another stand-alone next, which has also been hanging around in my mind for a long time— just imagine all that extra storage space I'm going to have in my head (I wish!). It's going to be a real action-led thriller with another female lead, a kind of middle-aged *Home Alone* with a *Thelma and Louise* vibe. Do sign up to my newsletter if you'd like to know when it's out.

Thank you to my editor, Natasha Hodgson, and book cover designer, Stuart Bache for their help in bringing Dead End to you. I'd love to hear your feedback so please do get in touch and let me know if you liked the read, you can email me: gwyn@gwynbennett.com

I would be very grateful if you could spare the time to leave a review on the Dead End Amazon page. Reviews are extremely important to authors, not only do they guide other readers, but I write for you and so hearing about your reading experience is a huge part of my motivation to keep writing.

If you would like to receive an epilogue chapter that tells you what happened to Abbie and Ben after this book finished, then sign up to my free Readers' Club and I'll keep you updated with news as well as competitions and offers. You can also get a free novella that introduces Dr Harrison Lane and his Ritualistic Behavioural Crime Unit— that's if you'd like to read about a hunky psychologist who works with the police to solve difficult crimes 😉

subscribepage.io/DeadEnd

If you would like to read Dead End or one of my other books with your book group or reading group, and would like me to join you online to answer your questions, get in touch with me and I'll see if I can pop along with Zoom or Teams. It would be great to meet you.

Finally, thank you again for choosing to read Dead End, I really do appreciate your support.

Many thanks and happy reading

Gwyn

www.gwynbennett.com

THE HARRISON LANE CRIME MYSTERIES

THE DR HARRISON LANE CRIME MYSTERIES
by GWYN BENNETT

To catch a killer you have to think like one...

Book 1 BROKEN ANGELS

A breath of sky broke through the canopy of trees in the small clearing. A wooden cross had been pushed into the earth, and four candles surrounded the boy. He looked as if he was sleeping, but the rotting leaves upon which he lay were his grave.

In the early hours, Head of the Ritualistic Behavioural Crime unit, **Dr Harrison Lane**, is called to a woodland to find the lifeless body of a young boy. Scrawled across his chest is a Latin satanic exorcism prayer and scraps of paper covered in quotes from the Old Testament are stuffed in his mouth. Who would want this innocent child dead?

Harrison is certain the killer has links with a religious group, and the clue lies in the twisted individual's childhood.

As he delves further, Harrison visits a cemetery and realises he's
been there before, dredging up a chilling memory from his past.
When he was a little boy, his mother, dressed in a black cloak, had
brought him there just before she died.

While Harrison tries to make sense of his traumatic flashback and
how it might be linked to the case, a child goes missing while on
his way to a leisure centre on a busy Saturday morning.

Can Harrison battle the demons of his own past and find the killer
before the life of another innocent child is taken?

*The Harrison Lane series is available on Amazon in paperback, ebook,
and audio.*

THE DI CLAIRE FALLE SERIES
DI CLAIRE FALLE SERIES

Someone's watching. Someone's Lonely. Someone's going to Die. Could it be You?

LONELY HEARTS

Meet Rachel, she loves animals and works at a dating agency bringing lonely people together – only somebody is watching her every move and she's scared…

Neil didn't see who killed him – but his murder brings DI Claire Falle on the case. What she uncovers leads her to discover a serial-killer is preying on the clients of the dating agency where Rachel works.

Can Claire work out the connection between all the deaths before Rachel becomes the next victim?

What is it in Rachel's past that haunts her?

As DI Claire Falle investigates the lives of the dating agency staff and clients, she is pulled into a tangled web of loneliness and deceit which will have devastating consequences for someone…

What readers are saying about Lonely Hearts

'What a twist! It absolutely had me on the edge of my seat.'

'Brilliant. If you want to get completely lost in a page-turner with an amazing twist, then Lonely Hearts is the book for you.'

LONELY HEARTS: CHAPTER ONE
RACHEL: 13TH OCTOBER 2016

The garden was illuminated only by thin leached light from the windows of the house; the curtains opened for that purpose. The dark, moon-less sky meant a thousand shadows had been born, but only one had made her heart pound, turning her skin cold and sending the blood pumping in her veins.

She knew they were watching again and cursed herself. How stupid not to have realised they wouldn't have just given up. Now she'd left herself vulnerable.

Her hands started to shake slightly as she locked up the shed, determined not to leave her animals unprotected. Her breathing was shallow. Muscles tensed for flight, as she listened for the slightest sound from behind: a bush parting, soft footsteps on the lawn, the breath of another on her neck.

Like last time, there was nothing.

Nothing except the endless drone of suburban London traffic and a baby crying in a house across the road, its high-pitched wailing summoning tired parents. She was surrounded by houses, by families, and couples, going about their evening routines: TV, computer games, reading, arguing, all oblivious to her rising fear and what might be about to happen.

Rachel shivered involuntarily, partly because of the cool October evening which had begun to penetrate the thin cotton jumper she'd flung on over her jeans earlier; and partly because of the tide of cold dread washing through her.

She pushed her blonde hair back from her face, pocketed the shed key, and spun on her heels to face the house. It was only ten paces, but the empty lawn gaped wide. Why were they here again? It'd been weeks since the last time and she'd convinced herself they'd gone, scared off by the presence of a man in the house. It was almost as if they knew she was alone tonight.

What if they were already inside? Slipped in unseen while she'd fed the rabbits.

Light poured from the open kitchen doorway in front of her, a threat lit up and welcoming to any passing stalker.

What should she do? Stay outside with the shadows in the open? Or trust the light and the doorway that will enclose her?

Fear won. Her legs started to move as flight and adrenaline took over. If she got into the kitchen, her mobile phone was on the table. She could almost see it from here.

Rachel walked. Each step an eternity. Nearly twisting her ankle as she missed the edge where lawn met footpath.

She was a few feet from the doorway, light bathed her pale face, making her blonde hair glow.

Her phone was just a breath away.

LONELY HEARTS: CHAPTER TWO
NEIL: 13TH OCTOBER 2016

Neil leant into the bathroom mirror, plucking the last grey hair from his dark eyebrows. The demanding youth culture of digital marketing wasn't his only motivation to hold back the years.

It was as he dropped his gaze to the sink, turning on the tap to wash away his age, that the knife entered his back.

He didn't see who killed him. It wouldn't have mattered much if he had because he was dead, and thus a useless witness, long before anyone found him.

As he careered headfirst into the bathtub, he knocked his bottle of Creed aftershave in with him, smashing and spattering the white porcelain with scent as well as blood.

The pathologist later commented that his was the nicest smelling corpse he'd ever had the pleasure to be acquainted with.

By the time Neil's mobile phone rang in the sitting room, Rachel's number flashing up on the screen, his heart had stopped pumping.

Neil would stay forever young.

LONELY HEARTS: CHAPTER THREE
CLAIRE: 13TH OCTOBER 2016

DI Claire Falle had an epiphany lying naked next to the man who'd shared her bed for the past three years. He would never make her happy, a fact backed up by the dull ache between her legs instead of a pleasurable post-orgasmic throb.

In truth, he'd bored her for months, but it had been convenient. The same reasons so many coppers get together, an understanding of the crap you have to deal with and the shit hours. Unfortunately, Claire no longer wanted convenience. She wanted passion and her own space, neither of which she'd been getting since Jack moved in.

He'd also been getting a bit too heavy lately, broody even. Jack had started talking forward, not just weeks or months, but years.

'This would be a good investment,' he'd said the other night. They were sitting on the sofa, dinner finished, watching *Game of Thrones*. It was one of those rare occasions they were on their own in the flat, without one of Jack's buddies over for a beer. All of a sudden, he'd just come out with it and handed Claire his iPad. Claire expected him to show her a savings account or the latest Kickstarter hit, but instead he'd offered up an estate agency site with an ad that said, "Great neighbourhood. The perfect family starter-home." Claire hadn't known what to say.

Thankfully, Khaleesi and her dragons took that moment to catch Jack's attention, and she was spared any further awkwardness.

LONELY HEARTS: CHAPTER FOUR
CLAIRE: 14TH OCTOBER 2016

The morning's rude awakening at the hands of her mobile phone saved Claire from any further embarrassing conversations about settling down. She resented the call, though; it was supposed to be her day off. She and Jack were planning to go to Great Yarmouth for a couple of nights. Even if she didn't want to play happy families with him, she missed the sea and could have done with getting out of London. The brown North Sea wouldn't have been a patch on the clear blues and greens of her Jersey childhood waters, but the fresh salty air would have been welcome. She needed to clear her head.

'We've got a murder. Get here as quickly as you can. Leave is cancelled. Sorry.' Detective Chief Inspector Robert Walsh's East End accent came at her down the phone, matter of fact. He gave her an address.

Jack stirred and opened one eye at her. 'Who's that?'

'Bob. I've got to go in. Sorry about today. Why don't you see if Matt's free?'

'Yeah, whatever.' Jack rolled back over.

She was relieved he wasn't going to create a scene. He knew the score with the job, but her lack of upset at not being able to spend time with him seemed to have gone unnoticed. She'd deal with what's going on in her head another time.

Claire disappeared to the bathroom and took a moment to gaze in the mirror while the shower heated up. She needed a haircut. Her auburn hair was looking scraggy around the edges. It had been a sharp mid-length bob. Maybe she'd try something different next time. More layers might last longer, although when next time was going to come was anyone's guess. She couldn't see herself getting time off for a haircut for a while, not with a murder inquiry on.

The shower dragged her into a state of full consciousness, and when she returned to the bedroom, Jack had fallen back asleep. His mouth was half open, black hair tousled, and he was making little snuffly snores like an upturned hedgehog. She took a moment to look at him, trying to rekindle the way she'd first felt about him three years ago, when just seeing him had made her want to unbutton his trousers. What had killed that passion? Familiarity? Too much of a good thing? Did she simply not find him intellectually stimulating? Had they crossed that line when you know there's nothing left to discover and what's there is simply not enough?

When they'd gone to bed last night Jack had farted, wafting the bed sheets at her, 'Smell the amber nectar.' He'd laughed. She'd got stroppy. Maybe she's prudish or doesn't have a sense of humour, but the laddish behaviour turned her off. She got enough of that at the station. At home, things should be different. Shouldn't they?

She thought about her mother and her parents' thirty-eight-year marriage. She couldn't imagine her dad doing that. Did her mother ever think like Claire? Ever feel the need for an affair just to know she's still capable of passion and lust? Claire couldn't see that either.

Claire had no urge to kiss Jack goodbye, instead, she slipped out of their bedroom and left him sleeping. Her mind buzzing with the prospect of a new case.

THE MAIN ROADS of Shepherd's Bush were already choked with traffic, and as she walked to where she'd parked her car, Claire could hear the rumble of the overground Tube trains. In the distance were the muffled shouts and mechanical noises of the massive building site that was once BBC Television Centre. It was being slowly transformed into apartments, restaurants, and a hotel. She'd hate to think how much even a one-bed flat would cost with their 24-hour concierge and underfloor heating. She'd heard a two-bedroom unit was nearly one million. If that's true, then there wasn't much chance of one of those unless you were already a TV celebrity. Besides, she could think of plenty of places she'd rather be than Shepherd's Bush. There's only so much landscaped gardens can do to detract from the overwhelming grey urban sprawl.

Claire reached her car, but only just managed to escape the parking space because the white van in front and VW Golf behind had boxed her in so tightly there was barely enough room to turn the wheel. The CD player switched on with the engine, and Adele kept her company for the journey.

It was easy to tell when she'd got close to the location of the murder. The London street changed colour, multicoloured residents' cars replaced, or blocked in, by the fluorescent yellow of emergency vehicles. Those at home were twitching their curtains. Those at work would return to a very different street to the one they'd left, but one which would temporarily be united in neighbourly gossip. People who'd not said as much as 'good morning' to each other in years would stop and chat about the terrible goings on.

Despite it being a Friday, a small crowd had gathered outside the flats where the murder took place. Among them Claire could see a couple of local journalists, already tweeting something, desperate to be the first with the next update. They won't have much to go on yet, and she certainly wasn't going to give them anything. Nevertheless, as she walked past and into the building, she saw their phones go up and heard the electronic clicks of their cameras.

'DI Falle, can you tell us who it is?' They knew she wasn't going to, but guessed they were hoping she'd turn round for a better shot. She wouldn't give them that pleasure. Her colleagues were bad enough as it was about the media attention she gets. Some sleazy tabloid had named her 'Baton Babe' last year. Armed only with her truncheon, she'd risked her life to overpower and arrest some knife wielding nutter as he'd threatened a playground full of terrified kids. They wouldn't have given a male copper that tag, would they? Yet in the same sentence as commending her bravery, they'd commented on her 'arresting good looks' and great figure. It wasn't fair. She'd worked hard to be seen as an equal, and they smashed that down with one badly written article.

A young PC directed her up to the third floor where Scenes of Crime Officers had taken over half the corridor. She donned the protective clothing and went in search of Bob.

The flat was nice, expensive TV and sound system, quite minimalist in other ways, especially the galley kitchen. She guessed it was probably a bachelor pad for a young but well-paid professional.

A pack of cleaning materials and cloths lay scattered on the floor just outside the bathroom. Claire quickly surmised that the distraught Eastern European woman being calmed down in the corridor was probably Neil's cleaner who'd discovered his body.

Bob spotted Claire and beckoned her towards the bathroom. Inside, two Scenes of Crime Officers were working: marking, measuring, photographing, and taking samples. The corpse was still upside down in the tub. He was only wearing boxers, so it was easy to see just how much blood had drained down the plughole, with more of it sprayed around the walls. There was one large puncture wound in his back, the bloodless skin giving the impression of cut pastry.

'Looks like the attacker stabbed him in the back while he was standing, and he then fell into the bath.' Bob didn't waste time with pleasantries. She could see him logging and assessing the scene like a well-programmed scanner.

'Why didn't he see them in the mirror?' Claire was standing in the doorway and it was clear the large mirror above the sink gave a good view of the whole bathroom.

'Tap was still running when the cleaner got here, so perhaps he had his head down over the sink. Maybe he knew the attacker. There's no sign of forced entry.'

Claire nodded in thought. 'Mirror could have been steamed. What's that smell?'

'Creed. Expensive stuff.' Bob motioned to the smashed bottle that could just be seen under the corpse.

'Nice.' She took another look at the scene, recording the

details: the tweezers on the floor by the sink, the row of expensive hair and body treatments. This was a man who took pride in his appearance.

She looked at the upside-down corpse again. She couldn't see his face, but from the toned body she could tell he was a young man. For a moment Claire allowed herself to see him as a person, not a case. Then her eyes moved on.

The drips of blood running down the white tiles reminded her of a poem she used to love as a child. Something about two raindrops having a race down the windowpane. She could even remember the book, *When We Were Six* by A A Milne. But this wasn't a scene for a child's eyes. The drops of blood had dried and congealed in place. Race over.

When it was clear in her head, she backed out and took a look around the rest of the flat. A mobile phone had been dusted for fingerprints and was being bagged ready to be given to the investigating team.

'Three missed calls,' Margaret Taylor, the senior SOCO, said to Claire. 'All from the same woman.'

'Thanks.'

In the kitchen, she saw one plate on the side next to a single wine glass.

'Looks like he ate alone,' she said to Bob, who had come up alongside her.

'Unless the killer took away their plate and glass knowing we'd find their DNA!'

Claire frowned and nodded. These days the level of information on the Internet and in TV crime dramas meant even the less cerebrally endowed criminals could make their job harder.

'The flat belongs to a Neil Parsons,' said Bob, leafing through some letters and paperwork. 'Looks like our bathtub man likes the camera,' he added, nodding at a gallery of photographs showing a handsome young man with various gorgeous women and groups of drunken men. In every photograph, Neil was the centre of attention.

Claire saw the face of their bathroom corpse for the first time. Twinkling blue eyes, all-year round suntan, and meticulously coiffed hair. Good looking, but in a self-absorbed kind of way.

'Maybe his ego was his downfall,' she replied.

'Crime of passion. I'll bet fifty quid on it,' said Bob.

Claire raised her eyebrows at his certainty. Then something drew her attention to the small desk by the window. Neil's laptop sat waiting to be collected for evidence, but it was the papers that caught her eye.

'SoulMates Dating Agency. You wouldn't have thought someone like him has a problem meeting women, would you?' She flicked through the printed pages of profiles. Smiling women all hoping to meet their Mr Right. They'd be disappointed if they were pinning their hopes on Neil. Some pages had ticks or crosses on them.

'Any sign of drugs?' Claire asked to the room.

'Nothing so far,' one of the SOCOs, the thin pasty one with eyes like a weasel, replied.

'Let's get back and get set up,' Bob said to her, already heading out the flat.

Claire took one last look around. The place was crawling with SOCOs, hard to see it as a home and not a crime scene right now. She'd come back again later.

'Did he drive a car?' she asked the uniformed officer at the door.

'We're looking for it,' he replied. 'Got an Audi key but parking's a mare round here so it could be a couple of streets away.'

'OK, thanks.'

She left, knowing in a few hours she'd be reacquainting herself with Neil on the autopsy table.

WANT TO CONTINUE READING? *You can buy Lonely Hearts on Amazon.*